Summer's breath came in shallow gasps as she sat still, not feeling she could move even if she wanted to. She was like a bird frozen in the mesmerizing stare of a snake, knowing it was about to be eaten alive but not able to make a move to save its own life.

She moaned and closed her eyes as his lips stroked the sensitive skin then moved to the base of her throat where he licked softly and gently. She didn't realize that she was still clutching the handkerchief tightly in her hand until she felt his strong fingers pry hers open to pull it away so that he could seduce her palm with his thumb.

"Relax, baby." He moved his lips up her neck and to her ear. "You're so tense. Just relax."

As he spoke he pushed her back gently into the plush pillows and began to nibble her ear lobe. He gave a lick just behind her ear and shock waves ran down her spine.

"Oh, God," she breathed, "what are you doing to me?"

"What someone should have done to you a long time ago, Summer Jones," he whispered. "Teach you what it means to be a woman."

HOT SUMMER

JUDY POWELL

Island Spice
BOOKS

ISLAND SPICE BOOKS
Published by
Lyons Publishing Ltd.
6-2400 Dundas Street West, Suite 502
Mississauga, Ontario, L5K 2R8
Canada
www.lyonspublishing.com

Copyright © 2005 by Judy Powell

All rights reserved. No part of this book may be reproduced or transmitted in any form, electronic or otherwise (mechanical, photocopying, recording, or stored in a retrieval system) without the prior written consent of the Publisher. Such action is an infringement of the copyright law.

Canadian Cataloguing in Publication Data
Powell, Judy –
    Hot Summer - 1st. ed.

    ISBN 0-9738590-0-8
    1. Blacks—Fiction. I. Title.
    PR9265.9P678H67 2005   823'.92   C2005-904127-7

If you have bought this book without a cover, you should be aware that this book is stolen property. It was reported as "unsold and destroyed" to the Publisher, and the Author/Publisher have not received any payment for this "stripped book".

All Lyons Publishing imprints are available at special quantity discounts for bulk purchases for sales promotions, premiums, fund-raising, educational and institutional use. For details, write to the office of Lyons Publishing: Lyons Publishing Limited, 6-2400 Dundas Street West, Suite 502, Mississauga, Ontario, L5K 2R8, Canada.

Cover Design by: www.mariondesigns.com
Book Layout by: Lisa Gibson-Wilson – www.renmanserv.com

Printed in the USA

*Dedicated to the memory of my dear mother and friend,
Evelyn May Powell.*

Your life was an inspiration. I will never forget you.

Acknowledgements

Special thanks to my dear friend, Byron "Bobby" Treasure, for being a great source of inspiration. You kept me focused and helped make this dream a reality. I thank you, also, for your invaluable contribution of background information on the Reggae music industry.

To Hotclue, thank you so much for all your support and advice – you are a true friend. To my ladies, Sharon and Dorothy, your encouragement can never be forgotten. And to the members of Love Designers Club, thanks for making me a part of the family.

To my dear Aunt Tiny, thanks for all the love and support you gave me while I was working on this project.

To all those who have encouraged me to reach for my dreams, I've done it – thank you!

Chapter 1

Summer picked up the tray of drinks and, balancing it gingerly on her raised right palm, turned towards the patio. It was only her fourth day at work but already she had begun to look forward to the daily display of beauty at the restaurant as the setting July sun cast red and gold hues over the waters of Lake Michigan. The day before, she'd been able to slip away to the balcony for a few moments to drink in the colours and breathe in the warm breeze that blew over the lake.

Taking a break would be out of the question today. It was Friday and the restaurant was full of Chicagoans as well as tourists, all determined to enjoy the beautiful summer evening.

On reaching table seven Summer gave a polite smile and began to place drinks beside each of the three clients as well as at the unoccupied place at the table. Two men - one African-American, the other Caucasian - sat with an elegant honey-coloured woman with flowing black hair and scarlet nails. She'd been told they were waiting for a friend and had been asked to bring an extra drink, a Piña Colada. She guessed another woman would be joining the group.

As the table was in the most private corner of the patio Summer was pleased to find that she didn't have to shout to be heard. She straightened and, still smiling, said, "Would you like to place your orders now?"

The men smiled back but the woman totally ignored her. Instead, she stretched her perfectly manicured hand for her glass and took a sip.

Then she turned haughty eyes to Summer. "You brought me the wrong drink."

Summer's smile faltered. "I'm sure you told me you wanted a virgin Strawberry Daiquiri?" Her voice held just a hint of uncertainty.

"No, I didn't. I told you to bring me a Strawberry Daiquiri and a virgin Piña Colada."

The woman put the glass down and sat back in her chair with a look of annoyance.

"I'm sorry. Let me change that right away."

Summer reached for the glass but the dark-skinned man put his hand on hers and gently pushed it away. He was laughing.

"Come off it, Monisha. Give the girl a break. I heard you order a virgin Strawberry Daiquiri so don't go changing your mind now." He leaned back in his chair and grinned at the woman. "You do this every time we go out. Now I've got Mike as witness."

Monisha's eyes flashed daggers at him but he only laughed and blew her a kiss. She pouted for a moment longer then, as if suddenly bored with her game, she shrugged and turned her attention back to the frothy drink.

With a barely audible sigh of relief Summer flipped her book open and waited for the guests to order. She hadn't written the drink order down. After all, there were only three of them. Still, after what had just happened she decided she'd better take notes.

She knew people like Monisha, women who suddenly found themselves with a little power and wanted to use it at every opportunity. She'd been on the job only four days and couldn't afford to mess things up. She definitely wasn't going to give this woman a second chance to chew her out.

"What's your house special?" The man they'd called Mike was flipping through the menu.

"Today we have chicken with black-eyed peas and yellow rice served with Okra Gumbo," she said brightly, glad for the diversion. "There's also Peach Cobbler for dessert."

"Sounds good." He nodded and handed the menu to her. "I'll have that."

"I'll go for your Seafood Gumbo with red beans and rice," said the other man. "The gumbo here is always good."

"And you, ma'am?" Summer turned to the bored-looking woman who sat drumming her long fingernails on the table.

"Bring me two orders of baked Snapper with yams and fried plantains," she said, stifling a yawn.

Then, as Summer began scribbling on her pad, the woman stopped her.

"No, change that. Bring me just one order of the baked Snapper. Make the other one Oxtail and beans with rice."

Summer didn't bother to look up but simply scratched out what she had written on the pad and started again. The two men chuckled.

"Don't get yourself all tied up again, Monisha," Mike teased. "If the order gets messed up, next time it will be all your fault."

Ignoring the banter, Summer thanked them and headed back to the kitchen.

"Hey, Summer, how's it going out there?"

The cook's heavy body shook as he stirred an aromatic concoction in a huge iron pot. He laid the large spoon on a saucer, reached up for one of the copper pots that hung above his head, then yelled, "Hurry it up with them carrots, Lisa. You're holding me up."

A slim girl wearing a chef's hat and a white apron quickly brought a tray of chopped carrots and the heavy-set man emptied it into the bubbling stew.

He turned back to Summer. "So, how is it?"

"It's okay, Brian," Summer shrugged. "Busy like crazy but nothing I can't handle."

"Well said, for a new girl. You picked the busiest time of year to start working here. It can't be easy on you but you seem to be holding your own pretty good. You're covering Maria's tables too, right?"

"Yeah," Summer nodded. "She couldn't have picked a worse day to call in sick, but it's okay. I'm hangin' in there."

Summer rested her tray on the counter and picked up another one laden with food. "Table four, right?"

"Yup. Just get that out there and come right back. I've got two more trays coming up."

Brian slammed a saucepan on the burner. He looked across at the younger man who was stacking dishes into the machine. "Keep 'em coming, Jason. We're gonna run out soon."

Summer grabbed the heavy tray, backed out of the hectic kitchen and headed for table four.

As she walked carefully with her load she spied Ted Jackson standing by the door, watching her. The manager had been skeptical about hiring her to replace a server who had recently retired. She lacked experience, he'd said, but she'd convinced him that she was a fast learner and was good for the job. He took her on board but kept watching her like a hawk since hiring her. All his employees had been with him for at least four years. Except her. So far she hadn't messed up but she knew she had to be on her p's and q's until he was totally comfortable with her.

She'd thought this job would have been a walkover but soon realized that it required speed, a great memory, skill at handling heavy trays, and a placid spirit in the face of irate customers.

With Mr. Jackson's eyes on her Summer was the perfect hostess. She carefully served each dish at table four, smiled pleasantly and asked if she could be of further assistance. They were a cheerful group, five women dining together, obviously good friends. They thanked Summer for her help and, with a nod, she headed back to the kitchen.

It was almost half an hour before Brian called Summer to collect table seven's tray. She'd been so busy dealing with the other eleven tables that she'd totally forgotten about that group. She quickly grabbed the tray and set out for the patio.

She plastered a smile on her face and steeled herself for the complaints.

The orange of the sunset had softened to a rose coloured twilight and as Summer approached the table in the far corner of the patio she realized that the fourth person had arrived. The shadowy figure was partially hidden by the artificial palm leaves which were part of the decor; the figure was definitely too tall to be a woman.

A well-muscled, ebony-skinned man sat in the corner. The dimness made it difficult to see his eyes but a strip of light from a nearby lamp illuminated a slip of moustache over a chiseled mouth.

As Summer approached, the strong lips parted in a sudden smile then the man threw his head back and laughed out loud. The unexpected laughter caught her by surprise and she found herself smiling involuntarily. When she got to the table the slight smile was still on her lips and she opened her mouth to quickly issue an apology for the delay.

Before she could get a word out the woman swung her eyes round.

"So - you finally grace us with your presence? Is this the kind of service you offer here? Just so you know, it's terrible."

Summer was taken aback by the harsh comment and her face grew hot with embarrassment. She spoke quickly, the words coming out far less elegantly than she had intended.

"I'm very sorry, ma'am. The restaurant…it's so crowded on a Friday. I really apologize for your wait."

Monisha's scowl deepened. "How hard can it be to get some food to four people in a reasonable amount of time? God, you would think it's rocket science."

"Ma'am, again, my apologies," Summer said, struggling to keep her voice calm and her face pleasant, "but Fridays are extremely busy for us during the summertime and we're short one server today. Please bear with us."

"That's not my problem," Monisha said coldly. "We've been waiting for over half an hour and that's not acceptable.

Some waitress you are." Under her breath she added, "God, where do they get these people?"

Suddenly, the man in the corner spoke. "Monisha, that's enough. Let's not create a scene here."

But it was too late. Summer had had enough. Her feet ached from running back and forth for the past six hours and her arms were tired from holding heavy trays. And now this woman was getting personal. The control she had been fighting so hard to maintain finally snapped.

She deposited the tray of food on a nearby table and folded her arms across her chest. "How dare you speak to me like that? If you're not satisfied with my service then speak to the manager. Please. But don't sit there throwing insults at me. I won't accept that from you or anybody."

Summer's breath was tight in her chest and with every word her voice got harder. "I'm neither your pet nor your servant and I expect respect and courtesy just as you expect it from me."

Without waiting for a reply she picked up the tray again then turned back to the table. "Now, if you don't mind, I'd like to do my job."

She ignored the woman who sat glaring up at her and pretended not to notice the chuckles from the men who had been there earlier. She avoided the eyes of the newcomer who remained silent in the shadows. Her face was rigid and her movements quick. In seconds she had set the plates on the table. With her face still grim she said, "Enjoy your meals."

Without another word she marched back to the kitchen, the empty tray under her arm.

Summer burst through the swinging doors and slammed the tray down on the counter so hard that five pairs of eyes turned to her in surprise.

"Hey, hey, what's up?" Brian rested his knife down and frowned as he saw her expression. "What's wrong?"

"I'm so ticked off I could just scream!" Summer's chest heaved and she clenched her fists tightly by her side.

Lisa had stopped chopping carrots and Jason put his dish towel down and turned towards her. Clem, Brian's assistant and Carla, one of the servers, stopped mid-conversation and stared at her in anticipation. They were all eager to hear what had happened.

"Back to work, all of you," Brian growled then grabbed Summer's elbow. He pulled her towards the back entrance. "What happened out there?"

"There was this woman…she just got on my last nerve!"

"They come in all types, Summer. You know that. You've just got to know how to deal with them."

"I know all that, Brian, but this one just got on the wrong side of me. I had to put her in her place. She was just too much. Can you believe she had the nerve to tell me off because she had to wait half an hour? It's Friday, for God's sake. Who the hell doesn't have to wait a little while for their food?" Her voice rose as she spoke. "I just felt like ripping that weave right off her head. That woman…"

"Alright, Summer, just calm down. You're going to run into lots more like her so just suck it up." Brian's firm voice silenced her. "We've got lots more people to feed. Now grab this tray and go get table three."

Summer grunted in frustration but turned to do Brian's bidding. At that moment Ted Jackson stepped through the door, his face stern. Summer's heart sank and she slowly put the tray back down on the counter.

"Miss Jones, what just happened out there?"

"I'm sorry, Mr. Jackson?" Summer stalled.

"Don't play dumb with me. You know what I'm talking about. You just insulted one of our patrons."

"I can explain…"

"There's nothing to explain. I saw everything. You were rude to our guests." He folded his arms across his chest and scowled at her. "Do you think I built my business that way? Obviously you have a serious temper problem but you'd better get it under control or else you won't be working here for long."

Summer's heart raced at the manager's last remark. It had taken her a while to find this job and she could not afford to lose it now. Damn her for her quick temper, she thought. It was always getting her in trouble.

"Mr. Jackson, I'm sorry. I just lost my cool for a minute but it won't happen again. I promise."

"You're sure that's a promise you can keep?" His voice was calmer now but his face did not soften.

"Definitely. I really need this job." Summer lowered her voice and tried to sound humble and subdued. "I'll make sure to keep my temper in control from now on."

"Good." The manager seemed convinced. "And you can start by going back to table seven and apologizing."

"What?" Summer's mouth fell open. She closed it quickly then started again. "What did you say?"

"You heard me. You either apologize or you no longer have a job here. You insulted some very important people - regulars at this establishment, big spenders. That table has been reserved every Friday for the past five weeks for Lance Munroe and his group and I'm not about to lose that business."

At her questioning look he continued. "He's not just any customer, Miss Jones. He's one of Chicago's most successful record producers. And, as luck would have it, he arrived just in time to witness your deplorable behavior." He shook his head. There was a pained expression on his face. "And the woman you insulted, don't you know who she is?"

Summer shook her head in bewilderment.

"That's Monisha Stone. What rock do you live under? Who in Chicago doesn't know Monisha Stone? She's the newest R&B singer from this city."

"I...I haven't had much time to keep up." She heard a snigger behind her and knew Jason and Clem were enjoying every minute of the episode.

"I can see that. But anyway," Mr. Jackson turned away and headed back through the swinging doors, "you know what you have to do. Get on with it, please."

He left Summer standing, silent and fuming, in the doorway.

"Summer." Brian's voice brought her back to the present and she turned towards him.

"Yeah?"

"You okay?"

She sighed then smiled wryly. "Yeah, I'm okay. Just not looking forward to humiliating myself."

"Don't worry about it." The big man put a hand on her shoulder and squeezed. "Just do it, get it over with, and move on. You want to keep this job, right?"

"You know I do." She sighed again. "Alright, I'll do it. But I hope to God I never set eyes on that woman again as long as I live."

As she turned to go Brian stopped her. "Hey, Summer."

"Yes?"

"You were joking when you said you didn't know who Monisha Stone was, right?"

"No, I wasn't. Who says I have to know every singer in this city? Knowing them won't put money in my pocket."

Shaking his head, Brian grinned then turned back to the chicken on his chopping board. "Girl, you need a life."

She shook a playful fist at him then flounced through the door.

The apology came hard for Summer. She felt she would choke on every word. As she spoke she stared at a spot above the woman's head, refusing to make eye contact with her tormentor. She held her body rigid and inside she was seething, but she kept her voice calm and steady and forced herself to speak until she had exhausted the words she had quickly rehearsed.

When it was finally over she looked down and found herself staring straight into the amused dark eyes of Lance Munroe.

A slight smile softened his firm lips and as he lounged in his chair, watching her through half closed eyes, she had the distinct impression that he was laughing at her.

She felt hot blood rise to her face and she bit hard on her lower lip and clenched her fist at her side. After seeing the way he was looking at her she felt angrier, even more than when she'd been in the middle of her apology to the woman who now sat staring at her, smiling smugly.

Totally ignoring the woman and the two men who sat on either side of her, Summer focused her glare on the man in the shadows.

"Do you find this funny?" she demanded, her heart pounding hard in her chest.

The man's lips parted in a slow smile and he drawled, "As a matter of fact, I do."

Something about the way he spoke the words made Summer catch her breath. Strangely, her anger suddenly dissipated and her raging emotions were replaced by a feeling of confusion then anticipation. She'd been so ready to blast him with words that would have shriveled any man. Instead, she was as tongue-tied and breathless as a school girl, and all because of six simple words the man had spoken.

No, not six simple words - six huskily and softly spoken words that had stopped her dead in her tracks; six words expressed in a strangely melodious voice that sent tingles up her spine. What in heaven's name was happening to her?

She opened her mouth to speak but, finding herself totally at a loss for words, she snapped it shut and scowled at the smiling man. Without another word she turned and stalked off.

Chapter 2

"But Mom, it wasn't my fault."

"Summer, remember it's your mother you're talking to. I know you better than you know yourself, child. I'm sure you wouldn't have found yourself in that position if you'd kept your temper in check."

"But I was real calm, Mom," Summer said earnestly.

"Really?" The older woman seemed unconvinced.

"Well, okay, my control slipped, but just once. I just couldn't stand there and let that woman talk to me that way - no matter who she is!" Summer pouted, wishing her mother would just accept that she wasn't at fault.

"Child, I know you were upset but there are times when you just have to swallow your pride and err on the side of peace."

"Mom, I'm not like you." Summer frowned. "I'm not the 'turn the other cheek' type. I just can't let people walk all over me."

"Hush, child. It's got nothing to do with people walking all over you. Of course there are situations where you have to defend yourself but you have to make that decision with a mind that's under control, not one that's red hot with temper." She wagged her finger under Summer's nose. "You'd better keep that temper of yours in check or else it's going to get you into some serious trouble one day."

Summer smiled wryly. "I'm already there."

Her mother smiled back. "No, not yet. This was just a warning. Now take heed and change your attitude, young lady."

"I'll try," Summer said in a subdued tone, then grinned mischievously at her mother.

"Naughty girl," she laughed and pinched Summer's cheek. "You're always pulling my leg. But you'll learn – one day."

Outside of a few distant cousins Edna Jones was the only family Summer had. Her father had long since passed away, the victim of liver disease which had resulted from years of alcohol abuse. That had been eleven years ago when she was only thirteen years old. But for Summer it had been eleven years of relief from the abuse that her father used to mete out to her mother whenever the alcohol turned him into the monster she had grown to fear.

Her mother had cried at the funeral but Summer hadn't shed a tear. She just stared at the stiff, lifeless body of the man who had raised her and thanked God for finally taking him. At thirteen she had already endured years of watching her mother suffer and she raged inside at her father's cruelty. She used to beg him to stop; she promised to be a perfect daughter to him if only he would stop hurting her mother. His expressions of shame and regret came easily and his promises were frequent. But he never stopped.

Then her fear of him turned to hatred. She stopped pleading with him and instead, became cold and silent in his presence, her eyes the only part of her that spoke. One day she would kill him, she thought. From early on she had lost her child's innocence to an adult awareness of suffering and pain and a woman's consciousness of the latent power of a man to control the mind as well as the body.

Never, she resolved then, would she love a man so much that she could not walk away from him. No man would ever have the power over her that her father had had over her mother all those years. For her there could be no love so great that she could not tell a man to get the hell out of her life.

"Summer, did you hear me?"

"Yes, Mom?" Summer blinked, her mother's voice suddenly bringing her back to the present.

"I was asking you about your thesis. How is it coming along?"

"Oh, sorry, Mom. I was a million miles away."

"I could see that."

"It's been rough going because I have so little time to dedicate to my research. You know, I took this waitress job because the hours were flexible and I thought it would've freed me up a lot," she shrugged, "but I guess my timing was off because the restaurant has been really busy. The manager even asked me to work extra hours a couple of times. That wasn't really in my plans when I took the job."

"But you said you wanted a part-time job so you could have enough time for your graduate studies." Edna looked confused. "So you're full-time now?"

"No, still part-time, but it's just that sometimes I'm called in to do extra hours and it really throws my study schedule off."

As she saw her mother's frown she quickly added, "Don't get me wrong. The extra money is always welcome. It's just that I don't want to lose focus now. I'm just one project away from my Master's and I can't afford to let anything slow me down."

"Of course you're right, dear." Her mother sighed then closed her eyes and leaned back on her pillow.

"Mom, are you alright?" Summer leaned forward and put a hand on her mother's brow. "Is the pain back?"

"No, not the pain. Just felt a little dizzy."

"Want me to get some smelling salts?" Summer roseto leave the room but her mother stopped her.

"No, dear. Just give me a moment." She breathed heavily. "I'll be alright in a second."

"Oh, Ma, why did this have to happen to you?" Summer's voice trembled as she spoke. "You've been through so much already!"

"Such is life, child. We just have to make the best of what life has to offer."

"But it's not fair."

"Nobody ever promised us that life would be fair, Summer." Edna patted her hand. "We've just got to take the blows, pick ourselves up and keep on going."

With tears in her eyes Summer hugged her mother's thin body and whispered, "You're so brave. I just don't know how you do it."

"I'm not brave, child, just practical."

"Oh, Mom."

Summer sat on the bed, put her arms around her mother's shoulders, and rocked her back and forth as she stared out the window.

They were on the fifteenth floor of the Serenity Nursing Home on Martin Luther King Drive and from that height she could see the afternoon sun reflected on the shimmering blue water of Lake Michigan.

This was Edna Jones' home and had been for the past six years, ever since she'd fallen ill. She'd been diagnosed with Multiple Sclerosis.

At first she had experienced only slight numbness in her left arm when she woke each morning. She hadn't worried too much about it at the time and had simply attributed it to the arthritis which plagued her from time to time. But the numbness spread to her left leg and then to her lower back and, giving in to her daughter's expressions of alarm, she went to the family doctor with her complaint. Tests were done but nothing conclusive was determined and after a while Edna became accustomed to the numbness and simply ignored it.

Then one morning she woke up to find that the muscles on the left side of her face had gone dead. She could neither blink her left eye nor wrinkle the left side of her forehead and when she spoke only the right side of her face moved. She was immediately placed in the care of a neurologist who put her through a battery of tests - a blood test, an electrocardiogram, Magnetic Resonance Imaging to check for lesions on the brain, and a sPiñal tap.

After two months of tests she was diagnosed with Multiple Sclerosis, a debilitating disease which could range from mild and merely annoying, to severe and crippling. To Edna's dismay and to her daughter's horror she was told that she had the severe form of the disease. She would gradually lose control of her muscles and would probably even lose her sight. She was also told there was no cure.

Always practical, the forty-nine year old woman prepaid her daughter's college tuition then checked herself into a nursing home. Summer had pleaded with her mother to let her nurse her back to health but Edna was determined that her daughter should achieve her dream of becoming a journalist. She convinced Summer to live on the Chicago University campus for all four years of college, studying during the school year and working during the summers. The only time she left campus was to visit her mother.

Now, six years later, Summer had completed her Bachelor's degree and was in her second year of the Master's Programme in Communication. This time she couldn't look to her mother for financial assistance so she funded her education through a partial tuition scholarship and a federal grant. She no longer lived on campus so, in addition to her studies, she had to find time for a part-time job that could cover the rent for her tiny studio apartment and the rest of her bills. She lived frugally and was just able to survive.

This didn't bother her. She'd never been into flashy clothes, jewellery or partying. She had goals in life and knew that the sacrifice she made now would allow her a more comfortable life in the future.

Her greatest concern right now was her mother. She wished there were something she could do to ease her suffering. Although the doctors were making no promises they had mentioned surgery as a possibility to stem her decline but that would cost a lot of money.

That evening Summer was uncharacteristically quiet at work. Normally upbeat, she felt like she had lost some of her spark. Brian noticed right away.

"Hey, girl. Got a lot on your mind?"

Summer gave him a weak smile.

"I'm okay, Brian. Just one of those days," she reassured him, trying to avoid too many questions.

She'd never been very expressive about her feelings and tended to keep personal problems to herself. Since childhood she'd had to work out her problems on her own and, no matter how friendly Brian was, she had no intention of sharing her pain with him.

The truth was, she was very worried about her mother's condition which seemed to be worsening. Edna had lost the use of her legs and had been confined to a wheelchair over two years ago. But now she was having pain in her eyes, too. She also complained of dark shadows that floated constantly across her vision. Summer feared that these were signs of the onset of blindness.

"Sure you're okay?" Brian's voice broke into her thoughts.

"I'm sure," she nodded. Then with a smile she demanded, "Now where's that tray for table five?"

Summer busied herself with serving the meals. Gradually, her grey mood lifted a little and as she worked she smiled pleasantly with the guests. It was Monday so things were slow and she was even able to engage in light conversation with a few of them. She'd been on the job only a week and a half now, but already she had established relationships with some of the faithful ones who came to the restaurant practically every night.

She had just learned the name of a young couple she'd seen in the restaurant at least three times. They seemed so much in love that she couldn't help smiling at them whenever she served their table. Tonight they introduced themselves as Kevin and Carolyn Madison and explained that they'd gotten married just two weeks earlier and were still trying to get settled in their new apartment in Hyde Park.

"You've chosen a great place to live," Summer told them. "You're close to downtown and all the night life and since you're right by the lake you'll be able to go jogging or biking. Many young professionals live in Hyde Park - you'll make lots of friends."

"That's what we heard," Carolyn replied, "that's why we decided to live there. But also," she paused, then said shyly, "because the area has some of the best schools. We want to have lots of kids."

"Maybe not lots," Kevin smiled at his blushing wife and took her hand in his, "but at least three. We love kids."

"Aw, that's so sweet," Summer teased and they all three laughed good-naturedly.

The brief conversation with the Madisons put Summer in a slightly pensive mood. She normally considered herself a tough cookie, definitely not the emotional type. She didn't know if it was because they looked so blissfully happy together or because they seemed to be looking forward so much to having children. She only knew that when she turned away from their table, still smiling, her eyes were misty with unshed tears.

She brushed at them furtively, praying they hadn't noticed. God, she thought, they'd probably think I'm weird. These days nobody cried over young couples in love - what the hell was wrong with her?

She sniffed and, dragging her emotions back under control, lifted her head again. Her heart jerked violently as she stared into the piercing eyes of Lance Munroe.

Oh my God, she thought, had he been sitting there all this time? Had he seen her wipe her eyes? She prayed that in the subdued lighting of the restaurant he hadn't seen her brief display of emotion. God, she moaned inside, this was more embarrassing than having to apologize in front of him.

Their eyes were locked together for only a split second but to Summer it seemed like aeons. She dragged her gaze from his face and hurried back to the safety of the kitchen.

To Summer's dismay she was again assigned to table seven for the night. She had taken refuge in the kitchen at the sight of him but she couldn't hide from the man all night. She was normally anything but a wimp so she couldn't understand her sudden nervousness at the thought of serving him again. Come on, Summer, she chided, get a grip. She took a deep breath, straightened her back just the way her mother had taught her, and marched out to table seven.

"May I help you, sir?" Her voice was sugar-sweet as she held the pen to her order pad and waited.

"Hello, again."

His voice had the warm, rich smoothness of molasses. His dark gaze traveled slowly over her face, down the rest of her, then came back to rest on her now rigid mouth.

How dare he scrutinize me like this, she fumed inwardly. She felt she could almost taste the arrogance of the man.

"How're you doing tonight, little spitfire?" The rich bass of his voice was beautiful to her ears but the obvious amusement in his tone made the hair on her nape stand up.

She stood even straighter and fixed a cold stare on his dark face. "I'm very well, thank you, sir. May I take your order?"

To her surprise he laughed out loud, a deep, husky laugh that made her think of the low rumble of thunder in the distance. Unable to stop herself she thought, the man's voice is beautiful.

As she watched his face she had to admit that he was beautiful, too. His skin was dark as coffee and his white teeth glistened against his lips. His hair was cut low and faded at the sides - it seemed that it had been brushed long and hard until the natural waves shone black on his head. His broad forehead and thick brows shielded dark eyes fringed with thick lashes. His strong African nose flared over firm lips above which a thin, perfectly shaped moustache had been sculpted.

But, despite the attractive picture he posed, what really fascinated Summer was the deep dimple in his left cheek. It gave him a boyish, playful air which totally disarmed her. How could she stay angry with someone who looked so mischievous?

He leaned forward in his chair, a look of keen interest on his face, and asked, "What's your name?"

Caught off guard by his sudden question she blurted out, "Summer...Summer Jones."

"Summer Jones." The way he said her name made it sound strange, almost exotic.

"Lance Munroe." He extended his hand to her as he rose.

Summer stepped back involuntarily and stared up at the man, totally ignoring his outstretched hand. While he had been seated she hadn't noticed just how tall he was. Now, as he towered over her five feet four inch frame, she could see that he was well over six feet tall.

Suddenly realizing that he was still holding his hand out to her, she took it and immediately felt his latent power as he enveloped her hand in a firm grip. As he shook her hand he gave her a delicious, dimpled smile. "I'm pleased to meet you, Summer Jones."

She did not return the greeting but simply dropped her gaze to his chest and pulled her hand none too gently from his grip. "Aah...are you ready to place your order now?"

"Summer, Summer," he chided playfully, "so businesslike. You're the type who never gets distracted from her work, right?" He sat down again and looked up at her.

"I do my job." Her curt response was given with the intention of shutting him up. She was good at that. Many men had suffered from her sharp tongue and she was prepared to use it on this one, no matter how smooth and charming he thought he was. He was an arrogant one to think that he had succeeded in getting on her good side. It hadn't worked. She still remembered how embarrassed she'd been as he'd grinned at her that night. She would never let this man have the advantage over her again.

"Now," she said firmly, "are you ready to order, sir?"

"Fine," he smiled, "I can see you're not ready to be friends. I'll place my order now."

"Yes?" Her pen was poised over her order pad.

"For starters, bring me some of your natural fruit punch, but tell them to go easy on the bananas. I love my juice pulpy and rich but not too thick."

"Yes?" She did not take her eyes from the paper as she wrote.

"I'll have your Pepper Pot Soup, baked chicken, and collard greens with cornmeal dumplings. That's it, thanks."

"Will anyone else be joining you?" She stared pointedly at the empty chairs around the table for four.

"No, I'm alone."

"I see," she said, and wondered why her heart suddenly skipped a beat. Her strange reaction perturbed her and she frowned.

"Is something wrong?" He looked up at her curiously.

"No," she replied quickly, "nothing's wrong. I'll be back with some bread rolls in just a second."

She whirled quickly, almost bumping into a server whose tray was laden with drinks. Her breath caught in her throat but the man skillfully swerved to avoid her and, without pause, continued on his way. She breathed a sigh of relief that Lance hadn't had the pleasure of seeing her in yet another embarrassing situation.

When Summer returned with the soup he was peering at sheets of paper under the dim lights of the lamp overhead. As soon as he saw her he pushed the papers aside and leaned back in his chair, waiting on her to serve him. He looked so smug that she almost felt like a maiden in a harem serving her master his meal. She set the bowl down more sharply than she had intended and a little of it splashed over into the plate beneath it.

"Careful," he said, and shifted the soup plate slightly so that she could rest the basket of bread rolls beside it. As she pulled her hand away he picked up his spoon and took a sip of the soup.

"Yeah, mon, this is just how I like it." He closed his eyes, savouring the spicy broth.

Summer was about to leave but, on hearing his comment, paused and watched as he took a second sip. He was obviously enjoying the food immensely. She had intended to be cold and businesslike with this man but her curiosity got the better of her.

"Excuse me," she said, conscious that he was so focused on his soup that he hadn't noticed that she still stood there.

"Hmm?" He looked up then set the spoon down and dabbed at his mouth with a napkin.

"I'm sorry to disturb you, but…are you from one of the islands?"

"Islands?"

"I mean, the Caribbean. From the first time I heard you speak I noticed that you had an accent and then when you said 'yeah, mon' just now it made me think of how those Caribbean people talk."

"Those Caribbean people?" He raised one eyebrow, smiling.

"You know what I mean," she said, exasperated. She knew he was making fun of her description. "People from the islands like Jamaica, Barbados, Antigua?"

"Well, don't we know our geography," he chuckled and Summer didn't know if she should get angry or give in and laugh with him.

"For your information, I know those islands. I've been on a cruise."

"You've been on a cruise and that makes you an expert on the Caribbean, right?" He was grinning openly now.

"I didn't say that. I'm just trying to tell you that I'm familiar with how the people there talk. And anyway, my grandfather was an English teacher from Barbados so I have connections – well, sort of."

Summer smiled as she recalled her beloved Grand-Dad. "He always used to speak 'the Queen's English', as he called it, and was always correcting my grammar. Now I can't even speak Ebonics without feeling guilty."

She tilted her head and looked down at the man before her. "Now, are you going to tell me, or aren't you?

"Tell you what?"

"If you're from one of the islands!"

"Okay, okay," he laughed, "don't hit me over my head with your tray. You have a short fuse, you know that?"

She didn't answer, but put a hand on her hip and waited.

"Alright, since you're so curious, I'm a naturalized American and have been since I was thirteen years old. I've spent the last twenty years of my life living in Chicago's south side; South Holland, to be exact. However, as you guessed, I'm originally from the Caribbean."

"I knew it." She grinned, exultant. "Which island?"

"Jamaica."

"I could have guessed. It seems like everybody in Jamaica says 'yeah, mon'."

"I guess it would seem that way to tourists but Jamaicans don't even notice it. But anyway," he leaned forward again, obviously forgetting the soup which he had relished just a little while before, "now it's my turn."

"Your turn?"

"Yes. You know my name, where I grew up, my origin. Now it's my turn to learn a bit about you."

"Well, there's not that much to tell," she shrugged.

"Regardless, tell me about Summer Jones."

She had to think quickly; she didn't want to divulge too much of her personal life. "I'm a final year graduate student at Chicago University, just trying to hang in there till I can complete my Master's thesis, graduate and start on my career path."

"And what path is that?"

"For my Bachelor's Degree I did a double major in English and Journalism but right now I'm doing my Master's in Communication. I love anything to do with talking or communicating with people. I would love a job with a PR firm."

"Sounds like you made the right choice. You certainly have the talking part down pat."

Summer recognized the jibe but decided to ignore it. She realized that the man who sat before her was very perceptive and was reading her like a book. He already knew how to touch the buttons that would get her heated up and she couldn't afford to let him have such control over her. She would stay calm, she thought, and manipulate him instead.

"It's not only that I love communication in whatever form - verbal or written - but I also love interacting with people. That's why I decided to study communication. It gives me a chance to broaden my scope and my understanding of different cultures."

"I see." His look was enigmatic as he asked, "Now tell me - what does waitressing have to do with communication or even journalism? Could it be that you're secretly observing people interacting in a restaurant setting? Sounds like a probable subject for a thesis."

"No, I'm not observing people for my thesis. I'm simply trying to survive while I complete my studies. And what the heck is wrong with being a server, anyway?"

"Hey, calm down. Don't get so sensitive." He put his hands up as if to defend himself from her ire. "I never said there was anything wrong with it. I simply asked your real purpose here because, if I were a Communications Major, I would've looked for a job that could enhance my knowledge of the subject in some kind of way, say, working with a newspaper or a PR company or even with a non-profit organization."

"Yeah, and you think it's so easy to get part-time jobs in those organizations? Well, it's not. I've been all over Chicago trying to get myself a job like that. And where did I end up? Right here in this restaurant. Nobody wants to hire someone without experience, not even for a part-time position. I tried, but it didn't work. So here I am - Waitress Summer Jones and proud of it. I'm making an honest day's pay for an honest day's work and damned if I'm going to let you make me feel ashamed of it!"

"Damn," he whispered, "you are one hot chili pepper, d'you know that? It doesn't take much to tick you off."

"I'm sorry," she muttered quickly, realizing she had fallen into the very trap she had been trying so hard to avoid. "I was rude and I'm sorry."

"That's okay. You have the right to speak your mind. But it seems to me that you're very sensitive about your job without even realizing it. Do you enjoy working here?"

"Yes, of course," she answered quickly, caught off guard by his question. Then she said more calmly, "Well, actually, I'm not enjoying it too much because it doesn't challenge me. The only good thing about it is that I get to meet lots of people although I don't get a chance to talk to them much," she paused, feeling slightly embarrassed, "except for now, of course." Then she added quickly, "Because it's slow today."

"Well, Miss Summer, let me just say one thing. I think your talents are being wasted here. It would be one thing if you were here for a purpose, such as conducting research for your thesis, but I think it can only do you good to be working in an environment that can provide you with experience in your area of interest. It may help you submit a great thesis. Do you know what I mean?"

"Yes, I do, but where am I going to find a job like that?" she asked, exasperated. "It's not that I haven't been looking. But in the meanwhile I have bills to pay."

"Here." Lance dug into his pocket and pulled out a thick, leather wallet. He pulled a black and gold card from it and handed it to her. "Take my card. I have a project coming up and a Communications Major would be ideal for the job."

Take it," he prodded as she hesitated. "It's not going to bite you."

She took the card and, without looking at it, folded it into her palm.

"You have my number," he said "so if you're interested we'll do an interview and you can get the details on the project while I get more information about you and whether you suit my needs."

"I don't think this would be right for me," she began, but he cut her off.

"You're not being forced to do anything you don't want to. Just keep the card. You may get tired of all this," he waved his hand at the people in the restaurant, "and want to try something new."

When Summer just stood there, her tray in one hand and the card in the other, he looked down at his soup then back at her. "I don't mean to be rude but I think I'd better get back to my soup now."

He dipped his head and slurped a spoonful of the soup that she was sure had grown cold. Serves him right, she thought ungraciously as she flounced away, still gripping the card tightly in her hand.

Chapter 3

"What do you mean, thirty days? I can't find a place in thirty days!" Summer's voice was sharp with frustration.

" 'Course you can." The landlord's face was impassive. "There are lots of places in Chicago and if you don't want to stay in the city there's always the suburbs."

"Yes, but those rates are going to be way more than I can afford. I won't be able to find another studio apartment like this, Mr. Williams. That's why I jumped at this one when you offered." Summer rubbed her forehead to ease the tension. She couldn't deal with a headache just now.

"You know you got a really special price because of my sister-in-law," the plump man shrugged, "because you'd helped her out so much that time when she was sick. That wasn't the real price on this apartment, you know."

"I know that and I appreciate it. But can't you see your way just to extend my lease?" She knew she sounded desperate but she didn't care. "I'll be graduating in just a few months and then I'll be able to get a good job and pay you more."

"No, no," he shook his head insistently and his jowls trembled with each shake, "this has nothing to do with you or the money. I gave you a good price, didn't I? I'm a fair man - I keep my word. But I told you, my daughter is coming back to Chicago and needs the place."

"But - so soon?"

"Yes. She just graduated last week and decided she wants to start job hunting right away. I can only give you thirty days past the lease and even that's pushing it. She and her stepmother don't get along at all." He rubbed his brow and muttered, "My life is going to be a living hell as long as those two are under the same roof."

"But, Mr. Williams…"

"No, don't say anything else." He put his hands up to stop her and the eyes behind the thick glasses were resolute. "It's done, so just start looking for somewhere else. I'll give you a great recommendation but I just need you outta here by the second week of August."

After James Williams left Summer went and sat down heavily on her bed. She looked around the small studio apartment which had been her home for the past two years. The place was small but comfortable. Outside of her bed and chest of drawers the only other pieces of furniture in the room were a small oak table on which a computer sat, a four-shelf book case and a small sofa. An eating counter with two bar stools separated the bedroom from the tiny kitchen. An abstract painting adorned the wall above the television set and a standing lamp illuminated the corner by the window. The apartment was neat except for the papers which were strewn all over the kitchen counter. A heavy dictionary sat on top of the pile of papers.

Well, so much for working on her thesis this evening, she thought. After her conversation with Mr. Williams she would never be able to concentrate on schoolwork. She might as well just pack up her papers for the night.

With a sigh she rose slowly, went to the counter and gathered the papers into one stack. After placing the dictionary on top of them she went over to the closet and pulled out a pair of khaki Capri pants and a white cotton shirt. She pulled white strap sandals from a cardboard box and grabbed a white baseball cap. She felt she couldn't stay inside the apartment one more minute. She dressed quickly, grabbed her purse, and headed for the elevator.

The soft breeze from the lake was just what Summer needed to clear her aching head. She sat on a low wall and watched people jogging, rollerblading and cycling by. Others walked along the path, some of them briskly for the exercise, while others simply strolled, enjoying the warm summer evening.

She enjoyed watching the couples, young and old as they walked hand in hand, sometimes pausing for an embrace or a kiss. As a child she would often wish that her own parents had shared such a loving relationship but all she had ever seen them do was fight. No matter how hard she tried she could not recall any occasion on which she had seen them embrace or even exchange loving words.

Eventually Summer had grown to accept the relationship that her parents had - one in which her father clearly dominated his wife who, despite his abuse of her, loved him immensely. Pleading with her mother to reject the tyrant was useless. She felt it was her duty to stay by his side.

Summer, on the other hand, had grown farther and farther away from the parent she had adored as a young child. She felt that her father had betrayed her and had trampled the love she'd had for him. She felt she could never trust another man with her love and resigned herself to the fact that she may never be one of those couples walking hand in hand along the shore of the lake. Beautiful to see, she thought, but definitely not for me.

She turned her back on the people along the shore and stared instead at the wide blue lake. She didn't know what mysteries lay in the depths but its surface was placid and beautiful. Sometimes the lake reminded her of herself. None of her college mates, none of the few people she considered friends, had ever guessed the turmoil that lay beneath her composed demeanour. She'd always stayed in control of her emotions except when her fiery temper had gotten the better of her. She was grateful for the way she was - practical, unemotional, and tough.

By the time she got back to her apartment building it was almost eight o'clock. The days were long in the summertime and darkness was just beginning to fall. She was heading for the elevator when she remembered that she hadn't checked her mail for the past three days. She went back around the corner to the mail room and retrieved a handful of envelopes and papers. She guessed it was all junk mail, as usual.

When she got to the apartment she threw herself down on the sofa and went through the stack. As she flipped through she tossed them one by one in a pile on the floor: life insurance solicitation - junk, credit card solicitation - junk, membership to local gym - junk, sale flyer from Furniture Land - junk.

But the next one was not junk. It was from Chicago University. Strange, she thought. She'd received all her registration materials already and was not expecting anything else. She quickly opened the brown envelope and read, 'Dear Ms. Jones: We regret to advise that you will not be allowed to submit a graduate thesis to the board until you have cleared the outstanding balance of five thousand two hundred and fifty dollars in tuition fees.'

Summer felt her heart jerk and her mouth fell open in disbelief. Thinking that she must have misread she went over the sentence again, slowly. No, she'd read it right the first time. But there must be some mistake, she thought. How could she have an outstanding balance on her tuition? All that should have been covered by her scholarship and federal grant.

She got up from the sofa, walked over to the open window and stared out with unseeing eyes. This couldn't be happening to her, not now. She was being kicked out of her apartment and would be faced with a significant increase in rent; her mother's condition seemed to be worsening and might even require expensive surgery; and now this.

With a shake of her head she reigned in her turbulent thoughts and decided to go to the university first thing in the morning. There had to be an explanation for this.

"That's what I pay you for, Derrick, to get the job done. Now, do it." Lance's voice was stern as he spoke into the telephone. He lounged, shirtless, in the plush leather sofa. He shifted his lean body to hang long legs over the arm of the chair. "No more excuses, Derrick. It's been almost three months. Don't call me until you have good news."

When he'd hung up he covered his face with a long-fingered hand and groaned. What misery to be saddled with incompetent employees, he thought. Derrick Dunn was a somewhat shiftless cousin whom he was trying to assist by providing honest employment. He had promised his aunt that he'd keep him under his wing and out of trouble. The twenty-nine year old had already gotten in trouble with the law and Lance knew that another such occurrence would kill her.

He'd been looking out for the younger man since he was twelve and Derrick was eight. Sometimes he got tired of playing rescuer but no matter how many times he'd had to save Derrick's skin he knew he would always be there for him. Family meant too much to him for him to abandon one of his own.

Lance rose and drew the blinds back from the large bay window. He blinked at the bright sunlight that streamed in. Although it was only seven-thirty the sun was already hot on his skin. He stood there for a moment enjoying the heat as it baked his chest while he stared down from the forty-third floor at Lake Michigan below.

He had a lot to do today but he was not in the mood to hit the road early. It had been a long night in the studio - he hadn't left until two in the morning and was still a bit tired. There was no way he was going to leave the apartment before ten o'clock - he felt like taking it easy.

He turned and strolled leisurely across the spacious living room and pushed the swinging doors that led to the kitchen. A cup of strong Blue Mountain Coffee would do the trick, he thought. He switched on the percolator and munched on a granola bar as he waited. A short while later he went back into the living room, mug in hand, and switched on the state-of-the-art stereo.

The rhythmic beat of Freddie McGregor's Reggae hit, "Just Don't Want to be Lonely," filled the room as Lance leaned back, rested his feet on the hassock and sipped hot black coffee.

The smell of the Jamaican coffee took his mind back to the tiny village of Porters Mountain where his grandmother used to grind the home-grown beans and boil the strongest coffee he'd ever had. She would grate a little nutmeg into the brew which gave it a distinctive spicy flavor he never forgot.

The thought of the spice brought back the memory of the feisty young woman who, twice, had waited on his table. He remembered how her curly hair had sprung, reddish brown and wild, from under her hat. High cheekbones accentuated her heart-shaped face and a mole by the side of her mouth drew attention to the full lips she kept in a tight line when she was angry. But it was her eyes that fascinated him most - she had big, dark-brown eyes fringed with luxuriously long eyelashes, eyes that flashed like flames when she got angry.

A slight smile softened his lips as he remembered the first time he'd seen her. He hadn't paid much attention to the slim, caramel-skinned girl who had come to the table bearing the tray of delicious dishes. His interest was sparked, however, when he saw how she met Monisha's glare with an equally bold stare, and when she stood up to the singer and spoke her mind he'd felt real admiration for her fearlessness.

He'd gone back to the restaurant out of sheer curiosity, wondering if she were always so fiesty or if she'd been putting on a show for him. Women had been known to do worse; they found all kind of ways to throw themselves at him.

He had become famous five years ago when he got his big break with Patricia Lee's album and ever since then he'd been the target of female fans. He tried to keep a low profile and, for the most part, had succeeded. He was grateful he wasn't a recording artiste so his face didn't appear on CD's or in videos.

As a record producer people knew his name more than they did his face but once they realized who he was the women would go to great lengths to attract his attention.

Somehow he knew this woman was different. Whether she'd known who he was or not, he had no idea. He felt confident, though, that even if she had, it would not have mattered. It was clear that she was used to speaking her mind and would not be intimidated by anyone.

He smiled and shook his head as he took another sip of the coffee. The girl was something else, he thought, recalling how she had practically told him off the last time they met. He licked his lips slowly as he thought about her. He was looking forward to meeting this woman again.

Summer stared back at the administrator in disbelief, "So why didn't anyone explain this to me?" Her voice trembled with anger. "At least I would've been prepared."

"Ms. Jones," the woman's voice was calm and cool, "when you got the scholarship you were advised that it would cover tuition for eighteen consecutive months of study. It's not the fault of the board that it's taken you longer than that to complete your studies."

"But I had to take a leave of absence because my mother was sick."

"I understand that, but in doing so you forfeited three months of scholarship money. Now that the eighteen months have passed you'll need to pay tuition for this semester."

"But I don't have the money!"

"I'm sorry, Ms. Jones, but you won't be able to register until the payment is made." The grey-haired woman turned back to her computer and began to tap furiously, as if demonstrating that she was extremely busy and should not be disturbed.

Summer closed her eyes for a quick moment and willed herself to stay calm. If she didn't maintain control she was going to give this woman a piece of her mind and then it would be all over. She clenched her fists, opened her eyes, and spoke through gritted teeth.

"I'd like to speak directly to the registrar about this."

The woman looked annoyed and said, "I don't see how that would help. She is not going to tell you anything different from what I'm telling you now."

"I said I would like to see the registrar." The pitch of Summer's voice was beginning to rise and the older woman looked startled, then rose with a humph.

"Just a moment," she said, annoyance plain on her face.

She turned away, went over to a desk in the far corner of her work area and picked up the telephone. She spoke in hushed tones as Summer watched then returned to the counter and said, "Mrs. Houstetter will see you in a few minutes. Please have a seat." She pointed to a row of chairs against the wall.

"Thank you." Summer nodded, none too pleased with the woman's impersonal manner but grateful that she would be able to plead her case at a higher level.

When she walked into Mrs. Houstetter's office she saw immediately that this was a personable woman. Paintings of garden scenes lined the walls and pictures of family members were on the shelves just above her desk. The small, white-haired woman rose upon her entry and came forward to greet her with a smile.

"Ms. Jones, how are you?" The woman extended a small hand and Summer shook it, feeling like a giant as she towered over the woman who could not have been more than four and a half feet tall. She was surprised at the warm reception and, despite her feelings of frustration, smiled back at the registrar.

"I...I'm fine, thank you."

"Please, have a seat." She was ushered to a chair across from a magnificent oak desk.

"Thank you," Summer murmured as she sank into the deep leather chair and placed her purse on her lap. She gripped the handle tightly, calmed by the pleasantries, but still very aware of her uncertain position.

"Now, Ms. Jones, I understand that you have a problem with registration for this semester?"

Mrs. Houstetter looked at her across the wide desk. Her large spectacles and pointy nose made her look like a wise little owl.

"Yes, and I hope you can help me."

Summer was surprised at how breathless she sounded. She was normally bold and outspoken but this time she had so much at stake. She was so close to her Master's Degree that she couldn't let anything stand in the way of the achievement of her goal.

By the time Summer finished her meeting with Mrs. Houstetter she was convinced that luck was on her side. The registrar had listened to her predicament with what seemed like sincere sympathy and, after further discussion, had agreed for Summer to pay her final semester's tuition fee by installment. She made it clear to Summer that this was not the norm - the standard was for full payment to be made prior to registration for any classes. However, in this case, an exception would be made in light of the unfortunate misunderstanding with the terms of the scholarship. Summer would be allowed to register right away but would be required to make payments at the end of each month for the next five months, with the understanding that all outstanding balances should be cleared prior to graduation which was six months away.

While on the train Summer took stock of her situation. By the time she got home she was depressed all over again. She flung herself down on the bed and stared up at the ceiling. She had twenty-seven days to go and then she'd be out on the street unless she could find a way to earn more money. On top of that, she would have to find an extra thousand dollars each month to make the payments on her tuition. As for her mother's surgery she just prayed Medicaid would cover the cost in full.

Suddenly her mind flashed back to the conversation she'd had three days earlier with Lance Munroe. The man was arrogant and his mocking tone annoyed the heck out of her but he had mentioned a job opportunity and, although the very thought of humbling herself to ask him for a job galled her, she was now in a desperate situation and might have to take him up on the offer. Her pride could neither feed her nor pay the rent.

She jumped off the bed and went to get her purse. Now that she'd made up her mind to do it she was overwhelmed with curiosity at what the job entailed. Right now she would do just about anything as long as it paid her double what she was getting. She decided to call him right away.

Summer had been rummaging through her purse for a full three minutes before she accepted the fact that she'd lost the man's business card. She flopped down onto the sofa. A deep frown creased her brow. Now where in heaven's name could she have put the thing, she wondered. She remembered taking it from him and walking back to the kitchen with it still in her hand. She could have sworn that she'd gone straight to her locker and put it in her purse. Or had she put it in the pocket of her uniform?

She racked her brain, not understanding why she found it so hard to remember a simple thing like that. Maybe she had a mental block concerning anything to do with this man? No, she thought, he was annoying and arrogant but he was not so bad that she would have to block him out of her mind.

On the contrary, there were some things about him that she found very pleasant to recall - the way his lips spread slowly in a smile she could only describe as seductive, the way his eyes moved deliberately over her face as if to caress every inch of it, the way his deep voice made her shiver inside.

She sat up with sudden realization. She was attracted to this man - yes, she, Summer Jones, committed bachelorette and career student who never had time to waste on men and relationships.

She'd finally met a man who peaked her curiosity and stimulated her emotions so much that she was actually looking forward to seeing him again. But of all the men in the world, why would she be attracted to the one who got on her nerves? Well, it didn't matter anyway, she thought, because she'd never let him know how she felt. She would never be so stupid as to give him one more thing to mock her about. She'd just let this thing die a natural death.

Chapter 4

Next evening Summer arrived at work thirty minutes early and ensured that table seven was among those to which she was assigned for the night. She wanted to speak to Lance Munroe about the job and she now knew that this was his regular table. She watched as diners came and went but he never showed up. She was very disappointed when closing time came without any sign of Lance.

"You okay, Summer?" As usual, it was Brian who noticed that something was wrong with her. "You've been on edge all evening and you don't look too good."

Summer's defences immediately went up. She fought between her need for privacy and a sudden desire to express her distress at her worsening predicament. She hesitated as she looked up at the big man who stood ready to go through the door.

"Alright, I know I'm a nosy son of a gun," he said, "but you look like you could do with someone to talk to right now. What say we go have a drink and you can tell me all about it?"

"I...it's nothing, Brian. I just need to go home and get some rest."

"Don't give me that, Summer." It was the first time she'd seen him look so serious. "I've worked with you almost every day for almost two weeks and I've never seen you like this. I know you're a tough cookie but, come on, you're human."

"Well..." Summer was still hesitant, then she said, "Alright. I could do with a friend right now."

"You have one right here. It's only ten fifteen. Let's go over to the Brass Turkey. We can talk over a drink."

Summer nodded wordlessly, collected her purse and followed him out the door.

Brian was a good listener and Summer found herself sharing her anxiety at her precarious position. She even told him about the possible job offer with Lance Munroe and her disappointment at having lost his card and then not seeing him at the restaurant that night.

"I'm getting really desperate, Brian. I've never been in a situation like this before." She didn't realize she was nibbling a fingernail until he pulled her hand away from her mouth.

"Hey, calm down." He covered her hand with his big one. "I might just be able to help you."

"But…how?"

"My cousin, Tina, works in the building where Lance lives. He's in the Water Tower building downtown. She told me she ran into him in the elevator once…"

"Yes, yes," Summer cut him off, "but how can she help me? Can she tell me which apartment he's in?"

"'Course she can. All she has to do is check the register of residents and then…"

"Can she get me his phone number?"

"I'm sure of it. I'll talk to her first thing tomorrow."

"Thanks, Brian. You're a life saver." She breathed a sigh of relief. "I just need to get in touch with him real fast. I need that job like yesterday."

"I know, honey." Brian smiled then looked at her gravely. "I'm gonna miss you."

"But you've only known me ten days."

"I know, but now I'm so used to having you around. You spice up the place. If you leave it's going to get all boring again."

"Oh, Brian," she soothed, "we'll still be friends."

"Yeah, right," he said sarcastically then they both laughed.

Next day Brian was true to his word. She had the telephone number by two o'clock that afternoon. She paced up and down nervously, trying to work up the courage to make the call. Finally, she sat on the edge of the sofa, picked up the phone and dialed.

He was not home. As the voice recording chipped in she thought desperately, 'What am I going to say? He doesn't even know me. He's going to be so pissed'. Then at the sound of the beep she said calmly, "Mr. Munroe, this is Summer Jones who you met at The Southern Belle. I'd like to know more about the position you mentioned. Could you give me a call as soon as possible?

She left her phone number and then hung up and sat staring at the clock on the wall. Well, she thought, she'd done it. She had asked Lance Munroe for the job. And she had called his home number. She knew he'd be wondering how she had managed to get it but she would never tell, even if it meant losing her chance at the job. She would never let Brian get in trouble because of her.

Next time she looked up at the clock it was two-thirty. She'd been sitting there, daydreaming, for the past half hour. She jumped up and headed for the bathroom. Her mother had a three-thirty appointment with the ophthalmologist and, if she didn't hurry, she'd be late for it.

The doctor's office was painted dusky green and there were plants all around the spacious reception area. A huge fish tank stood against the far wall and the other walls were covered with paintings of river scenes. The coffee table in the middle of the room was green marble streaked with white. Clearly, the decorator had used nature as the theme. Summer had no objection - it made her feel peaceful. Right now she could do with some calm to steady her jangling nerves.

She pushed her mother's wheelchair close to the fish tank and sat down beside her. "You feeling okay, Mom?"

"As well as can be expected." Her mother smiled back and patted her hand. "Now stop worrying your head about me. Whatever will be will be. No amount of worrying can change things."

"I'm your daughter. I'm supposed to worry about you."

"Well, since you put it that way, go ahead and worry. But just a little bit, okay? You have so much more to think about right now - like finishing up your studies. How's that going, anyway?"

"Oh, it's going alright," she said vaguely. "Once I finish the thesis then the only thing left for me will be graduation."

"I'm looking forward to that day." Pride gleamed in her mother's eyes and Summer turned away, pretending great interest in a magazine she'd picked up from a chair nearby.

Summer hadn't told her mother about the problems she was having with her apartment and her tuition fees. She felt that Edna had so much on her plate already that she didn't want to burden her with her own problems. As far as her mother knew she was busy with her studies and her job at The Southern Belle, and that was all. Summer was satisfied to keep her thinking that way - even if she ended up on the streets she would never add to her mother's stress.

Soon it was Edna Jones' turn to go in to see the doctor. Summer wheeled her in and sat quietly as the doctor shone lights into her mother's eyes and had her read letters from a chart. Dr. Ogobo was one of the most respected ophthalmologists in Chicago. He'd been with the Chicago City Hospital for over ten years and had made a name for himself with what was dubbed as 'Miracle Surgery'. He had actually returned sight to four patients who had each been blind for years. Summer had the confidence that if anyone could help her mother's failing eyesight it was Dr. Ogobo.

"Ms. Jones," the doctor's heavily accented voice cut through her thoughts, "your mother has a condition called ocular degeneration which is often seen in severe cases of Multiple Sclerosis. What this means is that if surgery is not done the optic nerves will deteriorate until she loses her sight."

The doctor was blunt and matter of fact and, as Summer gripped the back of her mother's chair, she wondered if she had made the right choice for her mother. Then she realized what the doctor was doing. He was giving her all the facts, painful as they may be, so that she could make the best decision for her sick mother. In not softening the blow he was forcing her to be practical.

"How much time do we have, doctor?" she asked weakly, as her hand rested gently on her mother's shoulder.

"Without surgery, anywhere from six to twelve months." The doctor looked at her gravely. "I would recommend that you have your mother evaluated for surgery and then make arrangements for the procedure."

"But are there any risks?" Summer tried to keep her voice steady, not wanting to upset her mother, but the words came out with a slight tremble.

"With surgery there are always risks," the doctor replied. "In your mother's case the risks are even greater because of her weakened condition. Outside of the risk to her life there's also the danger of the surgery failing and her losing sight completely."

Summer drew in her breath sharply but remained silent.

The doctor continued, "But without the surgery she'll probably lose her sight anyway, maybe as early as six months from now."

"Excuse me."

Both Dr. Ogobo and Summer jumped when Edna spoke.

"If y'all are finished talking about me as if I'm not here, I'd like to say something, please."

"I'm sorry, Mrs. Jones." The doctor smiled apologetically. "Please, go ahead."

Thank you." Edna's voice was quiet but firm. "I realize how risky it is for me to do surgery in my condition but it's either that or live the rest of my life in darkness." She looked up at her daughter. "Right now I'm more concerned about the quality of my life than the length of it. With my condition, life is uncertain anyway. I want to do the surgery."

Without a word Summer nodded. She was afraid of putting her mother's life at risk but she would never deny her this only hope.

"We'll do it, doctor." She now spoke firmly, decisively.

Doctor Ogobo nodded then sat down to take them through the details of the procedure.

By the time Summer returned to work two days later she was an emotional wreck. She was trying to come to terms with the fact that, even with surgery, there were no guarantees for the preservation of her mother's eyesight. What made it worse, surgery was actually going to put her mother's life at risk. Then she found out that Medicaid only covered half the cost of the procedure.

On top of all that, things were getting desperate for Summer. A week had passed since her landlord had given her notice and, even with a real estate agent helping her, she hadn't been able to find a reasonably priced apartment. As for her tuition fee, the first installment was due in three weeks and she still had no clue where she was going to get the money.

She'd waited anxiously for the past three days but Lance never returned her call. She threw her purse into the locker and slammed the door shut. Regardless of her desperation she was so angry that she felt that if she saw him right this minute she'd let him have it.

But he never came. Summer was on edge all night, seething because he'd totally ignored her call but desperately anxious for him to show. The combination of her distracted state coupled with her naturally saucy temperament proved to be a volatile combination.

"Waitress!" The shrill voice pulled her from her thoughts and brought her back to the reality of the restaurant and her duties at hand. She hurried over to a table where two elderly women sat.

She addressed the one who had spoken. "Yes, Ma'am, may I help you?"

"This soup is cold." The grey-haired woman pushed the bowl towards her. "I'm not paying for cold soup."

"Yes, ma'am, I realize it's now cold, but when I brought it to you over half an hour ago it was piping hot." Summer turned to her with a well-practised smile and waited patiently for her response.

It came quickly. The woman was abrupt. "Don't give me any backchat. The soup is cold and I don't want it. Take it away."

The other woman, obviously embarrassed, kept her eyes on her own bowl which was empty.

"And did you enjoy your soup, ma'am?" She jumped as Summer suddenly directed the question to her.

"Yes, thank you. Very much." She spoke with obvious sincerity.

"And yet you didn't touch yours, ma'am?" She turned her attention back to the frowning woman. "Was there a problem with it?"

The woman straightened her back and pursed her lips. "That is of no importance. It is sufficient to say that it does not suit me and I wish to have it removed."

"And why doesn't it suit you, ma'am? You ordered it." The bright smile that Summer pasted on her face masked her irritation.

"What insolence!" The woman's voice rose sharply. "I said take it away, and that is what you should do. I owe you no explanation."

"Very well, ma'am." Summer picked up both bowls and was about to head back to the kitchen when the woman stopped her.

"Aren't you going to take my order for a replacement?"

"A replacement?" Summer echoed as if confused. "But there was nothing wrong with the soup. I imagine what happened was, you were so busy talking that you allowed your soup to get cold. You do realize that if you order a second serving you will be charged for both orders?" Her tone remained pleasant but there was an underlying tone of steel in her voice. If this woman thought she was going to bully her, she thought, she had another think coming.

"How dare you?" The woman's voice rose and the people at the neighbouring table turned to stare at the scene. "I've been eating at this restaurant for years and never have I been treated so disrespectfully. I have a great mind to speak to the manager about this."

Summer's voice was low but firm. "It's your right to do that, ma'am. His office is the second door on the left." She indicated the direction with a nod then continued on her way to the kitchen.

Now I've done it, Summer thought. But in the end, she realized, she didn't care. Everything had gone wrong for her and she was at the end of her rope. Could things get worse?

Apparently, they could. Summer was heading back through the door with another tray when she heard Mr. Williams calling her name. With a heavy sigh she set the tray back down and headed for the office.

She pushed the door and entered. Mr. Williams was standing by his desk with his back to the window and a dark scowl on his face.

"I've just received a complaint about you, Ms. Jones." His voice was cold and unusually soft.

"What sort of complaint?"

"I think you know. Unless you've had more than one altercation this evening?"

Summer stared at him, unwavering, and said, "I don't know what you were told, sir, but I was just doing my job."

"I was told by a patron that you were rude to her, that you refused to replace her soup."

"And did she tell you why she wanted that soup replaced?" Summer's voice was strong in her own defence. "No, I didn't think she did. She sat talking until her soup got cold then she demanded that I replace it - for free. I simply advised the lady that she would be charged for both orders of soup."

"She said you were rude to her," he repeated as if he hadn't heard her explanation at all.

"If providing a customer with information about her bill is being rude, then I was. But that's all I did. And anyway," Summer frowned at her employer, "I would have thought that you'd appreciate my trying to prevent a customer from taking advantage of your restaurant. Suppose everybody were to do that? All the profits would be eaten up in free meals."

"I appreciate your concern, Miss Jones, but that's what I'm here for. There are certain things that you should refer to the manager and this was one of them."

"But I simply told her…"

"I know what you told her. Now what I am saying is that, in future, I want you to refer all such situations to me. Let me be the one to make such decisions." His tone softened slightly. "You never know - I may very well have decided to let this one slide just to maintain good customer relations. Mrs. Armstrong has been a regular customer for almost ten years. I can hardly afford to lose her over a bowl of soup. Do you understand?"

Summer did not speak but only nodded.

The man continued. "I was ready to dismiss you but after hearing your side of the story I realize that you had good intentions. However, this is the second time in two weeks that you've had run-ins with customers. I can't afford for my business to suffer because of your temperament."

He paused as if waiting for his words to sink in then said sternly, "You'll be placed on probation with immediate effect. Any further incident will result in your dismissal. Have I made myself clear?"

"Very," was all Summer said. She felt as if the strength had been knocked out of her and she had no fight left.

That night she went to bed by nine o'clock, which was very early for her. She lay still in the darkness. She'd been through so much that day that she was exhausted but, somehow, she just couldn't fall asleep. She had too much on her mind. It had been a terrible day, she thought. Her only consolation was that she hadn't lost her job.

It was clear, though, that her current job would never sustain her. She needed to find more work. She decided that first thing in the morning she would head down to the employment agency and submit an application for another part-time position. Her study time would be reduced even further but she had no choice. It was either work or sleep on the street.

With a sigh she rolled on to her side and lay facing the wall. The darkness was like a soft blanket, comforting her. Somehow, instead of making her feel better, she suddenly felt vulnerable and alone. A fat tear drop slipped from the corner of her eye and slid across her cheek to dampen the pillow beneath her head. A second tear drop followed, then another. Before she knew what was happening she had buried her face in the pillow and her body was shaking with uncontrollable sobs.

She cried hard for several minutes. Finally, she drew in a trembling breath and wiped the tears away with the back of her hand. She had surprised herself with the sudden outbreak. This was not like her - she couldn't even remember the last time she had shed tears like that. She guessed that she'd been so overwhelmed with her problems that she had finally lost control.

Well, she had broken down for a moment, but that was all over now. She had no time for tears. She needed to get her thoughts together and prepare a plan of action.

Against her wishes her thoughts went back to her last encounter with Lance Munroe. Then she thought of the offer he had made and her brow wrinkled in a frown. She thought of how she had anxiously checked her voicemail when she got home, inwardly praying that there would be a message from him. But still, there was nothing.

The disappointment had been like a bitter taste on her tongue but then it turned to anger. She was angry at the man who had thrown her a lifeline then pulled it away by totally ignoring her cry for help. But she was even angrier at herself for being so stupid as to believe that he'd had any interest at all in her well being.

After all, who was she to him? Nothing but a struggling waitress he was trying to impress, she thought. He'd had no intention of giving her a job. For him it was probably just a way of getting her into his bed.

Her nostrils flared as she thought of him – a typical man with only one thing on his mind. God, the arrogance of him, she fumed silently. He was a man she could find it very easy to hate.

Suddenly she couldn't lie down any longer. She felt the anger tightening in her chest and she got up off the bed and went to stand by the window. At that moment the phone rang.

Summer jumped. She wasn't expecting a call. It was probably someone from college, she thought, calling for last-minute help on a paper. They always did that to her.

She reached for the phone and put the receiver to her cheek. "Hello", she said brusquely, trying to convey her annoyance in the tone of her voice.

"Summer. Were you sleeping? It's Lance."

Her heart jerked with shock and pleasure when she heard the deep bass of the now familiar voice.

"Lance, is that you?" Even to her own ears she sounded inane. She sat down heavily on the sofa.

"Yes. I just got in from the airport and got your message."

"You were…away?"

"I've been in London for the past week trying to tie up a record deal." His voice sounded tired, strained. "I was trying to get so much done in the short time that I missed my flight. I should have been home eight hours ago."

"Oh. I'm sorry."

"That's okay, I'm used to this sort of thing. But that's not what I called about. What's going on with you? The message you left was straightforward enough but there was something in your voice…that wasn't the real you."

"The real me?" Summer frowned in the darkness. The man hardly knew her. "What are you talking about?"

"I'm talking about the bold, aggressive you."

"Aggressive?" she said, still confused.

"Will you stop repeating what I'm saying? Are you sure you're awake?" He chuckled softly. "You sound like you're in a daze."

"Yes, I am," she answered, then added quickly, "awake, I mean. I wasn't sleeping."

"Good, because I want to know what happened to the spitfire I left in Chicago a week ago. Your message made you sound like a meek little lamb and I know you better than that."

"You do?"

"I do. So...what has changed?"

"I..." Summer hesitated, suddenly embarrassed. She sighed. "It's a long story." She was silent, not knowing where to start.

Lance rescued her when he spoke. "I want to see you tomorrow. Will you be working in the morning, say around ten?"

"No, I'm off tomorrow."

"Come down to my office for ten o'clock then. We'll talk there."

Summer felt the tension in her body begin to dissipate and her spirit lifted as hope returned to her. "I'll be there..." she began, then stammered, "I'm sorry...but I don't know where your office is."

"I gave you my card." His response was curt.

"I...lost it."

"I see. So that's why you called my apartment. If you'd left the message at my office I would have gotten it days ago. My assistant relays all my messages when I'm travelling." There was a slight pause, then he said, "By the way, how did you get my home number?"

"Aah..." Summer felt her heart sink as she struggled to find an answer. Was she going to lose her last hope? Could she risk telling him the truth? Her sense of duty won and she decided to keep her promise never to reveal her source. "I'm sorry...but I can't say."

"I see." There was another pause then he said, "Get a pen and I'll give you the address for my office."

After Summer hung up she went and sat on the bed and tucked her legs under her. She didn't know whether to feel elated or depressed. She had finally received the call she'd been waiting on for so long and now she had an appointment with Lance for the next morning. However, her joy was tempered with the way Lance had become formal at the end of the conversation. He hadn't sounded angry but something in his tone had changed. She hoped it wouldn't affect his position about offering her a job.

As she unfolded her legs and slipped under the covers she breathed a prayer that things would go well for her next day.

Chapter 5

"You're late, Miss Jones."

"I'm sorry. The cab driver got confused when I gave him the address and we ended up on the other side of the city."

"If there's one thing I don't like it's tardiness." Lance's annoyance showed on his face.

"I said I was sorry." Summer tried hard not to frown or raise her voice. She couldn't understand why he was being so particular. It was only ten-fifteen, for goodness sake.

Still, she couldn't afford to annoy him so she simply said, "It won't happen again."

"Thank you," he said, as he beckoned her to a seat.

He sat down and leaned back in the black, leather chair and his relaxed yet alert posture hinted at underlying strength. He wore a dark blue business suit with a red silk tie and he held a gold pen loosely in his long, dark fingers.

Summer had never seen him in this attire, not even when he had come to the restaurant with his colleagues from the music industry. Wow, she thought. She'd heard he was successful but now he certainly looked the part.

She glanced quickly around the office, trying not to stare openly, but impressed by its opulence. Her high heels sank into plush carpeting as she walked towards the proffered chair. The sofa and all the chairs in the room were of soft black leather and the huge desk behind which Lance sat gleamed under the lights overhead. There were three huge paintings on the wall, one of Lake Michigan and the other two of island scenes - fishermen with their boats on the seashore and a rustic market scene.

Sculptures of rich black wood stood in the four corners of the room - the bust of an African, a Rastafarian with cigar in hand, and two female torsos made even more sensual because they were headless.

But what impressed Summer most was an illuminated glass case in which several trophies, awards and gold records were displayed. One of them even looked like a Grammy award. She was curious but guessed that this was not the best time to ask.

"So..." he leaned forward and rested his elbows on the desk, "your message indicated that you were reconsidering my offer. Did I understand you correctly?"

"Yes, you did." Summer suffered a little under his scrutiny but, despite her embarrassment, she pressed on. "I...a lot's happened in the past week and...I need a job." He leaned back again and clasped his fingers across his chest as he looked at her. His brow was knitted in a frown. "What exactly has happened in such short space of time? A week ago you wouldn't even consider my offer, and now this. What's going on?"

"I...I'd rather not say."

"I see." He stared at her until she felt like squirming. Then he said, "In the same way you'd rather not say how you got my home number?"

Summer could feel her face get hot. "Aah, you could say that," she muttered.

"I see."

"Will you stop saying that?"

"Saying what?"

"'I see'. You keep saying that and yet you don't see. You don't understand a thing about me." Summer's voice came out sharper than she'd intended but she was stung by his reminder that she'd had to retract her initial rejection of his offer.

He stared at her in silence, his lips twitching slightly. She didn't know if it was out of anger or amusement. She guessed it was the latter and could have kicked herself.

Then he said, "Alright. I can see you have a lot on your mind but you choose not to share your worries. No problem. I actually admire that in a woman."

He smiled, his voice sardonic. "The fairer sex isn't famous for keeping their troubles to themselves."

Summer grimaced at his words but said nothing.

"But that's beside the point," he continued. "I imagine your purpose for coming here is to understand what the job is about and to determine whether you'd be interested, right?"

"That's correct." Her composure restored, Summer decided to be as formal with him as he was with her.

"Fine. In brief, I need someone with strong communication and writing skills to assist me in creating a unique public relations campaign for the artistes I'm working with. I don't want to work with a PR firm on this particular project. I need this to have a different feel - I want it to be intimate, close to home, close to the heart. I want to get to the real person behind the performer."

As he spoke his voice grew more animated. "And that's why I need someone like you - young, open to diverse cultures and personalities, passionate. I want someone to whom my people, whether American or from the Caribbean, can relate. From the first time I met you I thought you possessed the qualities I was looking for."

Lance's eyes sparkled in his dark face and his excitement was obvious. Summer was surprised by the compliment but she was also affected by the enthusiasm in his voice. She leaned forward in genuine interest.

"It sounds great so far but I'm still not one hundred percent sure about what I'd be doing. Could you explain a bit more?"

"Of course." His lips softened in a warm smile which, coupled with his glistening eyes, made her heartbeat accelerate. She shook her head slightly, willing herself to concentrate on his words and not on his rugged face.

"I have a goal and that's for the public, and especially the fans, to get to know the real side of my artistes. Several of the people I work with have serious image problems. The Reggae singers are typically viewed as gangsters and drug dealers, and the R&B singers...well, let's just say there are some attitude problems." He grinned boyishly and she smiled back. She'd had first hand experience with this so she knew what he was talking about.

"Now," he continued, "what I want to do is reverse those negative impressions by getting people to see the other side of my people. Remember, some of these impressions may be true and some false. But whatever the case, what I want the public to recall is the positive side of these musicians."

He looked thoughtful. "I'd be the first to admit that creative people - in this case I'm talking about singers - are typically not very good business people. What I mean is, they sometimes let their personalities dominate their decision making. If they're spitfires like you," at this he smiled, "they let everyone around them suffer, including the fans. Then they suffer and the business suffers. If they're from the inner city then speech patterns will, of course, be typical of that area and if it's too pronounced, for some members of the public this can be an issue."

"Now don't get me wrong," he put his hands up, "I'm not saying we should make these people into something they're not. I simply want someone to work closely with my group, be with them on a daily basis, get to know them, get into their psyche, then communicate their human, positive side to the world."

As he spoke he stood up and turned to stare out of the big bay window behind his chair. She stared at his broad shoulders and couldn't help admiring the way the suit fit his muscled frame perfectly.

"What this means, Miss Jones, is that you will spend a lot of time with the singers, rappers and Reggae stars and you will get to know them so well that you'll be able to find the positive aspects of their lives, create stories and articles around that, and feed positive news to the agencies and to the media. You'll be my own little in-house PR agency, but you'll have the advantage of speaking as an insider."

He turned back to her and smiled. "You may even have to give tips to a few of them, take them under your wing, so to speak. But many of them are really nice people underneath it all." He smiled at her raised eyebrows. "Yes, even the bitchy ones. Once you get to know them and they get to know you you'll have fun, I can promise you that. And, at the end of the day, that's the essence of what I want from you - for you to know them so intimately that the rest of the world can see the diamonds that would otherwise never come to light."

"Well," Summer let her breath out in a whoosh, "that was some job description. But thank you, because now I know just what you're looking for."

She looked up at Lance who stared down at her and she knew her face mirrored his excitement.

"To tell the truth, I couldn't have stumbled on a more perfect job. It combines my studies in journalism with my communication studies plus," she stressed the last word, "it allows me to work closely with the persons I'm profiling. As I told you before, I love working with people and that's why I didn't want to end my studies at just journalism. I didn't want to be a news anchor or a reporter in Iraq. I'll leave that to the Christiane Amanpours of this world.

She sighed. "Me, I want to get into peoples lives and souls. I want to know what makes them tick. I'm nosy that way." She grinned up at her prospective boss and he smiled back.

"Sounds like I made the right choice." He raised an eyebrow. "Now, Miss Jones, the question is, when can you start?"

"As soon as possible, if you don't mind."

"I don't mind at all. I want you here first thing tomorrow – eight-thirty, sharp - so I can debrief you about each of the artistes you'll be working with."

He paused and looked at her questioningly. "I must admit I'm a bit surprised that you're available to start so early. Don't you have to give notice at The Southern Belle?"

"Actually, no," her voice turned sheepish, "I got into some trouble - nothing illegal, of course - and I was put on probation. Mr. Williams won't miss me if I leave. He's scared I might make him lose customers."

"Something to do with your temper, I assume?"

"Yes," she admitted ruefully then quickly added, "but it wasn't my fault. But anyway, I'll give him a call as soon as I get home. He'll have a replacement before the day is out. Trust me."

"I don't doubt that. But let me just say this," he said, looking at her with serious eyes, "just like your previous employer I will expect you to keep a tight reign on that temper of yours. Situations are volatile enough with these musicians without you adding to it. I want you here to help solve problems, not create them."

"I'm very aware of that and I promise you, you'll have absolutely no problem from me." She spoke earnestly, not bothering to hide her eagerness. "In fact, you won't even know I'm around."

"I doubt that," he said with a grunt.

"This job will be perfect," she bubbled on without responding to his comment, "and it will definitely give me the experience I'm looking for. Oh!" She stopped suddenly and clapped a hand over her mouth.

"What is it?" Lance frowned at her sudden change of expression.

"I just thought of something," she said, crestfallen. "I may not be able to take the job if it's full-time. I still have six months to go before graduation and I still haven't done my thesis yet."

"Is that all you have left to do? Your thesis? No classes to attend?"

"Yes, it's only the thesis, no classes, but it's a big part of my overall grade." Her disappointment was almost tactile. "I can't graduate unless I submit it and I need at least twenty hours a week to get it done."

"How far along are you?" He sounded genuinely interested.

"Well," she stalled, slightly embarrassed, "not very far. I'm just doing some general research now but I still haven't tied down my topic. And what makes it worse," she sighed, "my thesis proposal is due next week."

Lance walked around the desk and sat on the edge with his arms folded across his broad chest. She was glad she was seated because a sudden weakness made her knees tremble.

As he looked down at her he shook his head. "Miss Jones, in some ways you're pretty sharp but in others you are so slow. Don't you see that I'm providing you with the opportunity to not only earn a decent living but also to complete all the requirements of your thesis? What better study to do than the one I've thrown in your lap?"

"Oh…my…God!" Summer's eyes widened. "Oh my God, you're so right! How could I have been so stupid?"

Tears filled her eyes. It was too good to be true. Here she was, almost at the point of being thrown out of her apartment, at risk of not graduating if she didn't pay her tuition, and up to her ears in frustration at not being able to come up with a solid subject of study for her final paper. And in the space of thirty minutes sitting in this man's office it was all resolved.

She turned her eyes up to him. The movement loosened a teardrop and it ran down her cheek and splashed onto her folded hands. "You're a life saver."

Lance seemed nonplussed at her sudden show of emotion and he stood up quickly. He was obviously bewildered by the sudden change in her. He cleared his throat and said, "Miss Jones…there's no need for tears. We're simply creating a situation which is mutually beneficial - you earn more money and complete your thesis while I get the PR coverage I want for my team. Please..." he went over and placed a hand on her shoulder, "don't cry."

When he said that Summer felt like crying even more. This was so different from how she'd always seen him. She couldn't believe this was the overbearing man she had cursed silently not so long before. Suddenly she felt ashamed. She ducked her head and dabbed at her face with a tissue as more tears ran down her cheek.

"Summer, please." His voice was gentle, almost pleading. Suddenly he pulled her upright to stand before him. Her purse fell to the ground. He wrapped strong arms around her quivering body and pulled her to his broad chest. Heaving sobs shook her body but he held her close, stroking her wild curls and whispering softly in her ears. "It's okay, it's okay. Everything's alright now."

It took a full minute before she rested quietly with her cheek against his silk shirt, all her tears spent. She felt drained but at the same time refreshed, washed clean like the leaves after a shower of rain.

As he gently stroked her cheek she sighed and relaxed into his body, breathing in the fragrance of his cologne and his warm body. She didn't know if it was the strength of his arms, the seductive aroma of his cologne or her feeling of euphoria at having her problems resolved. The only thing she knew was that she raised her head to look up into his dark brooding face and then her hands, of their own accord, rose to rest at the back of his head. Those hands now purposefully pulled his head down until his face was mere inches away from her upturned one.

Summer closed her eyes, wiped all thoughts from her mind and gave herself up to the waves of desire that washed over her. She applied more pressure to the back of his head and her greatest wish for that moment came true. Lips so firm but oh, so mobile, pressed against her eager ones. She moved her mouth gently against his then moaned softly as he placed a large hand on the small of her back and drew her against his hard body.

Before she knew what was happening he had taken control. As her hands fell away from his head and came to rest on his lean hips, he cupped her head and tilted it ever so gently until his lips had full access to her willing mouth. His tongue flicked against her bottom lip until she opened to him with a groan.

He took the opportunity she gave him and probed deeper until their tongues met and became as one in a sensual exotic dance. He pulled back and nibbled teasingly on her lower lip then went back to exploring her depths.

The kiss must have lasted only a few seconds but to Summer it seemed like an eternity - a wonderful, delicious eternity in Lance's arms.

When he finally released her she was shaken to the core. She sank slowly into her chair as he turned and walked back to his own.

"Thanks for coming, Miss Jones." His voice was husky as he leafed through the papers on his desk. "I'll see you tomorrow at eight-thirty."

Summer nodded then rose and headed for the door. There she paused and glanced back. Lance did not look up from his papers. Without a word she pulled the door shut behind her.

Chapter 6

Summer was miserable. It was seven-fifteen, she was getting ready for her first day of work with Lance and she was scared. What must he think of her, she thought. She'd broken down in tears in front of him then had thrown herself on him like a wanton. He must think her either an emotional ninny or a slut.

"Oh, no," she groaned aloud, wondering if she'd messed up her chance at her dream job.

She sat in front of the mirror and slowly traced her lips with wine coloured lipstick. She had picked out a burgundy suit and this lipstick was the only one that went with it. Although she didn't often wear make-up today she wanted to look her best. She'd seen how Lance dressed and didn't want to embarrass herself by not fitting in. She dusted her cheeks and nose with loose nut-brown powder then applied light mascara to her lashes. Finally, she added a little eye shadow then she was ready to go.

By seven-thirty Summer was out of the house and heading for the L train. Now that she knew the way to Munroe Productions she didn't need to rely on a taxi cab. In fact, she'd found the cab ride expensive and was definitely not planning on spending that kind of money everyday. She was sure that, even with a pay raise, she wouldn't be able to afford such luxury. She'd save the cab rides for specific occasions, she thought, such as if she happened to be running late or if it rained. Now that she realized what a stickler Lance was for time she would have to make every effort to be punctual.

She arrived at exactly eight-sixteen. The office was on the fifteenth floor of a forty story building on Canal street. As she rode the elevator she took deep breaths and checked herself in the mirror on the walls. She was glad she was alone so that she could scrutinize herself freely. Well, I guess I look alright, she thought, not exactly high fashion, but alright.

The elevator door opened and she walked down the corridor to the glass doors with black and gold lettering. As she entered the receptionist looked up and smiled at her.

"Good morning, Miss Jones. Mr. Munroe told me to expect you."

As the attractive woman spoke she rose from behind the reception desk and walked around to extend a hand to Summer. "My name is Chantal Snow. Welcome to Munroe Productions."

Summer was surprised at the warm reception. Although Chantal had been pleasant enough when she'd come the day before she had looked so sophisticated in her chic, obviously expensive suit, that Summer had immediately assumed she was a snob. Now it seemed that she'd been wrong, at least from what she'd seen so far today.

She smiled back and took the woman's hand. Chantal was at least three inches taller than Summer and her make-up was perfect. Her satin-smooth cheeks were dusted with soft rose-coloured powder, a perfect complement to her maroon eye-shadow and plum red lipstick. Her jet-black hair was cut short and immaculately coiffed, giving the impression that she had just stepped out of a hair salon.

Summer felt a little intimidated by this glamorous woman; she knew fully well that she looked nothing like that. But then she gave herself a mental shrug and straightened her back. She was not here for a beauty contest. She was here to execute a project and she was going to do a damn good job of it.

"Thank you," she said brightly. "I'm glad to be here."

"Please follow me. I'll show you to your office."

My office, Summer thought with a smile. She liked the sound of that.

She was taken to a small room lined with shelves full of books, video tapes, DVD's and CD's. She even saw what looked like old movie reels. A desk was in the middle of the room and it was obvious that it had been cleared to accommodate her. It was totally bare except for a desk unit that held half a dozen pens and pencils, a note pad and a small Dictaphone.

Outside of the desk and chairs the only other piece of furniture was a credenza on which she saw stacks of photographs and magazines - Rolling Stone, Vibe, Honey and Ebony.

"Here you go, Miss. Jones," Chantal said. "Mr. Munroe left instructions for you to be provided with the files of the eight people you'll be working with. Please make yourself comfortable while I retrieve them from the main library. I'll be back in a minute."

Chantal left and Summer walked over to read the labels on the video tapes. 'Summer Tour 2003', 'Times Square 2001', 'Irie Reggae Party 2005', she read. She saw CD's of various singers some of whom she knew, others she'd never heard of. She went over to the credenza and flipped through some of the magazines. She wondered which of the singers profiled in the books were from Lance's group. Well, she'd know soon enough. Based on what he'd told her she would soon be spending a lot of time with them.

Chantal returned and placed a stack of files in the middle of the desk. "Here they are," she said. "You're to spend the morning going through these files so that you'll have all the necessary background information on your group."

"You mentioned eight persons. Is that the total group that Munroe Productions handles?"

"Of course not," Chantal laughed. "We manage thirty-two singers, some of them well established and well known and others, up and coming artistes who we're trying to get established in the music industry."

"Oh, I thought I'd be working with all your singers."

"Oh, no," Chantal shook her head, "only the ones we've had problems with. Mr. Munroe says that's why you're here - to help us get them back on track."

"Oh." Summer picked up one of the files and read, 'Super Cool'. She looked up at Chantal who still stood in the doorway and asked, "And Mr. Munroe - am I to see him today?"

"Actually he'd mentioned wanting to be here when you arrived, I guess to get you started on the right foot, but he was suddenly called to a press conference with Rolling Stone Magazine. He should be back some time this afternoon." Chantal smiled at her reassuringly. "Don't worry. I won't leave you to yourself. I'll check up on you from time to time and, of course, you know where to find me if you need anything."

Summer breathed a sigh of relief as the receptionist went through the door. At least she wouldn't have to face Lance for the next few hours. She had no idea what she would say to him next time they met. The memory of the kiss was still vivid in her mind - the wild beating of her heart when his warm lips touched hers, the way she felt helpless and pliant in his powerful arms. She had relived the moment a hundred times and her heart raced every time. She just hoped that, by the time he returned, she would have regained her composure. No matter what had happened between them she was determined to remain professional.

Then another thought crossed her mind and she paused, an open file in her hand. Chantal was a very attractive young woman. Could there be anything going on between her and Lance? Lance was a handsome, successful man. He could get practically any woman he wanted and she knew that many women would think nothing of throwing themselves at him.

Like I did, she thought bitterly, and cursed her moment of indiscretion.

Anyway, she had no intention of letting that happen again, and even if he and Chantal were involved that was certainly none of her business. She picked up the file again and forced herself to concentrate.

Some time later there was a knock on the door and Summer looked up, startled. The door opened and Chantal peeked in.

"It's ten-fifteen. I just wondered if you'd like some coffee or tea?"

"Ten-fifteen already? I feel like I just got here."

"Well, it's been close to two hours."

"I guess I was so taken up with these files that I didn't notice the time. I'd love a cup of tea. Do you have a break room?"

"We do, but I can bring a cup for you. Tea with sugar?"

"Yes, please. That's so nice of you. Tea with sugar would be great."

"I'll be right back."

When Chantal disappeared Summer looked back at the folder in her hand - it was Top Cat's file. He was a twenty-one year old rap star who had grown up in Chicago's south side. He'd had a couple of big hits including his latest album, 'Just a Kid from the South Side'. Munroe Productions was grooming him to be the next Fifty Cent - young, brash, and hounded by teenage girls all over the country.

He was popular with the young kids but he was also known to have a bad drinking habit. There had been a demonstration on State Street - parents were concerned about the type of role model Top Cat was; they were afraid their children would be influenced by the young rebel. Summer thought of what it would take to improve this tarnished image. She'd have to be very creative but she felt she was up to the task.

By midday she'd gone through five of the files and had taken copious notes. She'd also begun to formulate a tentative plan of action for each person. This, she would flesh out as she got to know each of them better.

When she heard a knock at the door she looked up with a smile. Chantal had been so nice to her. She'd probably come to get her for lunch, Summer thought. She had really misjudged the woman.

"Come in," she called out and started packing up the files on her desk.

"Aren't you going to have lunch, Miss Jones? It's almost one o'clock."

At the sound of the deep masculine voice Summer's eyes flew to the door. Her heart thumped wildly as she saw Lance standing in the doorway. He seemed even more handsome than ever in a black business suit and striped tie. She felt her face suddenly get hot and she stammered, "Oh…Mr. Munroe. I thought it was Chantal at the door."

"Ms. Snow had to go on an errand." He entered the room as he spoke. "It's about time you got to know the rest of the staff. Well, at least the ones who are in office today. They're in the lunch room."

His presence was intimidating in the small office. She sat staring up at him, the memories of his arms, his lips, his strength flooding her mind.

"Well, are you going to just sit there?" He looked amused.

She shook her head quickly and rose. "Let me just grab my purse."

As he strolled out the door she grabbed her bag and hurried to catch up.

There were half a dozen people in the lunch room. Lance told her that the additional five people were out on assignment for the day. He introduced her to Fred Billings, the chief accountant, a kindly-looking gentleman who looked like he was in his fifties. Jennifer French, the office manager, looked almost the same age. Both the engineer, Sean Patrick and the studio manager, Jonathan Brown, were young men; both seemed to be under thirty years old. Abe Williams and Sasha Perez were road managers and the two seemed to be the youngest of the group. Summer would guess that neither one of them was older than she.

After the introduction Lance directed her to the long table on which various cold plates were laid out. There were sandwiches of chicken salad, tuna, roast beef and turkey, as well as cans of soda and bottles of juice and water.

"Help yourself. I'd like to meet with you at one-thirty so you have about forty minutes."

When Lance left Summer picked up a cold sandwich platter and sat down at an empty table.

"Hey," Abe called, "don't sit over there all by yourself."

"Come join us." Sasha tapped the chair beside her.

"Thank you." Summer smiled and slipped into the chair.

Lunch was pleasant but, in Summer's mind, much too brief. She was dreading the moment when she would be back in Lance's office - alone. She didn't know what to expect. She was afraid he would reprimand her or at least make some reference to her less than circumspect behavior.

To Summer's surprise Lance didn't make any reference to the incident at all. On the contrary, he simply spoke to her about her salary and benefits package and asked her to finish going through the files as he wanted her to accompany him on a press conference next day.

When she put down the last file it was five-thirty. Chantal had bid her farewell fifteen minutes earlier and had asked if she wasn't ready to leave but she was determined to complete her task so that she would be free for tomorrow's press conference.

When she finally closed the last file she was filled with satisfaction. She collected her purse and left the office with a contented smile on her face.

That night Summer called her mother at the nursing home, eager to share her good fortune.

"Mom you'd never believe what happened to me."

"What? Did you win the lotto?"

"Come on, Mom, you know I never buy that stuff. When it comes to luck, I don't have any."

"I know you don't gamble. I was just teasing," Edna chuckled into the phone. "So what great thing has happened to you? Don't keep me in suspense, girl."

"Alright, alright," Summer said but paused just long enough to torture her mother with the anticipation. "I got another job."

"Really? I didn't even know you were looking for one." Edna's voice held a hint of uncertainty. "So how are you going to manage that plus your job at the restaurant?"

"Oh, I forgot to tell you. I don't work at The Southern Belle anymore. I'm now at Munroe Productions – full-time."

"But…I don't understand." Edna sounded even more confused. "You always said you couldn't take a full-time job, that you needed the extra time to do your school work. So how are you going to manage?"

"That's the beauty of it, Mom. With this job I'm killing two birds with one stone. This job is actually providing me with material for my thesis, so everyday I go to work I'm adding to my research. At this rate, I'll be done in no time."

"I'm happy for you, child. That sounds great. But what exactly are you doing at this new job?"

"Oh, I'm sorry," Summer laughed, "I was so excited I forgot the most important part. I'm working on a public relations project for Munroe Productions, a recording company. I'm responsible to come up with human interest stories on eight of their artistes in order to help create a positive image for them. In a nut shell, I'll be spending a lot of time with these singers so I can get to know them and share their positive side with the public."

"Well, it certainly sounds interesting." Edna sounded relieved. "You should have fun with it."

"I'm sure I will, Mom. And I can learn so much. I'm just glad I ran into Lance at the restaurant."

"Lance? And who's he?"

"Oh, I'm sorry," she giggled nervously then almost kicked herself for sounding like a silly school girl. "He's the owner of Munroe Productions. I met him at the restaurant one night and he offered me this job."

"He just met you and offered you a job? I don't think I like the sound of that."

"Oh, Mom, you're always so suspicious. The reason he offered me the job was because I mentioned my studies in journalism and communication and he just happened to need someone with that background. It's like this job was made for me, Ma."

"Well, you sound very excited so I won't discourage you. I'm sure you'll do a great job."

"I'll certainly try my best," Summer sighed happily.

Then her thoughts went to the main issue with her mother and her mood changed to one of concern. "Have you heard anything further about the surgery?"

"No, dear, they're still waiting on the test results."

"But you did those tests over a week ago."

"I know, but they did say it would take at least ten days to get the results. Just be patient, dear. We'll know in good time."

"I wish they would just hurry up. I can't stand this waiting."

"I'm anxious, too, but worrying about it won't make things go any faster. Just focus on your new job right now. In just a few days we'll know if my body is up to this surgery or not."

Summer sighed again. "Okay, Mom."

There was a pause then she said softly, "I love you, Mom."

"I know you do, dear. And I love you, too."

When Summer hung up from her mother she dialed Brian's number. Suddenly, she needed someone to talk to and he had always lent a listening ear. This was definitely one of those times when she wished she had a best friend.

Lance hung up the phone, covered his eyes with a large hand, and leaned back in the plush leather chair. It had been a long day. It was nine in the evening and he'd just hung up from a Kingston record manufacturer. He urgently needed fifty thousand forty-five's for immediate distribution in Europe and Japan. After much negotiation he'd gotten the manufacturer to agree to a rush job and, with that agreement, records would be shipped to London and Tokyo within three days. The situation had been uncertain but he'd pulled it off. Now he was beat.

He swung his chair around to face the bay window with its view of the Chicago skyline and the dark waters of Lake Michigan. He loosened his tie, put his feet up on the window ledge and leaned back, enjoying the silence of the deserted office.

Sometimes these evenings alone in the office were his most peaceful and often his most productive ones. Without the distraction of the staff and the constantly ringing telephones he could concentrate on his work without interruption.

Somehow, though, this evening was different. He felt distracted and decided to call it a night and head for home. He wondered at his lack of concentration. Then he remembered Summer Jones...and the kiss that had taken him totally by surprise.

A slow smile spread across his lips as he recalled how her lithe body had molded into his and how her normally tight mouth had melted into soft lips that trembled beneath his own. He'd felt her soft breasts pressing against his chest and, at that moment, he lost control. A sudden wave of passion had rushed through him and he'd remembered pulling her close and returning her tentative kiss with one that reflected his desire for her. She must have felt the same attraction because she'd responded willingly, almost eagerly. He loved her passion and momentary abandon. The spitfire was human, after all.

His thoughts were rudely interrupted by the telephone. Its ring seemed especially loud in the stillness of the empty office and he jumped, startled. He wondered who would be calling the office at that hour.

"Hello." His voice was scratchy from lack of use.

"Lance?" It was a woman's voice, husky and breathless, a hint of anxiety in its tone. "I've been trying to reach you at home and on your cell phone but I kept getting your voicemail. I just decided to try your office as a last resort. I couldn't imagine you'd be there so late. You work so hard…"

"Jennifer." Lance cut her off abruptly. "Why'd you call? Is everything alright?"

"Not really, and that's why I called because I think you should know, with you taking care of her and everything."

"Know what?"

"Michelle is in the hospital."

"What happened?"

"It's the same problem, Lance. I'm so sick and tired of this damn sickle cell thing. I can't stand what it's doing to my baby."

Lance felt his head begin to throb. A tension headache was coming on.

"How is she?" His voice was tight and low.

"She's in a lot of pain. This attack was really bad. It started in the afternoon and I took her up to the hospital right away. I was there from almost three o'clock. I just got home half an hour ago."

"And you're just calling me?"

"I wanted to call you from the hospital but I was in such a hurry I forgot my cell phone at home. But I tried calling you as soon as I got in. I just couldn't find you." Jennifer gave a tired sigh. "I kept leaving messages on your voicemail and when I wasn't getting any reply I finally decided to try your office."

"Yes, I heard all that before," he said impatiently. "So the baby is at the hospital all by herself?"

"Yes, but don't worry. The nurses are watching her for me. The matron has my number in case of anything."

"Did they have to put her on saline this time?'

"Yes, and you know how she hates the needles. She cried the whole time but they had to do it. Her eyes almost looked green, it was so bad." There was a pause then she said, "And she was asking for you, Lance."

"Oh, God," he groaned, and began rubbing his temple again. "I'm going to see if I can get a flight out tomorrow."

"But you're so busy. You really think you can make it?"

He sighed then said, "I was supposed to have a press conference tomorrow but I'll leave a note for Chantal to cancel it. I'd just mess it up anyway, thinking about Michelle. Don't worry. I'll be there."

"I'm sorry, Lance. I didn't mean for you to come. I just wanted you to know what was happening. You know I don't like to trouble you when you're busy…"

"Jennifer, stop it. Please. If you hadn't called I would have been very angry. You know that. Now just calm down and get some rest. I'll call you in the morning to let you know what time I'll be in. Just tell Michelle…" He drew in a deep breath as the migraine attack worsened. "Tell Michelle that I'll be there."

"Okay, Lance. I'll see you tomorrow. Bye."

"Yeah, bye."

As soon as Lance rested the receiver back into the cradle he began to dig around in the desk drawer where he kept a bottle of pain killers. He found it and quickly downed two Ibuprofen capsules, washing them down with the last of the water in the bottle on his desk.

Whenever he was under stress the migraine attacks would come, swift and severe. Sometimes they were so intense that he felt almost blinded by them. He leaned back in the chair and breathed deeply, willing the pain to go away. He forced his mind to go blank. Then he tried thinking about crystal clear water bubbling over rocks in a stream. After long moments the throbbing gradually subsided and he was finally able to open his eyes again.

With a groan he rose, grabbed his jacket and briefcase and walked out the door.

Chapter 7

Summer hoped that Chantal didn't see the disappointment on her face. The receptionist was telling her that the press conference had been called off and, in fact, Mr. Munroe would not be in for the day. Summer didn't know which news had affected her more - not getting to do the press conference, or not getting to see Lance.

With a start she realized that Chantal was still speaking to her.

"I'll take you down to the main library now," she was saying. "Mr. Munroe asked that you use the day to view some of their past interviews - we have them all on tape. That will help you to see a little of what the public knows of them so far. If you get through them quickly enough you could even watch some of their stage performances."

Oh, well, Summer thought, at least she would be fully occupied for the day.

She wondered what business had taken Lance out of town so suddenly. Chantal hadn't mentioned the reason for his absence. She could only guess that it had something to do with one of his singers.

The morning was uneventful but interesting. Summer watched interviews and performances until her eyes burned. Still, she was satisfied that she was able to gather lots of notes from the tapes. She planned to add these to the files she was creating for each of her assigned singers.

The only break Summer took was to sip a cup of herbal tea that Chantal brought in at ten-thirty. She was so absorbed in her task that she didn't realize how the time had passed. She was surprised when her stomach growled. She looked at the clock. It was one-thirty. As if timing her, the phone rang. Chantal was on the line.

"Oh, sure," Summer responded to Chantal's offer to bring her lunch. "That will help me get through this even faster. Thank you."

Summer put another tape in the VCR, picked up her note book, and prepared to write. This interview was with Monisha Stone. The singer, elegant and beautiful as ever, handled herself very well. She had an aura of sophistication that was arresting.

Summer could imagine the impact the diva had on men if she, a woman, couldn't take her eyes off Monisha's immaculate face. She seemed so self-assured that Summer wondered why Lance had even included her in the list of artistes she'd be working with. This woman didn't need her help. In fact, Summer doubted that she would take kindly to her offering any form of advice.

There was a knock on the door and Summer switched off the tape, ready to dive into the turkey sandwich she had ordered. She stood up and was stretching luxuriously when a man entered the room with her sandwich and soda in hand. Summer froze mid-stretch.

"Who are you?" she blurted out.

"Derrick Dunn, at your service."

With a flourish he placed the food on the credenza then turned to her with a wide smile. "So you're the new girl who's gonna make waves with the media, huh?"

"Excuse me?" Summer used her coldest tone – she'd been known to freeze even the most forward man with it. This time, she quickly realized, it wasn't working. The man barely seemed to notice her aloof attitude.

"So what's your name, honey?"

"My name," Summer said, frowning, "is Summer Jones. And may I ask who you are and what you're doing in my office?"

"I told you already. I'm Derrick. Lance's cousin." He stretched out his hand to her and she took it reluctantly, too polite to ignore it. "Pleased to meet you...Miss Jones."

He gave her a lopsided grin. He looked her over slowly from head to toe then gave a low whistle. "I'm very pleased to meet you."

She pulled her hand away from his grasp and frowned at him. If this man didn't stop, she thought, Lance's cousin or not, he was going to get it.

She was just about to give him a biting response when he looked questioningly at her then said, "Hey, don't I know you from somewhere?"

"I'm sure you don't."

"I mean, seriously. This isn't a line. I've seen those mean eyes of yours before."

"Mean eyes?" Summer was indignant.

"Okay, that may have been a bit strong, but I've seen those flashing eyes..." he said then drew in a sharp breath. "You're the server from The Southern Belle. You and Monisha argued about the food. Yeah, it's you alright.

"So?'

"So, you're one hot mama when you're angry."

Summer clenched her fists to keep from slapping his grinning face. She'd thought Lance was bad but this one was arrogance personified. Instead of giving in to her desire to smack him she strode purposefully to the door and pulled it open. She stared pointedly at him.

When he didn't budge she spoke. "Thank you for stopping by, Mr. Dunn, but I really must get back to my work."

He put his hands up as if to fend off invisible daggers. "Alright, alright. I see you're a serious woman. I'll behave myself. Let me start again."

"Good afternoon," he said politely. "My name is Derrick Dunn. I hope you enjoy your meal. May I help you with anything else?"

"No, thank you, I'm fine." Summer's tone softened with his sudden change in attitude. "And yes, I was a server at The Southern Belle. I remember you now. But…" she looked at him quizzically, "…your hair is different."

"Yes, I had cornrows then. Got tired of it," he said with a shrug as he patted his low-cut hair. "I was really impressed with the way you handled yourself with Monisha. She can be such a…"

"Thank you," Summer cut in, not wanting to discuss the woman behind her back, "but let's not talk about her right now."

She went back to her desk and sat down. "Would you like a piece of my sandwich?"

"No, thanks. I already ate. In fact," he rose as he spoke, "I have to go now. Lance will be on top of me if he catches me lounging around."

"As well he should," she muttered under her breath.

Derrick paused at the door and turned. "I hope to see you again soon, Miss Jones."

Summer simply said, "Bye," but she softened her response with a smile. There was no need to be rude. Still, she didn't want him to linger. She wanted to cover a lot more ground before the day was done.

As soon as the door closed behind him she sat back in her chair, took a big bite out of her sandwich, and switched on the VCR.

It was after four o'clock when Summer surfaced from the main library and headed back to her office, her pad now filled with notes. On her way she stopped at the reception desk and greeted the receptionist.

"How's it going, Chantal?" She leaned over the counter and looked down at the woman tapping busily on the computer keyboard.

Chantal looked up with a start.

"I'm sorry," Summer said. "Did I startle you?"

"A little bit but that's okay. The office has been so quiet this afternoon that I decided to get some work out of the way. I was so caught up in what I was doing that when you spoke it brought me back with a bump."

Chantal leaned back and looked up at Summer. "I need a break anyway. I've been at it for hours. So, how were things in the library?"

"I got through a lot. Look at how many pages of notes I took." Summer held up the note pad and flipped the pages so Chantal could see. "I'll need to continue tomorrow, though. I still have four or five more tapes to view then I'll be all done."

"That should be fine, but be prepared to change plans suddenly if Mr. Munroe returns. He hasn't called the office but he'll probably be back first thing tomorrow." Chantal brushed a speck of dust from the computer screen. "His trips to Jamaica are usually pretty short."

"Jamaica? Is that where he is?"

"Yes. Didn't I tell you?"

"No. You only said he wouldn't be in office today."

"Oh." Chantal frowned slightly as if trying to recall their earlier conversation then she shook her head and continued. "Well, anyway, he called in to say he had to rush down to Jamaica - some urgent personal matter. I think Michelle must be sick again."

Summer's breath caught in her throat and she was barely able to choke out the question. "Michelle? Is that…his wife?"

"Oh, no, he's not married." Chantal laughed and, for the second time that day, Summer prayed that the receptionist couldn't read her usually expressive face. She was fighting hard to hide the relief she felt inside.

But her relief was short-lived. Summer felt her heart freeze at Chantal's next words.

"Michelle's his little girl. At least I think she is. He talks about her quite a bit. That's how I know about her illness. She's only three years old but she's been through a lot. She's got sickle cell anemia. Do you know what that is?"

"I'm...I'm sorry, Chantal. What was your question?" Summer felt slightly dazed.

"I was asking if you knew what sickle cell anemia is. That's what Michelle has."

"I've...heard of it. I don't know all the details but I know it causes a lot of pain in the joints."

"Yes, that's part of it. The reason why people with it have so much pain is that, instead of being oval their white blood cells are shaped with a curve, like the sickle the disease is named after. When the cells are moving through the veins they get hooked instead of just sliding past one another. That's what causes all the pain."

"How come you know all that?"

"Lance told me. He knows all about this sickle cell thing."

"Oh, I see." Summer's voice was quiet, contemplative.

Chantal didn't seem to notice. "You know another thing I learned? Only black people get this sickness. Oh, and people from some parts of the Middle East. Isn't that weird?"

"It certainly is." Summer tried to sound interested but her voice came out weak.

"You alright, Summer?" Chantal asked. "Did I gross you out with that sickle cell stuff?"

"No, no. I just started feeling a little woozy all of a sudden. Maybe I overdid it with the videos." She rubbed her eyes. "I'll be alright. I'll just go sit in my office for a bit."

"Yes, do that." Chantal's voice was edged with concern. "I'll bring you some water in a sec."

Summer turned quickly, glad for an excuse to escape, and bumped right into Monisha Stone.

"Will you look where you're going?" The elegantly dressed singer looked down her slender nose at Summer and glared.

Suddenly, her eyes widened in recognition. "What the hell are you doing here? Have you been following me around or something?"

"Definitely not." Summer's voice, so weak just moments before, was sharp and biting. "I don't need to follow you around. I've got better things to do with my life."

"Miss Jones works here, Miss Stone." Chantal's clear, serene voice cut through the tension.

"What? Since when?" Monisha raised her eyebrows and stared at Chantal in disbelief.

"Since yesterday." Summer didn't give Chantal a chance to respond. "Do you have a problem with that?"

"If I have any problems," Monisha's voice was cold as she looked Summer up and down, "I certainly won't be discussing them with you."

She turned to Chantal, dismissing Summer with a toss of her head. "Tell Lance I'm here to see him."

"I'm sorry, Miss Stone, but Mr. Munroe is not in office today." Chantal's voice was even but Summer thought she saw a slight smirk. "Would you like to leave a message for him?"

"No. I need to talk to him right now. Where is he?"

"I'm sorry, but I can't say."

"You can't say or you won't say?"

Chantal did not respond to the question, but continued calmly, "You could try him on his cell phone. You have his number, of course?"

"Okay, I'll call him. But I came all this way to see him about something important. When we talked last night," Monisha's stress on the last two words was not lost on Summer, "he didn't mention being out of office today. This isn't like him."

"Maybe something urgent came up." Chantal tried to appease her. "I'm sure you'll hear from him soon."

"I'd better. I don't like wasting my time coming all the way over here for nothing. And what's more," she flashed angry eyes at Summer, "he's got a lot of explaining to do."

Without so much as a farewell she whirled and went back through the door, her high heels clicking loudly on the tiles.

Summer and Chantal watched the dramatic exit then turned to look at each other. Suddenly, they both burst out laughing.

"Oh, my God," Summer squeaked between guffaws, "she's a trip."

"You're lucky," Chantal wiped tears from her eyes as she struggled to regain composure, "you're just getting to know her. I've been dealing with her for almost a year."

When they finally calmed down Summer turned as if to go then said, in as casual a tone as she could manage, "By the way, are Lance and Monisha an item?"

"Not that I know of," Chantal shrugged. "I know he's been out with her a few times but I don't know if that means they're together. Looks to me like Monisha is the one doing the pursuing. I doubt they're into anything serious." She paused. Then, as if rethinking her statement, she said, "Then again, when it comes to men you never know."

That night as Summer thought back to all she had learned that day she didn't know whether to feel hopeful or depressed. From the way Monisha had spoken she'd assumed that the woman and Lance were involved, but Chantal seemed to have doubts about that. But then, she'd also learnt that Lance had a child in Jamaica. That news was devastating. She wondered if he was still involved with the child's mother.

Then again, she asked herself, what was all that to her? It was none of her business what the man did with his life. She was nothing to him and he was nothing to her. Alright, she was attracted to him, she admitted to herself. And yes, they'd shared one impulsive kiss. But that was it. Who was she to be lying in bed, moping over a man who probably didn't even remember she existed?

He was out of her league and out of her reach. She realized that fully now. She rolled onto her stomach and sighed in resignation. From here on she wouldn't let his charm and sex appeal distract her from her task. She set her mouth in determination as she thought of how she would change her attitude towards him then wondered why her heart still beat wildly at the thought of him.

Chapter 8

"Jamaica? You never told me I'd have to go to Jamaica," Summer blurted out as she leaned against the door she had just closed behind her. She had been summoned to Lance's office for a quick conference but was totally confounded by this new development.

"I never thought it would be an issue. It will only be for a couple of weeks." Lance shrugged then waved her to the chair in front of him.

She remained where she was, still too surprised to respond.

"Do you have a problem with travelling?" He looked at her quizzically.

"No, no, it's not that." Summer put her hand to her eyes. She wondered how she could get out of this situation. "I...you just caught me by surprise. I never expected that I'd have to leave the country."

"And would that be a problem? Leaving the country?"

"No. I guess not." She sighed and looked at Lance. "You just caught me by surprise, that's all."

"Miss Jones," Lance frowned, "it's obvious that you're not comfortable with the idea of going to Jamaica. What, exactly, is the problem?"

"No, no, there's no problem." Summer spoke in what she hoped was a reassuring tone. "It's just that I wanted to tie up my move to the new apartment. But I'll just have to hurry up, make my selection and sign the contract. I want to get all of that out of the way before I leave town. That's all."

"You're sure?" Lance looked at her skeptically.

"Yes. I'm sure." She nodded then quickly dropped her eyes to the paperweight on his desk so that he wouldn't see the lie in her eyes.

Lance was silent for a while then he said, "Sit down, please. I want to give you the details of your trip."

By the time Summer left Lance's office thirty-five minutes later her flight to Jamaica was booked and she had her list of pre-trip assignments, as well as details of what she would be doing while on the trip.

According to him they'd be going to Jamaica to do a video shoot, recordings for the latest album he was producing, as well as meet with a local promotions company. Lance felt that this was also an excellent opportunity for her to get to interact with the artistes in their own territory and really get to know their personal side. He expected her to return with meaningful stories and lots of information to feed the press.

Summer had a lot to do before leaving for Jamaica. The trip was only ten days away and she had to complete all the summaries she had been working on for her eight assigned artistes and submit them to Lance for review. She also had to organize a press conference for the launch of Monisha's new album, as well as work with the agency on an article to appear in Vibe Magazine. On top of that she would have to complete her apartment search and then move.

But despite all she would have to accomplish in ten days she was not worried about her work. Her greatest concern was her mother. Edna Jones had not yet been scheduled for surgery and Summer had no desire to go far from her mother's side. She worried that if she left town her mother would have to face surgery alone. It was not as if she had siblings who could be there in her absence. She was all her mother had.

At the same time she desperately needed to keep this job. She would be moving soon, which meant a deposit plus the first month's rent would be required. Her first tuition payment would also be due in less than two weeks. And, most important for her, she needed to have some funds to assist with her mother's surgery. She definitely couldn't afford to lose this job. Not now.

"Hey."

Summer looked up to see Chantal peeking into her office.

"I have your e-ticket."

"That was quick." Summer smiled weakly. "Come on in. I could do with a little distraction right now."

"You alright?" Chantal entered the office and went to sit in the chair in front of her.

"I'm okay," Summer shrugged, "just a little overwhelmed with all I've got to get done, that's all."

"You sure? You look kinda down. I thought you'd be excited about going to Jamaica."

"I…I am," Summer replied.

"Yeah, right." Chantal was obviously unconvinced.

"Alright, alright. I'm not," she admitted, then added, "but it has nothing to do with not wanting to go. It's just the timing. I've got some personal issues right now, that's all."

"Oh. I'm sorry. Want to talk about it?"

"Not really…" she said the words reluctantly, not wanting to offend Chantal.

"Okay, but did you discuss your issues with Lance?"

"No, I didn't think it was appropriate."

"Maybe you should. If he's aware you're having problems maybe he'll go easy on you and not give you so much stuff to do, maybe even let you get out of this trip. Why don't you talk to him?"

"No," Summer shook her head, "I really don't think that's a good idea."

"He's not an ogre, you know. I've known him more than a year and I can tell you, his bark is a whole lot worse than his bite."

"Well…I'll think about it," Summer conceded. She still had no intention of sharing her private life with her boss. She just wanted Chantal to leave her alone so she could think.

Later that day Summer got the shock of her life when Lance stopped by her office, perched on the edge of the credenza and said, "I want to know what day you're planning to move. I'm making myself available for you to use me in anyway necessary."

Somehow, the way he said the words made Summer's face get warm.

"Oh, that's okay," she said quickly, "I wouldn't want to bother you."

"It's no bother. I want to make sure that you've got nothing hanging over your head when you're in Jamaica. You said your concern was about getting moved into your new apartment, right? Well, let me help you deal with that and get it out of the way."

"But you don't have to do that. I'll manage okay."

"Don't argue with me, Summer. You were obviously feeling overwhelmed this morning when I told you all you had to complete before your departure. You were the one who complained about having to move, on top of all that." He folded his arms across his chest, but his look was relaxed. "Now tell me…which day are you planning to move?"

She looked up at him then dropped her eyes again and toyed with her pencil. "Ah, I haven't decided yet. I just need to talk to my real estate agent to do the final selection and then I'll set the date."

"You haven't done any of that yet? What are you waiting for?" His tone was impatient.

"Well, I've been a bit busy lately," she responded quickly, annoyed at his lack of understanding.

"For someone who acts like she's always in control you certainly don't seem to be very organized," he continued, as if immune to the pointed look she gave him.

"I have a lot on my mind," she parried.

"Hmmph." He rose and strode towards the door where he paused and said, "Just make sure you tell me when you've finalized your move date."

When he walked out the door Summer stuck out her tongue at his retreating back then giggled at her childish behavior.

"Too bossy for your own good, that's what you are," she muttered but there was a smile on her face as she whispered the words.

That evening Summer was pensive as she walked down the corridor to her mother's room. She was going to have to tell her about the trip to Jamaica and she was nervous. The longest time she had spent away from Chicago and from her mother was when she'd gone on that week long Caribbean cruise with her graduating class; and that had been when her mother's condition had not been this bad. Now she would be leaving at a time when her mother needed her. She felt a wave of guilt wash over her and wondered if, somehow, she could back out without losing her job.

When Summer knocked and pushed the door open there was a bright smile on her face; it hid the turbulent thoughts that churned inside her.

"Hi, Mom. How're you doing?"

Edna Jones turned away from the window and returned her daughter's cheerful smile. "You're early."

"I wanted to surprise you. I thought maybe I'd come catch you with a man or something," she teased.

"Oh, you go on. Where am I going to find a man in here?"

"Well, you never know. Your Prince Charming might just show up at your door one day." Summer slung her handbag onto a hook by the door and turned to her mother. "Isn't that how it normally works?"

"Well, I wouldn't know. You're the one who's in fairytale land right now," Edna chuckled. "Imagine me with a man. Ha!"

"You never know." Summer bent and kissed her mother on the forehead. "So, what are you up to?"

"Oh, nothing much," Edna replied and waved her hand to the window, "just enjoying the view. Not much else to do up here."

Summer went over to stand by the window and, for a moment, she stood staring out at the reds and golds that streaked the blue water. She drew in a breath then spoke.

"Mom, I've got something to tell you."

"Yes. What is it, dear?"

"I may have to go away for a couple of weeks. To Jamaica."

"Jamaica? How's that?" Edna sounded surprised and Summer felt even more apprehensive.

"It's…it's my job. My boss asked me to go down there with the team." She hesitated then said, "I'm not sure what I'm going to do."

"What do you mean, Sugar?"

"Well, you're sick. You could get called into surgery any day now. I don't want to leave you like this."

"Oh, child, go ahead. You may never get the opportunity to do this again. Don't you worry yourself about me."

"But Mom, what if the doctor calls you for surgery when I'm gone? I have to be here."

"No, you don't. Didn't you tell me this is your dream job?"

"No job is more important to me than you are." Summer frowned at her mother.

"I know, dear. But this is such a great opportunity for you. I mean, with this you have the best of both worlds - a great job, plus a chance to travel. What more could you ask for?"

"I could ask for you to be better," she said sadly. "That's what I really want."

"Summer, come sit here." Edna patted the bed beside her. "Let's talk."

With a sigh, she went over and sat on the bed.

"Honey, I know you love me very much. You've always been there for me, even to the detriment of your studies and your classes." Edna took Summer's hand in hers and spoke gently. "But this time, baby, I want you to focus on yourself. I'm on my way out of this world, but you're just beginning the journey. You have your whole life ahead of you. Just this one time I want you to go for it."

"But, Mom…"

"No, no, let me speak. You've always put me first but now you need to do this for you." Edna reached into the top drawer of her night table and pulled out a big brown envelope. "These are the test results from the labs."

"Momma!" Summer jumped up and grabbed the envelope from Edna's hand. "You got the results and didn't tell me?"

"Hush, child. No need to get so excited. I only got them this morning."

Summer pulled out three sheets of paper and an X-ray.

"But what's all this?" Summer's voice was sharp with anxiety as she scanned the papers. "What did the doctor say?"

"He said the tests results were better than he expected. In fact, he was saying that the surgery may not even be necessary after all. He's going to run some more tests just to make sure but I'm hopeful." A smile softened the weathered face. "So you see, you can go to Jamaica after all. As I always say, just leave it all in the hands of the Lord."

Relief washed over Summer and she leaned over and hugged her mother tight.

"Oh, Mom, I'm so glad," she whispered, and there was a catch in her voice. She bit her lip, trying hard not to cry. She hated showing any sign of weakness. Lately, she'd started getting so emotional. She'd have to start getting tough again. This emotion thing would definitely not do.

When she left the nursing home that evening she felt light-hearted. It looked like, at last, her mother was moving into remission and her health would be improving.

As she turned the corner onto State Street she saw her reflection in the window of the Toys R Us store. Her face was all smiles. Had she been walking down the street, grinning like an idiot all this time, she wondered. She pursed her lips, struggling to keep a stern face, but it was no use. For the first time in a long time she was truly happy and there was nothing she could do to hide it. Oh, what the heck, she thought, and continued on her way, a trace of a smile still on her lips.

It was a whirlwind week for her, both at the office and at home. Her work days were packed with activities and by the time she got home in the evenings she was exhausted. Despite her tiredness she then had to pack boxes with books, clothing, cookware and china and she still had to find time to meet with her real estate agent to discuss the offer on the residence she'd selected.

To her relief the transaction was completed on Thursday and she left the meeting with the keys to her new apartment. She went into the office earlier than usual on Friday, as she had requested to leave early that day. She wanted to have everything ready for the Saturday morning move. She ducked her head into Lance's office and reminded him of her early departure. For a moment he looked at her inquiringly and she held her breath, hoping he hadn't changed his mind about letting her leave at two o'clock.

"You'd asked for this afternoon off?" He seemed unsure.

"Yes, I spoke to you on Monday and you said it would be fine," she reminded him. "I came in early this morning to compensate for the time I'm taking this afternoon."

"Oh, I know you requested time off. I just forgot that it was today." He frowned slightly then shrugged. "That's fine. I'd wanted you to accompany me to the meeting with the Action Agency but I'm sure I can manage without you - this one time." His smile was teasing.

"I'm sorry you forgot but I wouldn't have asked for the afternoon off if I didn't really need it. I have to move into my new apartment tomorrow so I have to get everything in order from today."

"You're moving tomorrow? You didn't tell me you needed the afternoon to get ready for your move." The frown returned to his face. "I thought I told you to let me know what day you were going to do that."

"I'm sorry, I forgot to tell you." Summer's voice was hesitant as she tried to read his face. "And anyway, I didn't know you were serious."

"Miss Jones," Lance leaned back in his chair and locked her in his steady gaze, "I don't say things I don't mean. In future, please take everything I say seriously."

He dropped his gaze from her for a moment as he reached over to pick up a glass of water. Summer used the opportunity to roll her eyes and fix him with a feisty stare of her own. Suddenly he looked back at her, and she quickly made her face serious again.

"I know you're a very independent woman and you probably feel you can do it all by yourself but there are times when you need to put pride aside and accept help when it's offered. It's all well and good to be cheeky," his faint smile made her realize that he'd caught her look, "but not at the expense of your well-being."

Summer smiled back at him, this time a bit sheepishly.

"So, what time is the move?" he asked.

"The truck will be at my place at nine in the morning but I'll be up at seven to start putting things out."

"I'll be there at eight. Make sure you leave your address and home number with Chantal before you go."

Without waiting for her response he picked up the telephone and began to dial. Summer withdrew from the office, pulled the door shut behind her, and let her breath out slowly. She was going to have a hell of a time concentrating on boxes of books with that man around.

By the time the doorbell rang at exactly eight o'clock next morning Summer felt she would have been ready to work with

Adonis himself. She'd gotten up at six to finish packing the final boxes. She had also been practicing her nonchalant 'I don't give a damn that you're here' look. She'd dressed as casually as possible - grey baggy sweat pants, grey t-shirt, sneakers and a black baseball cap. She had on very little make up and no jewellery except for gold knobs and a thin gold chain.

She was certainly not going to give Lance the pleasure of believing that she was in any way affected by his presence. If he thought for one moment that because she'd been so weak once before she was going to throw herself at him again, he had another think coming. She would show him that she was in total control of her emotions and he was absolutely nothing to her but an employer.

She walked quickly to the door and flung it open, a bright smile plastered across her lips. The smile froze then slowly dissolved as she stared up at the ruggedly handsome man who filled her doorway. He wore a navy blue polo shirt which was stretched across his broad chest. The short sleeves revealed his muscled arms. The shirt was tucked into jeans that hugged narrow hips and solid thighs and emphasized the height of him. His sandalled feet were long and narrow and Summer remembered the stories she'd heard about men's feet and their virility.

Her eyes flew guiltily back to his face and she stared at his firm lips which were curled in a quirky smile. She raised her eyes to his dark ones and saw that he was staring back at her, almost mockingly. He, too, wore a baseball cap. It gave him a relaxed look which was boyish and, at the same time, breathtakingly manly. Gosh, she thought, this isn't going to be as easy as I thought.

"Good morning." His deep voice broke into her thoughts. "Aren't you going to invite me in?"

"Oh, I'm sorry." She stepped back and allowed him entrance. As he passed her his arm brushed against her shoulder and she felt as if a jolt of electricity had hit her body.

She pulled away quickly and he looked down at her, his amusement obvious. Mercifully, he only smiled and walked into the apartment.

As Summer followed him she said, "Just go right ahead."

She needn't have bothered. By the time she finished her statement he was already surveying the bags, boxes and suitcases that filled the space. She was a bit disgruntled that, instead of waiting for her, he'd begun touching things as if he owned the place.

She knew her annoyance showed on her face when he looked back at her and laughed, "Hey, why that look? I'm not taking over, you know."

He approached her then stopped a few feet away and tucked his hands into the back pockets of his jeans. "Today I'm not your boss, just someone who's here to give you a helping hand. You're the one who's running the show, okay?"

Summer's face relaxed into a smile. How could she stay mad at him when he looked so charming? No, not charming, she corrected herself. Sexy.

When the movers arrived at nine o'clock Summer and Lance were ready for them. All her loose items which had still been stacked in a corner when Lance arrived were now in boxes sealed with heavy duct tape. Three men had come from the moving company and, since she didn't have a whole lot inside her studio apartment, the truck was loaded in no time.

She smiled inwardly when she saw how Lance took charge of the move, giving orders to the men and even giving directions to her. So, she thought, she was the boss, huh? Boss was written all over Lance. Apparently he just couldn't help himself.

The actual move took only a few hours. All the furniture, boxes and bags were in the new apartment by midday. Then it was time for the real work.

When the moving men left Summer and Lance worked together to get all the furniture organized then began unpacking boxes and bags. Summer took charge of the kitchen. She cleaned out the cupboards then began sorting her china and silverware. Meanwhile, Lance unpacked boxes of books and organized them on shelves that ran along the walls of the narrow hallway.

Next, he worked on the living room, hanging drapes and setting up the lamps while Summer moved into the bedroom where she started unpacking her clothes, bed linen and shoes.

She was so engrossed in her task of organizing the closets that she didn't realize that Lance had entered the room until she backed out of the closet and into him.

"Oh," she gasped as she felt the solid mass against her back. Rock hard arms encircled her waist and he held her close for a brief moment while she regained her balance. She turned in his arms and found herself staring at the triangle of hair that peeped out from his polo shirt. She rested her cheek against his shirt momentarily, basking in the warmth of his body against hers, enjoying the strength of his arms wrapped around her body.

Lance used a strong finger to tilt her face up towards his own. She watched, entranced, as he lowered his mouth slowly to hers.

Firm lips pressed gently against trembling ones, moving, teasing, caressing. The tension in her body melted away, leaving her soft and yielding in his arms.

As she leaned against his hard body all thoughts left her except the feel of him as he held her close. Her quivering lips parted with a sigh and as she opened to him he pulled her even closer and covered her mouth fully with his own. His kiss became insistent, masterful, and soon she found herself responding in kind. A soft moan escaped her throat as she surrendered to him. He slid his hand down to the small of her back as he relished her warm, willing mouth.

When Lance finally lifted his head Summer still clung to him, eyes closed tight. Her heart pounded so hard against her chest that she feared he could feel it, too. He pulled her close again, but this time he only gave her a soft peck on the forehead then put her away from him gently. He bent his lips to her ear and whispered, "You may open your eyes now, little one."

With a sigh she did so. She gazed up into his dark enigmatic eyes, trying to understand what lay within their depths, but when her gaze fell to his lips and she saw the amused curl of his mouth she quickly pulled away, annoyed that he could laugh at her when she was so overcome with emotion.

She glared at him and pushed hard against his chest, almost causing him to stumble, then stalked out of the room.

Chapter 9

"Welcome to Montego Bay, ladies and gentlemen. We thank you for flying Air Jamaica and hope you enjoy your stay."

As the plane taxied along the runway Summer peered through the window at the houses, large and small, tucked away on the green hills in the distance. The scene was different from the one she'd seen two years earlier when she had arrived on a cruise ship. Then, her very first view of Jamaica had been turquoise waters, white sand, and tourists engaged in all kinds of water sports - parasailing, water skiing and boating. This time she watched as local air traffic controllers guided the aircraft into position in preparation for the disembarkation of the passengers.

Summer's heart skipped a beat. No matter that this was a business trip - she was filled with anticipation and excitement at being on the island. She glanced over at Lance who sat in the aisle seat and saw that he was still absorbed in the sheaf of papers he had pulled from his briefcase. She guessed that he'd been back and forth between Jamaica and Chicago so many times that the arrival didn't affect him like it did her.

She turned her attention back to the window and watched as a vehicle came right up to the side of the plane and the technicians connected the portable stairs. She was glad that Super Cool, a young Jamaican singer, sat between Lance and her. She'd been afraid that she would have been forced to make small talk with her boss but she needn't have worried. Super Cool's chatter kept her fully entertained and Lance kept his nose buried in his papers for most of the four hour flight.

Summer was pleasantly surprised when they entered the airport's immigration lobby and was greeted by a gaily dressed group of singers who welcomed them to the island with a medley of local folk songs and a small glass of rum punch for each arriving passenger.

It was only then that she saw a change in Lance's distant mood. He relaxed visibly in the presence of the friendly group and even exchanged a few words with them in their local dialect. Summer couldn't help smiling when she heard them. Lance had converted from Chicagoan to island man just like that. She wondered if his attitude would change, too - she wouldn't mind if he became less cold and formal. She was tired of being called 'Miss Jones'.

The hotel had sent a bus to collect all their arriving guests. It took them one hour and fifteen minutes to cover the forty-five miles from Montego Bay to their hotel in Ocho Rios. Summer didn't mind the journey one bit. She sat right up front with the driver and drank in all the rural Jamaican scenery.

The tourist town of Montego Bay was teeming with visitors walking the streets in shorts and sandals, colourful shirts and wide-brimmed straw hats. At her expression of surprise at their numbers Simon, the driver, explained that this was how it was when a cruise ship came into port.

What made it worse, he said, was that it was the middle of the summer season and many visitors, tourists as well as Jamaicans living abroad, were taking advantage of their children being on vacation to visit the island. He explained that outside of the January-February winter season the summer months were the heaviest for visitor arrivals.

"We don' mind it at all," he smiled as he spoke in his heavy Jamaican accent. "The more visitors we have the more money we get. Everybody make money and we can sen' the children to school when September come. Yeah, mon, tourism is good for all of we."

Summer laughed and settled back in her seat to enjoy the view from this vantage point. Somehow she felt totally relaxed, almost carefree. She didn't know if it was the warm sunshine that baked the arm she rested on the window or the vividness of the colours all around her - the sky was so blue and the hills so green. All she knew was that she was in high spirits. She couldn't explain it so she just put it down to 'Island Fever' - maybe that's how you are when you live on an island, she thought. No wonder these people were always saying, 'No problem, mon'.

As they left Montego Bay they drove along the rolling green plains and golf courses of Rose Hall and went past the magnificent Rose Hall Estate where, Simon said, the owner used to control her slaves by threatening to place a curse on them. He told her how Annie Palmer, called the White Witch of Rose Hall by the locals, had had seven husbands and had killed them all, one after the other, with her witchcraft. She finally met her end at the hand of an old African witchdoctor, Tacoma, who killed her because she'd placed a curse on his granddaughter that drew her into a deep depression and finally led to her death.

Summer was so intrigued by the story that she kept plying Simon with questions until Lance, who had so far been silent, broke in. "You seem to be very interested in this witchcraft thing. Be careful you don't scare off any prospective suitors."

Summer turned in her seat and looked back at him. He was smiling at her in his usual mocking manner. Her breath caught in her throat at the sheer handsomeness of him and the retort which was at the tip of her tongue was suddenly lost in her confusion.

Like Summer, Lance had dressed casually for the trip. He wore a short sleeved cotton shirt and jeans. His head was bare and his short-cropped hair shone black and glossy in the rays of sunlight that streamed in through the window of the bus. No matter what Lance wore there was no hiding his commanding presence and arresting profile.

"Cat got your tongue?" His question dragged her out of her reverie and she replied quickly, hoping he couldn't see the effect he was having on her.

"Not at all. I was just thinking that a woman like Annie Palmer would make the perfect wife for someone I know."

"Ooh," Simon laughed at the remark, "is a really saucy sistah we have here."

"Yeah, Simon," Lance joined in the laughter. "See what I have to put up with?"

"But dat's good, sah. She hot jus' like the Jamaican girls. Das how I like it. A woman mus' speak up for herself, mon."

"I should leave this one with you for awhile, Simon. You'd be begging me to take her back in a week." Lance's voice crackled with laughter and the other people in the bus, Super Cool and a honeymooning couple, all joined in the laughter.

"Will you stop talking about me as if I'm not here." Summer frowned at Lance then turned to Simon who was covering his mouth with one hand, struggling to contain his laughter. It was no use. It burst out of him and he laughed so hard that tears streamed down his face.

Finally Summer gave in and laughed too. Then, trying to sound stern again, she said, "Okay, Simon, enough laughing. I need you concentrating on these winding roads, not laughing your head off."

"Alright, Miss." Simon quieted down but still chuckled as he said, "I don' want to scare you. Jus' relax now and enjoy the sunshine and the sea breeze. Alright?"

With a smile Summer nodded, leaned back in her seat and did as he instructed.

The rest of the journey was quiet and pleasant. They drove along the sea coast through fishing villages and small towns until the tall hotel buildings of Ocho Rios came into view. Within another ten minutes they were standing in the luxurious lobby of the Grand Caribbean Hotel.

The front desk manager greeted them with a smile and a glass of rum punch for each guest.

"What is it with these people?" Summer asked, shaking her head. "Are they all trying to get us drunk?"

The comment brought a smile to Lance's face but he remained silent.

As they were checking in there was a noise behind them and they turned to see Derrick coming towards them wearing nothing but a pair of baggy shorts and a towel draped across his shoulders. There were grains of sand on his sandalled feet and his shorts clung damply to him.

"Hey, guys," he called out loudly, "you finally made it."

He greeted Lance and Super Cool then turned appreciative eyes on Summer. She stared boldly back at him, her eyes daring him to make his usual chauvinistic remarks. On seeing her stern look he simply grinned and said, "Dang, girl, why so grumpy? This is Jamaica, man. The least you could do is try to look happy."

Not wanting to seem ungracious Summer pasted a smile on her face and replied, "Hello, Derrick."

"Now that's more like it," he said, and threw his arms around her in a big bear hug.

Lance stared at them questioningly then said, "You two know each other?"

"Yeah," Derrick responded as he released Summer. "I met this fine lady the day I came by your office for the documents. You're a lucky man. This girl is hot!"

Summer looked away, deeply embarrassed at the man's open praise. She wished he would shut up. Lance didn't respond but Summer stole a glance at him and saw that his face was stern. Then his face cleared and she began to wonder if she had only imagined it.

He looked at his watch and said, "Three o'clock. Okay, guys, we'll regroup at six for the dinner meeting with the managers from Rock Steady Promotions. I'm going to take a quick nap so I'll be fresh for later. I'd suggest you both do the same." He put his hand to his mouth and quickly stifled a yawn. "Getting up to catch a six o'clock flight is a real killer."

He picked up his bag then looked at Derrick. "I expect you to be there. On time."

"Yes, sir, Mr. Munroe, sir." Derrick straightened his back and saluted smartly then, relaxing his posture, he laughed and clapped Lance on the back. "Hey, man, I'll be there. You know me."

"I do." Lance did not smile back. "Just show up on time, alright?"

"Cool, man. No problem."

After Lance departed for his room Summer left Super Cool and Derrick in the lobby and took the elevator to her own room. She had a beautiful view of the ocean. As soon as she had deposited her bags in the closet she opened the glass sliding door and went out onto the balcony to drink in the view.

It was a warm sunny day and the afternoon sun glistened on the blue sea that stretched before her. Down below she could see people, black and white, lying on the white sand and playing in the water. Children shrieked and laughed as they played. Just watching them made Summer's tiredness disappear.

She thought of the hot pink bikini she'd brought and suddenly decided to go down for a quick swim. After this trip she didn't know when she'd make it back to Jamaica. Why not make the most of it, she thought. After all, they'd be heading for Kingston day after tomorrow so she might not get another chance to enjoy the beach.

Summer pulled her bag out of the closet and dumped it on the bed. She dug through and pulled out a pink t-shirt, a pair of white shorts and her hot pink bikini.

Within fifteen minutes she was walking on the hot sand, her sandals dangling from her fingers. It felt so good when the grains of sand slid between her toes that, as she walked, she stopped every few minutes to dig them deep into the gritty earth and feel the warmth envelop her feet.

She spied a gazebo with palm fronds for a roof. Guests sat around the counter on high stools and bartenders were serving cold drinks and liquor. Just what I need, she thought, and headed for the oasis on the sand.

As she downed a tall glass of lemonade Summer leaned back against the bar and watched the waterskiers go by. A snorkelling class was also in progress. The instructor was a tall, very black man with wide shoulders and an incredibly narrow waist. Each time he ducked his head into the water then stood up again he flashed his dreadlocks and sent drops of water flying in all directions. He smiled often with his group and his teeth flashed white in the sun. Summer stared at him, smiling involuntarily at his joviality.

At that moment the man looked straight back at her. His smile widened and he raised his hand in a wave. Feeling slightly embarrassed that he'd caught her staring she waved back feebly then ducked her head to suck on her straw.

"Hey, baby. What you doing down here with all them clothes on?"

As Summer turned towards the voice she rolled her eyes. There was only one person she knew who would greet her that way.

"Hello again, Derrick." Her tone lacked any warmth or friendliness.

"What you drinking?" He perched on the stool next to her and rubbed the back of his head with a towel. "God, that water's good."

"Lemonade," she said in a bored tone.

"That's it? Kinda soft for a girl like you, isn't it?"

"What's that supposed to mean?" Her voice was sharp.

"You know…college girl, sophisticated and all that. I know about all the drinking and partying that goes on at college."

"Listen. You don't know anything about me so don't make assumptions." She fixed him with a glare. "I don't drink, I don't smoke and I don't sleep around. So whatever you think you know about college women just don't go using that to brand me, okay?"

"Whoa, ease up, baby. I'm sorry. I didn't mean to come off like that." Derrick put his hands up in a defensive gesture. "I just think you're a beautiful woman and you come off as so independent. I really like that in a woman. Don't think I'm trying to put you down, baby. No way…I'm a fan."

"Oh…thanks." Not knowing what else to say Summer tried to change the subject. "So when did you arrive at the hotel? You look so settled here."

"I got in yesterday. Wanted to get here a little earlier than you guys to tie up some other business. That's taken care of so right now I'm just chilling on the beach." He relaxed with his back against the bar, his slight paunch exposed to the open air, and stared out at the blue water lapping against the sand.

"Doesn't get any better than this - good weather, good food, and a beautiful woman by your side."

At that moment the bartender approached with a pleasant smile and asked, "And what may I serve the lovely couple?"

"We're not a couple," Summer was quick to tell him.

"But you never know, know what I'm saying?" Derrick laughed and threw a casual arm around Summer. She shrugged it off and pushed her empty glass away.

"Let me have a Red Stripe Beer," Derrick ordered, "and bring something nice for the lady. What're you having Summer?"

"I'm okay, thanks."

"Aw, come on. Have a drink with me," he cajoled.

"I just had a drink."

"Lemonade?" he scoffed. "Have a real drink."

"What's wrong with lemonade?"

"Nothing, but you're on an island, honey. Live it up a little."

Summer sighed, "Okay, if you insist. I'll have a Piña Colada. Virgin."

"How'd I know you were going to say that?" Derrick laughed then turned to the bartender. "Piña Colada it is, my man. But hold the spirits."

As Summer sipped her drink and Derrick guzzled his beer he told her about the Reggae Sumfest Show that had taken place the month before. He gave such a vivid description of the various acts that Summer almost felt like she'd been there herself.

His skills at commentary surprised her and she soon found herself deep in animated conversation with the man who had so recently been nothing but a source of annoyance. By the time Derrick finished his account of the events Summer was responding enthusiastically. When he later invited her for a swim she gave in, more relaxed in his company.

"Well, come on then, girl. We don't have all day."

He jumped off the stool and raced away. With a laugh she ran after him. When he reached the water he kept on running then plunged into the gentle waves rolling in to the shore. Summer stopped short, suddenly remembering that she was still fully dressed.

"Come on," Derrick called to her. "What are you waiting for?"

"This." Summer pointed to her clothes. "I've still got all this stuff on."

"Well, get rid of them, woman." Derrick's grin was infectious. "Go change real quick and get in here or else I'm gonna come get you and drag you in, clothes or no clothes."

She took his threat seriously and scampered off to the nearest kiosk where she quickly ripped off her shorts and t-shirt. She handed them to the clothing check girl and accepted a large beach towel in exchange.

Within minutes she was back at the water's edge watching Derrick doing the back stroke. When he spied her still standing there, the towel draped loosely around her, he yelled, "I'm coming to get you," and began swimming to shore.

With a squeal she let the towel fall to the sand to reveal the hot pink bathing suit which was designed to accentuate her curves. Derrick pulled up short then whistled in appreciation and Summer felt her body tingle with embarrassment, but mostly with pleasure at his appreciative response.

She stepped gingerly into the frothy water at the shore line and was surprised at its warmth. She plunged in and swam towards Derrick. The warm water of the Caribbean Sea washed over her body and she reveled in its caress.

Summer had so much fun and the time passed so quickly with Derrick that she lost track of time. It was only when she heard a woman call to her child to come in for dinner that she remembered that she had an evening engagement.

"Derrick," she gasped, "the dinner. We need to go get dressed."

"Shoot, I forgot all about that." He stopped mid backstroke and began to tread water as he peered at her through the salty water running down his face.

"I'm sure it's late," she said. "I wonder what time it is?"

"Well, we won't know if we stay here. Come on."

He made for the shore and Summer swam after him. He waited for her to retrieve her clothes. She didn't stop to put them on. They both ran, dripping wet, to the hotel lobby where the huge clock showed five thirty-six. Summer groaned. She had twenty-four minutes to get dressed and be back downstairs for the dinner meeting.

Suddenly, before she knew what was happening, Derrick grabbed her arm, halting her in her tracks. He pulled her close in a strong embrace and bent his head to plant a wet kiss on her startled lips.

"Thanks for a lovely afternoon," he breathed against her face. He released her slowly and she stared up at him, still clutching her clothes and sandals in one hand and the beach towel in the other.

"How romantic." At the sound of the deep voice Summer turned to see Lance standing by the door of the lounge, fully dressed for the evening. He had a glass in his hand and looked totally relaxed as he stared at his two employees.

Summer felt a wave of embarrassment wash over her but she held her head high and refused to be intimidated.

Derrick broke the tension. "Hey, man. We were just heading up to get dressed."

Lance didn't answer. He took a sip of his drink and continued to stare at the dripping, sandy couple. The tension became too much for Summer.

"I'll be down by six," she muttered and walked quickly to the elevator.

Once inside she leaned back against the mirrored walls and let out a sigh. It was going to be a long night.

Chapter 10

Lance watched Summer's face as she spoke animatedly with the manager of Rock Steady Promotions. She was deep in conversation and seemed to be deliberately avoiding his eyes. He could understand that. She certainly had something to feel guilty about. He'd had a feeling that this girl, attractive as she was, would be something of a flirt. He leaned forward and took a sip of the fruit punch he'd ordered.

As the rich, fruity mixture slid down his throat he watched Summer from under hooded lids. She was wearing a cotton dress the color of burnt orange, the perfect complement to her copper brown hair. Her usually wild curls had been brushed straight and were pinned on top of her head in a neat bun. Her full lips, which curved attractively each time she smiled, were accentuated with rich color. Her perfume was soft and sweetly seductive. Lance thought she fit perfectly in the Jamaican setting - she was like a tropical flower just waiting to be plucked.

As he listened to the lively discussion it was obvious to him that Rock Steady's managers were impressed with Summer. George Morrison was listening keenly to her description of the strengths of the various artistes from Munroe Productions. Ann-Marie Garvey had seemed nonchalant at first but Lance knew that Summer struck a chord when he saw the woman pause in her note-taking to listen keenly to the description of the audience's reaction to Super Cool's performance the month before.

"Super Cool will be great on stage," Summer said, as she spread the artiste's publicity shots on the table. "He's young, talented and so cute. He's bound to be a hit with the girls." She smiled and Lance could see that it was having an effect on George.

"I'm sure we have a winner. So - what do you think?"

"Well, when you put it that way, how could we object?" George leaned back in his chair with a broad smile and shook his head slowly. "Miss Jones, you are one determined woman. When you want something there's no refusing you."

"Thank you, Mr. Morrison. I go after what I want, and I get it – well, most of the times, anyway."

"If you ever decide to leave my good friend over here," George stretched over and patted Lance on the shoulder, "give me a call. A woman like you would be a great addition to my team."

"Why, thank you," Summer responded breathlessly, obviously taken aback. "I'll bear that in mind."

Lance looked at her pointedly but said nothing. He could see that she was becoming flustered by his stare but he held her gaze until she dropped her eyes and picked up her napkin. As she dabbed lightly at her mouth Ann-Marie spoke, breaking the tension.

"Summer, the PR package you gave me...it has the latest shots of Super Cool, I assume? It's stuff we can use right away?"

"Of course," Summer looked up, obviously glad to get back to the conversation. "It's all up-to-date. In fact, I included a press kit so you don't need to create anything new if you don't want to. It's all done."

"Sounds good," Ann-Marie patted the folder and looked across at George. "Looks like a go, George?"

"A fresh new face on our show? You know these young girls go crazy over the young DJ's." George directed his attention towards Lance. "Now, Mr. Boss-man, let's talk money."

Summer stared at her reflection in the mirror then tried to soften the frown that creased her brow. Lance Munroe was insufferable. He'd hardly said a word all night but simply sat there staring at her with those dark, unreadable eyes. She knew he was angry with her. He hadn't come out and said so but his intense looks and his terse statements left no doubt in her mind.

And what right did he have to be angry with her, she huffed. She'd done nothing wrong. He'd acted like he had some claim over her and it irked her a lot. She'd always been independent and wasn't about to start letting any man run her life, boss or no boss. If he thought she was some kid he could intimidate with his scowl then he had another think coming.

She gave herself a mental shake then dipped into her purse and pulled out her lipstick. She slowly traced her lips with vivid color then smiled at her reflection in satisfaction. She'd had enough of hiding in the ladies' room. She wasn't scared of him. She was her own woman and he would just have to accept that, like it or not.

When Summer returned to the table the contracts were already signed and the visitors looked like they were getting ready to leave. As she slipped into her chair she heard the men talking about a recent cricket match. Ann-Marie was packing papers into her briefcase.

She looked up as Summer sat down then leaned towards her and whispered, "Are you alright? You were gone quite a while."

Summer gave the woman a smile and said reassuringly, "I'm fine. Thanks for asking, though."

Lance must have overheard Ann-Marie's question because he glanced sharply at her but within a split second he'd turned his attention back to George and she didn't know whether to be grateful that he was no longer staring at her or angry that she was of so little consequence to him.

After George and Ann-Marie had departed they sat in silence - he, sipping on a Strawberry Daquiri and she, toying with her purse.

Finally the tension got to her and she spoke. "Well, that went fairly well."

His reply was blunt. "No need to be modest. It was a damn good meeting and you represented the company really well. I think you already know that."

You could have said so, she thought, but only nodded with a slight smile. "I'm glad I got a chance to put my negotiation skills to the test."

He nodded but said nothing. They sat in silence for a while longer then Summer said, "Well, I think I'll head upstairs and rest up for tomorrow."

As she rose to leave he stood and nodded solemnly to her. Clutching her purse tightly she strode quickly away, feeling his piercing eyes on her back.

Summer lay back on the pillows in the king sized bed and flipped through the channels of the hotel cable system. She'd returned to her room still wound-up and tense. She needed to relax and thought TV would do the trick.

But as she flipped from channel to channel she became more and more frustrated. Over forty channels and nothing sensible to watch. With a hiss of her teeth she threw down the remote control and jumped off the bed.

She turned on the CD player and Sade's sultry voice filled the room. She reached behind and pulled her zipper down, then let the soft folds of burnt orange slide down her body to the floor. She stepped out of the dress and without even bothering to pick it up, walked across the plush carpet to the bathroom.

The hot water felt good against her body, both relaxing and stimulating at the same time. She could feel the tension melt away as the water hit her back and shoulders. She rubbed her hands over her warm wet body, pausing to knead the flesh in the small of her back. She stayed there for a long time enjoying the luxurious sensation.

Reluctantly, she turned the tap off, pulled the curtain aside and stepped onto the thick white rug. She stood naked in the steamy bathroom and drew a huge smiley face on the mirror then grinned at her own childishness. The shower had rejuvenated her and lifted her spirit. She felt like herself again.

Summer towelled off then wrapped her body in the luxurious bathrobe provided by the hotel. She slipped her feet into the complimentary bedroom slippers and wondered at how flimsy they were in comparison to the bathrobe.

She padded over to the glass sliding door and pulled it open. There was a rush of warm, tropical air and the sound of a steel band in the distance. It put her in an upbeat mood and suddenly she felt like dancing.

Summer left the balcony and threw the closet doors open. Late though it was, she was going out tonight. She rifled though her clothes and pulled out a pair of black stretch pants with flare bottoms and a black silk top with spaghetti straps. She threw the clothes on the bed then bent to pull out a pair of silver high heeled slippers.

Within twenty minutes she was fully dressed and heading for the elevator. Silver earrings dangled from her lobes and bangles jangled on her wrist. Her thick hair bounced around her head as she strode down the hallway. She could feel the stretch pants hugging her round hips and her full behind, and she held her back straight as she walked. She knew she looked good.

It was eleven-fifteen and the Mystique Nightclub in the lower level of the hotel was already packed with people. Reggae music pulsated from the huge speakers and people of all colours and ages were rocking to the rhythmic beat.

It surprised her when she saw some older couples on the dance floor. Then she remembered that many retired couples also came to Jamaica on vacation or on stopovers from the cruise ships. There were just as many tourists as Jamaicans in the nightclub. She could differentiate the visitors from the natives not only by skin color but also by the way they danced.

Wanting to blend in with the local crowd she adopted the slow, easy rocking style she observed. Bobbing to Bob Marley's 'We Jammin', she drifted away from the entrance and danced her way to the middle of the floor. She'd always found that, when alone at a party or nightclub, the best way to avoid unwelcome advances was to stay away from the outskirts and hide deep within the mass of dancing bodies. Here, in the heart of the crowd, she could lose herself to the music. As she swayed her hips and mouthed the words of the song, she moved to the rhythm of the throng around her.

Suddenly, an appreciative roar erupted from the crowd as the disc jockey changed the pace with "Electric Boogie–Woogie". As if directed by an invisible guide the crowd automatically formed lines along the dance floor and began to execute orchestrated moves so that a sea of people were now moving to the right, then all sliding to the left, then moving forward with a roll, then backward with a dip.

Summer knew the dance and all the moves that went with it. She fell into step immediately and was soon grinning just as broadly as everyone else around her as dancers missed their steps and bumped into one another, caught themselves, and quickly fell back into the rhythm. She never missed her step once and she noticed that several of the dancers were watching her every move in their efforts to keep in step.

A tall white man to her right almost tripped her up; he'd been watching the movements of her feet so intently that he did not step away in time and she stumbled into him. With an apologetic grin he grabbed her upper arms and righted her. She laughed back at him as he shrugged his shoulders as if in defeat then, still smiling, pushed away through the crowd.

After another ten minutes of music the DJ switched to Caribbean Soca and, for the first time, Summer felt unsure. She was not familiar with the fast-paced island music of steel pans, drums and horns but when she saw that all it required was rotation of the hips she quickly fell into step.

She watched, fascinated, as the locals gyrated their hips and moved close to each other then backed off, still dancing, only to move in close again. Many of them came in so close that their bodies rubbed in a twisting, erotic dance that made her own movements slow as she stared. But no-one seemed the least bit perturbed about what seemed to her to be extreme intimacy on the dance floor.

When a conga line of gyrating bodies formed she stood back and, with the rest of the dancers on the floor, clapped to the rhythm. The music went faster and the bodies bobbed quickly to the beat, then the music went faster still, until the line of bodies fell away and disintegrated into a laughing crowd of people.

It was then that the lights were dimmed and the deep husky voice of the DJ filled the room. "Now, for you lovers out there, a little bit of slow jam to get you in the mood." Marvin Gaye's "Sexual Healing" filled the room and couples moved closer together in embrace.

This was Summer's cue to exit.

She turned and came up hard against a broad silk-covered chest. She stepped back quickly, an apology already on her lips, but when she looked up she found herself staring into Lance's gleaming dark eyes.

Before she could speak he pulled her into his embrace. Strong arms encircled her waist, bringing her deliciously close to the masculine body. Her heart pounded hard in her chest and, even as she began to move with him she caught herself holding her breath.

"Relax." Lance breathed against her cheek then moved his right hand to her back. "Just let your hair down - for once."

Summer drew in a deep breath, trying to calm her nerves. She wished she hadn't. The masculine scent of him coupled with Marvin Gaye's sexy rendition had her body tingling with awareness. She felt relaxed and languorous, and yet so tense and aware all at the same time.

At that moment Lance rested a hand gently on her left hip and pulled her just a little closer then he rocked his hips to the rhythm and guided her body to follow. When she began swaying her hips slowly to the music his hand moved again to her back. She moved hesitantly against him but then, as the silky sounds caressed her, she began to match his every move.

Slowly but deliberately, she slid her arms up his chest and clasped her hands at the back of his neck. She moved against his body and felt the solid strength of him. As if drawn by an irresistible force she lifted her head and gazed into his dark smouldering eyes. His lips softened in a gentle smile and she felt her heart ache at the intensity of his look. He lowered his head and she closed her eyes, lips softened and ready for his kiss.

But it didn't come. Instead he rubbed his cheek against hers and pulled her closer, enveloping her in his warmth, drowning her in his sensuality.

It was almost one o'clock when Lance whispered, "We'd better go. We have a full day ahead of us."

She smiled, her cheek resting against his chest, her body relaxed and fluid against his. She nodded in assent and he took her hand and led her from the dance floor.

Lance was still holding her hand as he walked her to the elevator and when he pulled her into his arms as the doors closed she relaxed into him without any resistance. He held her there, not speaking, just caressing her back with hands that seemed to burn through the sheer silk of her blouse.

When the elevator door opened he released her and they walked down the carpeted hallway to her room. She slipped her electronic key into the door and, when the light blinked green, pushed it open and went inside. She held the door open, waiting for him.

Lance raised one eyebrow and smiled then entered at her unspoken invitation. A single lamp glowed by her bedside but, outside of that, the room was in darkness. As Lance paused inside the doorway she stretched her hand to grasp his warm fingers and pull him farther into the room. Her fingers trembled slightly but he didn't seem to notice.

"Are you thirsty?" she asked, her voice soft and husky in her own ears. She cleared her throat then continued, "I have some sodas in the fridge."

"Thanks, I'd like one."

"Just make yourself comfortable," she said then stammered, "I...I mean, please...have a seat." She gave herself a mental kick for sounding so lame and directed him to the small couch under the window. "I'll have your drink in just a second."

Summer knelt down by the small refrigerator and pulled out two cold bottles of a local grapefruit drink.

"Do you like Ting?" she asked as she rose and pulled two wine glasses from the cupboard above her head.

"Yeah, mon. That sounds good."

"Yeah, mon?" she giggled. "It always tickles me when you talk like that. You never say that in the office."

Lance grinned back at her. "I guess whenever I'm in Jamaica I just fall back into my old speech patterns. You really never lose it, you know."

As he spoke he leaned back into the couch and peered up at her through half-closed eyes. She turned away from his gaze and quickly opened the bottles and poured bubbling liquid into both glasses.

"Here you go," she said with a smile and handed him the drink. She sat on the edge of the sofa beside him but as far away as was polite. She put the glass to her lips and sipped the sharp cold liquid, feeling the bubbles bursting in her mouth.

She felt his eyes on her and gulped more liquid, then opened her eyes wide as it flooded her throat. Her eyes burned and she struggled to swallow but it was no use. Before she could cover her mouth she coughed violently, spraying her lap and the coffee table with soda.

Summer clapped her hands over her mouth, but too late. The damage was already done. Her eyes grew huge with distress and she looked across at Lance, hot with embarrassment.

"Are you alright?" He'd quickly rested his glass on the table and was leaning towards her, a large white handkerchief in his hand. She took it gratefully, still coughing. Then the spasms gradually subsided and she was able to look at him again. Her eyes were brimming with tears.

"Are you crying?" He looked incredulous, almost out of his depth, as he raised his hand and wiped away a tear with his thumb.

Summer dabbed at her eyes, sniffed, then looked up at him again, her lips curling into a grin. "Of course not, silly. I never cry. It's the coughing that made my eyes fill up with tears." Somehow, seeing him look so nonplussed had made her more at ease with him.

"Silly, huh?" He smiled back at her. "You're the one who gulped down a carbonated drink too fast and ended up losing the whole lot all over yourself. So, who's silly?"

While he was speaking Lance had rested his arm at the back of the couch right behind her head and had begun to gently stroke her nape with his thumb. Summer swallowed hard but couldn't get the lump out of her throat.

"I guess...I am," she said, her voice breathless.

"Yes," he whispered as he leaned forward to press his warm lips against the side of her neck, "you are."

Summer's breath came in shallow gasps as she sat still, not feeling she could move even if she wanted to. She was like a bird frozen in the mesmerizing stare of a snake, knowing it was about to be eaten alive but not able to make a move to save its own life.

She moaned and closed her eyes as his lips stroked the sensitive skin then moved to the base of her throat where he licked softly and gently. She didn't realize that she was still clutching the handkerchief tightly in her hand until she felt his strong fingers pry hers open to pull it away so that he could seduce her palm with his thumb.

"Relax, baby." He moved his lips up her neck and to her ear. "You're so tense. Just relax."

As he spoke he pushed her back gently into the plush pillows and began to nibble her ear lobe. He gave a lick just behind her ear and shock waves ran down her spine.

"Oh, God," she breathed, "what are you doing to me?"

"What someone should have done to you a long time ago, Summer Jones," he whispered. "Teach you what it means to be a woman."

He dipped his head and slid his lips back down her neck, over her collar bone and down to that oh, so sensitive place between the curves of her breasts. Here he paused and she held her breath, eyes shut tight, wondering if he was going to stop now. She prayed he wouldn't.

She was not disappointed. An involuntary gasp escaped her throat as he slipped a warm tongue down her cleavage, sliding it between the orbs and teasing her soft flesh until her body screamed and she felt she would die from the sweet sensation. She grabbed the back of his head and pressed him into her, wanting more of the pleasure, more of the sweetness.

She was rewarded when he turned his head to a soft, round breast and gently and sweetly licked at the smooth skin. He slid a finger along the top of her tank top and pulled the silky cloth down to reveal the hardened nub of her nipple. Summer felt a quick twinge of embarrassment then it was washed away in a tide of sensation as his firm lips and agile tongue settled over her center of pleasure and made her eyes open wide at the tremors that rocked her body.

She moaned again and arched her back, straining to give him all of her, wanting more of the sweetness that flowed from his lips.

"Please, please…" she moaned, but could say no more. As if he knew what she wanted, what she needed more than anything, he sucked on her nipple long and hard then circled it slowly with his tongue. She arched up towards him again and he responded to her silent plea. He took the nub gently between his teeth and nibbled expertly until she grabbed his head and pressed it hard into her soft flesh.

"Oh god, oh god," she moaned, "please…" Then her voice was lost in a gasp as he turned his head to the other breast.

When he finally lifted his head to stare deeply into her eyes she knew she was ready for anything he was willing to offer. In her whole life, never had she felt the way she had felt just now under his expert caresses. It wasn't that she'd never been kissed or caressed before but there was something different about this man, about the way he played her body like a guitar tuned by his own hands.

Lance lowered his lips to hers and she opened to receive him. His tongue flicked her lips then moved gently inside, first teasing then probing, while his fingers slowly stroked her belly. Her elastic waistband gave him easy entry and soon his fingers, those wonderful fingers, were caressing her hips, turning her into a mass of quivering nerves.

She leaned back even farther into the couch and slid her hand under his shirt. She caressed the smooth skin of his back, trying to give back some of the joy he was giving her.

When he broke the kiss and pulled slowly away from her she gazed up at him, still dazed.

"Summer," he said softly then stopped as she raised trembling fingers to slowly trace his moustache then his lips.

"Yes, my love?" she whispered as she lay her palm against his cheek.

He turned the palm to his lips and kissed it softly before gently resting her hand on her lap. "Summer," he began again and this time she could see through her cloud of emotions that he was struggling to find words. She felt her heart thump hard and she slowly pulled herself up into a sitting position.

"Lance. What's wrong?" When he didn't answer Summer felt her heart plummet and she suddenly felt like crying. She'd done it again, she thought. She could see it in his eyes. She had opened herself to him and now he thought her a slut.

She dropped her head and covered her mouth with her hand. A sob escaped her throat and he reached for her and pulled her into his arms.

"Please, my darling, don't cry." He held her tight against his chest and the strength of him quieted her. He held her away from him and looked down into her eyes. "I didn't mean to hurt you Summer," he murmured, "I'm really sorry."

"Hurt me?" she said, confused. "What do you mean?"

Lance frowned as he looked down at her. "If I didn't hurt you then why are you crying?"

She looked away. "Only because…I thought you were angry with me for throwing myself at you. Again."

"You crazy girl." He shook his head. "When did you ever throw yourself at me? I'm the one who's been taking advantage of you. And for that… I'm sorry."

"What are you talking about?" she asked, still bewildered.

Lance let go of her and straightened his body. "Summer, I'm a grown man. I know when a girl lacks experience. And I know you've got a lot to learn." He turned back to her and stroked her cheek with the back of her hand. "I don't want to rush you, honey. I don't want us to regret this."

"But you weren't rushing me. I wanted it…"

"You wanted it," he cut her off, "but you weren't ready for it. I want you to be absolutely sure, Summer, so let's take it slow."

With that he rose and stretched out both hands towards her. She rested her own hands in his and he pulled her gently to her feet and into his arms. He held her like that for a moment then pressed his lips against her forehead and put her away from him.

"Come," he smiled. "Walk me to the door."

When Summer had said goodbye and closed the door she leaned against it and let out a long sigh. She prayed she wasn't falling in love.

Chapter 11

When the telephone rang at seven o'clock for her wake up call Summer was far from ready to face the day. After Lance's departure in the wee hours of the morning she had lain in the bed for over an hour reliving every moment until finally sleep had claimed her. With less than five hours of sleep to refresh her she dragged herself up, groggy and irritable.

The only thing that brightened her mood was the thought that she would soon see Lance Munroe, the man she loved. Yes, she'd wondered at it and had been so scared, but now she accepted it. She was in love with Lance. No other man had taken her to the heights that he had shown her, no other had been able to steal her heart. The conquest had been easy for him but she didn't mind. If he could make her feel this good then she was his.

Summer swung her legs off the bed and padded over to the mirror. Ugh! she thought, I definitely wouldn't want him to see me like this. She raked her fingers through her wild hair and headed for the bathroom.

A cold shower did wonders for her. She was the first person from the group to get down to the lobby. She had dressed in a comfortable, yet attractive summer outfit – dandelion-yellow cotton shirt, white pants and a pair of yellow sandals. She had propped a pair of sunglasses on her head in anticipation of a sunny day and a broad-brimmed straw hat dangled from her fingers. Underneath this garb she wore a black and white polka dot bikini that she knew would turn heads when she walked along the beach. Today she wanted to look good for him.

Summer ended up waiting over fifteen minutes in the lobby before anyone in the group showed up. She was beginning to wonder if she was waiting in the wrong place when she heard a familiar voice.

"Whoee! Don't we look delicious."

Summer turned to see Derrick approaching. He wore denim shorts and a denim shirt which flapped open to display a white t-shirt stretched tautly over his belly. Even his sandals were made of some kind of denim material. Summer looked him over and stifled a smile. Poor Derrick, she thought. He was trying so hard to look smooth and sophisticated but no matter what he did he would never be as cool as his cousin.

"Hi, Derrick. How are you?" Her smile was warm as she greeted him.

"Wow, we're even pleasant, too?"

"I'm always pleasant." She dipped the corners of her mouth, trying to look hurt.

"Yeah, alright." Derrick punched her lightly on the shoulder. "I have to admit, you've turned out to be pretty nice." He flopped down in a wicker chair with cushions covered in tropical print. "Come sit by me. Take a load off."

"I'm fine, thanks. I prefer to stand."

"Is it me?" He pretended to sniff at his armpits. "I took a shower this morning."

"Of course not," she laughed, "it's just that I can see the beach when I stand here and that's a lot more interesting than sitting in the corner staring at the concierge's desk.

"Well, I won't argue with that."

"By the way," Summer looked at him questioningly, "where were you last night? I thought you were supposed to be at the meeting with us."

"Yeah, well, something came up."

"Something came up? In the few minutes between the time we ran in from the beach and the time we had to get back downstairs?"

"Didn't Lance tell you?" he asked.

"Lance didn't tell me anything," she said, confused. "When I got back down the Rock Steady people were already there so I just joined them and we got started right away. I never even got a chance to ask Lance for you."

"Well, let's just say he's not too pleased with me right now."

Summer's eyes narrowed as she looked at Derrick, waiting for an explanation.

He continued. "Lance was the one who told me not to come to the meeting. After you left us in the lobby he jumped on me, telling me how I needed to be more professional and not fraternize with the employees, how I should show more…"

"Fraternize with the employees?" she interrupted, frowning.

"Yeah, can you imagine he said that? As if we were from two different planets or something. Anyway, he told me you'd both handle the meeting by yourselves while I…" Derrick pretended to speak in Lance's deep voice, "…got myself out of this holiday mood and back to the business."

"I see," Summer said quietly, feeling deflated. It was not as if Lance's words weren't true. After all, she was an employee. Still, the impersonal description hurt. She wondered how Lance would have described the episode in her room. As far as she was concerned that was way past fraternizing.

"Hey, are you alright?"

She relaxed the grimace she felt forming on her face and tried to smile. "I'm fine. So…" she looked around the spacious lobby then back at Derrick, "…where is everybody, anyway? We aren't going to do this video shoot all by ourselves, are we?"

Derrick glanced at his watch then rose. "You're right. It's already a quarter after. Let me go call the others." He adopted a serious tone. "Let me start acting like a manager." Then he broke into a grin.

When he turned towards the house phones Summer sat down for the first time since she had come downstairs. Somehow the sight of couples frolicking on the sand didn't appeal to her anymore. Right now she didn't feel quite so 'on top of the world'. She drew in a deep breath, straightened her back and gave herself a mental shake. She wasn't going to let a simple comment ruin her day.

Derrick was heading back so she looked up and smiled. "Are they on their way?"

"Yeah, they're coming." He sat down beside her on the wicker sofa. "Seems like they went out on the town last night so nobody could wake up this morning. The whole lot of them went to Ambrosia. You've heard of it?"

"No, what's that?"

"It's a nightclub in the heart of Ocho Rios. It's really popular. You should check it out."

"But we'll be in Kingston by tomorrow."

"I know - but there's always tonight."

Within ten minutes Super Cool, Monisha and Abe entered the lobby. Derrick beckoned to them to come over.

"You guys wait here," he said, "I'm going to bring the van around front then we'll be on our way. We're already forty minutes late so we'd better get moving. The video crew's going to be waiting for us at Dunn's River Falls and you know they charge by the hour."

As he turned to go Summer grabbed his arm. "Wait. I mean, let me walk with you to the van. I need to stretch my legs."

"Sure, come on." They headed for the exit while the others helped themselves to the complimentary muffins and orange juice on a nearby table.

Derrick made long strides and Summer had to hurry to keep up with him.

"Derrick...how come Lance didn't come downstairs? Is he going to drive his own car?"

"No, he changed his mind about going." Derrick directed her to a navy blue minivan and reached forward to open the door.

"He's not coming?"

"Nope."

"Why not? I thought this was an important project."

"It is, and that's why I'm in charge." He grinned at her as he held the door open. "Hop in."

She climbed into the front seat and waited for Derrick to go around to the other side. As soon as he sat down beside her she blurted out, "So he's really not coming?"

"No, he's not." Derrick turned and looked at her quizzically. "Hey, you're not falling for Lance are you?"

"Of course not," she said quickly.

"Good, because he's got so many girls after him it's not even worth trying to get his attention. Too much competition. Know what I mean?" He smiled at her but she didn't answer.

She wanted to ask him when Monisha had arrived but felt she had said too much already. She was trying hard not to let him read her thoughts but she felt she was failing miserably. Thankfully, he just turned the key in the ignition and started the van.

When he got to the main entrance the group was already waiting outside for them. They piled into the van and set off on the short trip to Dunn's River Falls. Summer remained silent for most of the trip, listening to the light chatter of her colleagues. She tried to keep a cheerful look on her face but inside she felt like crying. She had so looked forward to the day; now it was as if all the excitement had been wiped out of it. She felt like a stupid school girl with a crush on her teacher.

Well, she thought, if Lance didn't feel it was worth his time to see her again she certainly wasn't going to waste hers thinking about him.

Dunn's River Falls was beautiful. While the video crew set up their equipment she walked along the warm sand until she got to the bottom of the waterfall. Children splashed in the shallow pool while adults tackled the rocks. Derrick had told her that the main attraction of Dunn's River Falls was the climb all the way to the top. It was just sloping enough for this to be done. People were holding hands, climbing together up the slippery rocks, laughing and screaming.

Suddenly, a short blonde man slipped all the way back down. They were having so much fun that Summer found herself laughing too. She hoped she would find time to do the climb herself.

By the time she ran back to the beach everything was ready for the video shoot. Monisha lounged on the sand in a bright orange bathing suit. A cocoa-coloured man lay by her side.

The first clip was a beach scene. Two young lovers caressed each other, totally oblivious to everything around them, lost in their love. Monisha crooned a sweet love song as she stroked her partner's cheek and gazed with loving eyes into his face. He stroked her hand in return then dipped his head to kiss a smooth shoulder.

At that point her voice rose at the punchline and she gathered his head to her as she sang, "Loving you is all I ever want to do". The camera zoomed in close as she sang of her love. When she closed her eyes and rested her head on the well-muscled chest the cameras came in even closer for a full facial shot then the sound of her voice faded away.

"Cut!" The video director was beaming. "Excellent work. Monisha, you're the greatest!"

"Why, thanks, Franklyn," she preened. "You know I aim to please."

"And that you did. You're such a professional." He stretched out his hand to help her up.

"Thank you." Monisha took the proffered hand and rose in one fluid movement.

"Come on, guys," Franklyn called to his crew. "Let's head for the rocks for the next scene. We're running behind so we're going to have to set up real fast."

When Franklyn walked away Monisha came over to where Derrick and Summer stood sheltering in the shade of the palms.

"Well, well. Don't you two make a lovely picture."

"We do, don't we?" Derrick grinned and put his arms around Summer's shoulders. She stiffened but caught herself before she embarrassed him by struggling.

"So what's up with you being at the video shoot?" Monisha turned her attention to Summer. "Outside of the managers, people from the office never usually come to these things."

"My job is to do PR," Summer replied, "and that entails being at all the video shoots and events in which Munroe Productions is involved. What that means is that I have to make sure that we take advantage of every opportunity for publicity."

"I know what PR is," Monisha huffed.

"Well, you asked," Summer shrugged. "All I'm saying is that it's my job to make you a star."

When Monisha looked at her askance Summer continued, "You may say you're popular already but you have no idea what the right kind of publicity can do for you. I could make you into the next Alicia Keyes."

Monisha's cold stare softened at that. "So you think I'm that big, huh?"

"No, but with my help you can be."

"Oh, really." Monisha looked offended. She flipped her ponytail over her shoulder and stalked off towards the production tent.

"Oops!" Derrick chuckled, "You got her good. What a dis'."

"No, it wasn't," Summer turned to him, hands on her hips. "Do you think I have time to waste feuding with the likes of Monisha Stone? I wasn't putting her down. She's a talented singer and no-one can take that away from her. All I meant was that talent, without promotion, would be lost in the crowd.

Lots of people have talent but it's the ones who are thrown in your face who make it big."

"Oh. I thought you were trying to mess up her head."

Summer smiled. "Don't look so disappointed. You'll get your cat fight some other time...but I won't be in it."

"Oh, come on." He turned puppy dog eyes to her.

"No, you come on. The crew is leaving us behind. Let's go."

The rest of the video shoot went just as smoothly as the first scene. The weather had been picture-perfect all day and they actually finished thirty minutes early despite the late start.

With all their work behind them the entire group disrobed and took off for the falls. Super Cool, Monisha and Franklyn joined a group of tourists and went climbing up the rocks while Abe and the two cameramen went scouting the beach for free and single 'honeys', as they put it. Summer sat with Derrick in the serene pool at the bottom of the waterfall.

Although she'd been excited about making the climb somehow she couldn't get herself into the right mood. No matter how hard she tried she couldn't put Lance out of her mind. She wondered if he was still back at the hotel.

"Derrick," she said softly, trying to screw up the courage to speak.

"Yup?" He opened one eye then yawned. "What's up?"

"Have you heard from Lance today?" she asked, deliberately avoiding his eyes.

"Oh, yeah, he called about twelve o'clock to see how the shoot was going."

"And...he didn't say anything about coming down here?"

"Nope. He's spending the day with Michelle. She just got outta the hospital so he's gone over there to spoil her, as usual."

Summer's breath caught in her throat. She felt her heart plummet and she lowered her gaze to hide her confusion.

Derrick rubbed his eyes and yawned again. "You know about Michelle, right?"

"Yes. I...I heard she has sickle cell anemia."

"Yeah. Poor kid. That's why Lance dotes on her so much. Just trying to make it up to her, I guess."

Summer nodded but remained silent. Her thoughts were in a turmoil. How could she have forgotten about Lance's other life - his Jamaican life? He had a little girl who was sick and needed him. Of course, that would mean he had a woman here, too - Michelle's mother.

She'd been such a fool to believe there could have been anything between the two of them. She would never be satisfied to be just one of his many women. She wanted all of him or nothing at all. Then I guess I'll have nothing, she thought, and suddenly felt despondent.

"Are you okay?" Derrick peered at her. "You just got so quiet all of a sudden."

"I'm fine," she said and gave him what she hoped was a convincing smile. She rose and the water streamed down her body. Derrick's eyes shone as he stared up at her. She stretched a hand out to him. "Come on. Let's go tackle this monster waterfall."

Chapter 12

Summer shook her head and sighed in regret. How was she going to get out of this? Derrick had asked her to go out with him to the Ambrosia Nightclub. Caught up in the moment she had accepted but now that she was back in her room she was loathe to leave again. She was just starting to feel the effects of her exhausting day. The video shoot had been hectic and the evening at the waterfall had been tiring.

But overall it had been a pleasant day. Climbing the rocks at Dunn's River Falls, laughing with Derrick, meeting other tourists, it had been a lot of fun for her...even the time when she'd been climbing and almost slipped and Derrick had to save her from a fall.

But what had made the evening even more pleasant was that Derrick had taken her to have dinner at the Ital Food Shack which was a Rastafarian restaurant not far from the Falls.

It was quite rustic. The building was made from logs and bamboos. It had a thatched roof and there was no glass in the windows, only blinds made out of plaited palm leaves. There were paintings of Jamaican scenes hanging on the walls and the room was decorated with carvings of fish, birds and people. Colourful woven baskets filled with flowers had been placed in the corners. The seats they sat on were made of bamboos tied together with ropes and the table was out of a rough hewn wood. The tables were lit by candles in small red glasses.

Summer had found the menu quite interesting. It was all vegetarian food but it made her mouth water before she even tried the dishes. There was Coconut Run-Down, Stewed Peas,

Callaloo a la Spice, Shake-me-up Cabbage and Pretty Girl Carrot Melee. Summer couldn't help laughing at the names as she ordered but she was not surprised when the food came and she found that it was delicious.

It was while they were relaxing with tall glasses of fruit punch that Derrick asked her out. He'd been so attentive to her all day that Summer didn't have the heart to say no. But now she was feeling so tired, not to mention depressed, because Lance had abandoned her. But, outside of feigning actual sickness, she didn't see how she could get out of it. She figured she'd just spend an hour or so with him then call it a night.

Summer got dressed and was all ready by twenty minutes after nine. She sat on the bed and turned on the television to kill time. Derrick had told her he'd pick her up at nine-thirty which, he said, by Jamaican standards was quite early to go to a nightclub. Normally the locals would head out between eleven and midnight but, since they were in a tourist town, he figured there'd still be a fair enough crowd that early and he'd said he didn't want to keep her out too late.

It was a Thursday night so Ambrosia was not too packed. The nightclub was small but sported a dance floor with television screens underfoot and there was one wall that had a huge screen on which those on the dance floor could watch themselves. The other wall had a mirror. There was a second floor balcony with tables and chairs and people sat drinking or just leaning over the rails, looking down at the dancers below. Three young men were in the middle of the dance floor executing intricate moves. Obviously, they were professionals.

Summer could feel the ground shake under her feet as she walked and the music pulsated from huge speakers around the room. The place smelled slightly of cigarettes and she was grateful that it was not overwhelming.

"Come on," Derrick said, "let's go over by the mirror. There aren't too many people over there."

He grabbed her wrist and pulled her through the crowd, making her bump into some dancers. He was going so fast.

She pulled back on her wrist. "Hold on, I'm coming," she said.

He looked back and grinned. "Sorry," he mouthed, and slowed his pace.

When they got over to the other side of the room he started rocking to the rhythm of Soul to Soul's 'Back to Life' and she fell into step with him. She loved the music. In fact, eighties music was her favourite.

After a little while the DJ switched from Disco to Jamaican Dance Hall music and Sean Paul's rough voice filled the room. Then they started playing Beenie Man's 'Zim-Zimmer' and a couple beside her began doing a dance that she could not figure out.

Summer stared so intently at them that Derrick laughed and put his mouth close to her ear. "They're doing 'Pon the river, Pon the bank'. It's a Jamaican dance."

Summer could only laugh. Then, she spied another couple with some even stranger dance moves. The man looked like he was running in one spot but he kept stopping and looking over his shoulder.

"That's a dance?" she asked.

"Yeah," Derrick said. "That one's called 'Gi Them the Run'. With that dance you're pretending to run away from the police; you're looking over your shoulder to see if they're catching up."

"What the…that's crazy. How can they make that a dance?"

He shrugged and grinned. "Ever heard of the 'Bogle' and the 'Butterfly'?"

"Yeah, I saw the 'Butterfly' in one of Janet Jackson's videos. And I know the 'Bogle' – you lean back and you move your arms around."

"Yeah, those were created right here on the dance floors."

"Y'all are something else."

Derrick just grinned.

Summer enjoyed herself so much that she forgot about planning to leave after an hour. In fact, it was when Derrick said, "Maybe we'd better head back now," that she looked at her watch and realized that it was after eleven o'clock.

She found herself saying, "We'll go in a little while. Come on. Teach me some dance moves." She waved her arms in the air then stopped abruptly as she noticed the couple beside them watching her and smiling.

"No, don't stop," the woman said. "You doin' good."

"Yeah," Summer muttered, "for a tourist."

Then she laughed with them and kept on dancing. She was concentrating on the dance move when she felt a hand on her shoulder and looked up, startled. It was Abe.

"Hey, Summer, I can see you're getting down, girl." He was laughing.

"Yeah, trying," she laughed back at him.

"I would never embarrass myself that way," Monisha said with a snort as she came up behind Abe.

"Well, I'm just having fun," Summer said, determined not to let the woman spoil her enjoyment.

"Yes, I can see that you guys are having a lot of...fun," Monisha said, staring pointedly at Derrick.

Monisha and Abe wandered off and Summer and Derrick went back to their dancing. Within moments they were interrupted again. This time it was Derrick who got a tap on his shoulder. Summer paused as he turned to a tall bald-headed man wearing dark glasses.

"Hey, Zeeko. Long time, man," he exclaimed, and both men embraced, clapping each other on the back.

"Yeah, man," the man said in a deep voice. "You not been around lately, eh?"

"Well, not this side of the island." Derrick nodded. "Just got here a couple of days ago."

"Come on. The rest of the guys are in the back," the man indicated with his head. "I know they'd want to hail you up."

"Oh...okay," Derrick said then took Summer's hand. "We're right behind you."

They followed the man to the back of the dance floor and went through a narrow passageway to a green door. He knocked and it opened to a slim light-skinned woman in a very tight red dress. She opened wider and, without saying a word, waited for them to pass through the door.

The room was a private lounge with lamps that threw soft lighting around the room, illuminating the deep red of the couch and the rich black carpeting. Two men lounged in the couches and another sat around a glass table smoking what looked like a very fat stick of tobacco but Summer knew it was anything but that.

"Hey, who this just drop from the sky?" The stout man in the couch sipped his drink and nodded to Derrick.

"Derrick, my youth," said the one with the joint, "long time no see."

"Yeah, man," Derrick said, "but I'm here now."

He pulled Summer over to an empty chair.

"I see you have a lovely girl with you, man. Your wife?" the fat man asked.

"No, she's my friend," Derrick replied. "Summer, these are my longtime buddies from school days. That's Michael over there," he said pointing to the one smoking, "that's Cliffie" he nodded towards the plump man, "and that's Germaine."

Germaine sat silent, still staring at Summer without a word. She nodded to him but felt uncomfortable under his intense look. He was well-dressed in a suit and tie and gold rings flashed on his fingers. Without his having spoken a word she knew instantly that she didn't like him.

The tall man who had brought them into the room came over to her and said in his deep voice. "And I am Zeeko."

"Yes, I know," she replied. "I heard Derrick call you that."

"Cool," he nodded then went over to sit at the glass table. Summer's eyes widened as he pulled out a piece of paper, sprinkled what looked like dried leaves into it and rolled it up. He lit it and stretched his hand out to Derrick. "Dis one have your name on it, man. Come take a draw."

"No, man," Derrick said. "Thanks, but I not into them stuff, okay."

The man lifted his eyebrows at Derrick. "Boy, you getting soft."

"Jus' cool, man," Derrick said. "I jus' not into them kinda things right now. No more rude boy stuff for me."

The man nodded. "Cool. Your choice, brethren. You missing out, but is your choice."

Summer glared at Derrick.

He cleared his throat. "Guys, it was nice linking up with you but I have to make a run now. I have the lady out kinda late so…nuff respect." He took her hand and she rose.

"Cool. No problem, man," Zeeko said. "We'll see you 'round the place."

Cliffie nodded and Michael continued smoking. Germaine never took his eyes off Summer and never said a word.

She was very quiet as they left the nightclub and walked back to the car. Her entire mood had changed. What she had just seen was a reminder of the sordid side of life and a revelation of another side of Derrick.

As she buckled her seatbelt Derrick turned to her. "Summer, you okay?"

She nodded but stared straight ahead.

"Summer, please talk to me."

She looked across at him. "About what?"

"I know you're upset, and I'm sorry."

She didn't reply, but just raised her eyebrows.

"I'm sorry I took you in there. I shouldn't have. That's a part of my life that's in the past."

She remained silent.

He continued. "I have to admit I was a part of that crowd but not anymore. It was a mistake to have taken you in there. Forgive me?"

Derrick seemed so distressed that she nodded. "Yeah, it's okay. I understand."

"So you forgive me?" he asked again.

She stared back at him for a moment then sighed, "You're forgiven."

He grinned then switched on the ignition and they drove off.

Summer leaned back in her seat and closed her eyes, enjoying the balmy breeze blowing in through the window. It smelled slightly salty, like the sea. She was beginning to drift off when Derrick broke the silence

"If I didn't tell you earlier, you look lovely tonight."

"Thanks," she replied, with her eyes still closed, "but I'm so tired right now I'm sure I look crazy."

"Of course not," he said. "You do a man's heart good. You're a beautiful woman." He reached for her hand and, before she could pull it away, began stroking her palm.

"Derrick, I…" she began, then said sharply, "Remember you're driving."

"I'll be alright," he shrugged as he manouevred the steering wheel with his free hand. "I like you a lot. You know that, don't you?"

"I don't think we should…"

"Yes, we should. I like you and I think you like me, too."

"Derrick," she said sternly, "I don't think we should go there." Then, feeling guilty at her abruptness she said, "Please, Derrick, let's just…not rush into anything."

"Alright, honey," he acquiesced, "I'm not gonna rush you. I'll leave it alone – for now." He patted her hand before letting it go.

Summer hurriedly thought of another subject, just to get him off her. "I have a question for you."

"Yeah, baby? Anything."

"I want to know more about Super Cool. I have to come up with a human interest story about him and I don't even know where to start. Can you tell me anything about him, what he's like outside of when he's performing?"

"No problem. I was the one who found him in a talent search six months ago. He's a cool youth. He's from a rural part of Jamaica. Linstead, it's called. He's from a poor family, but he's an ambitious kid."

"And he seems to be a pretty nice guy," she said.

"He sure is. He really wants to make a success of himself but he's humble about it. Still goes home a lot, every chance he gets. He travels with us now but when he's not doing that he goes to stay with his Mom in Linstead. His sister lives there too, with her child. He's got a brother in the army. His Mom's a small farmer."

"A small farmer?" She feigned exceeding interest, hoping it would keep his mind off her.

"Yeah, she grows vegetables and stuff. She takes them to the Linstead Market on the weekends. That's how she put her children through school."

"Really?"

"Yeah, and she's real nice. I've met her a couple of times. Kind of stern, but real funny woman."

"I would love to meet his family, get some tidbits about him. That would be a great way to start," she said, now genuinely interested.

"We can do that," Derrick glanced at her with a smile.

"But how?"

"I can stop at their house on our way into Kingston tomorrow. We can leave earlier and I'll make a stop there so you can talk to his Mom."

"That would be great."

"I'll just tell Super Cool in the morning so he can give her a call and let her know we're coming."

"Sounds good to me," she said then asked, "Can he be there, too?"

"Sorry," he shook his head as he pulled into the parking lot of the hotel, "he has to go in early with the rest of the crew. They've got lots of work to do. We're lucky we don't have to be there till in the afternoon."

"Then I'd like to stop there."

"No problem," he said, then pulled into a parking space and switched off the engine. There was a tender look on his face as he turned towards her. "I look forward to spending tomorrow with you, my sweet."

Summer groaned inside but just pasted a smile on her face. "Uh, yeah. Me, too."

Chapter 13

By eight-thirty next morning Derrick and Summer had left the hotel and found themselves in the middle of a traffic jam in the heart of Ocho Rios.

"God," Derrick groaned, "I forgot everybody would be heading for work at this time of the morning."

Summer paid hardly any attention to him as she drank in the sights of the hustle and bustle of the tourist town. The streets were filled with cars and every so often there would be a taxi darting through the traffic with its horn honking, creating even more confusion on the road. They were almost always caught by the police patrol on bicycles because it seemed like the only vehicles moving forward were the ones on two wheels.

"Hey, whatever happened to police cars?" Summer laughed.

"We've got those, too," Derrick replied, laughing with her, "but it's just that in Ocho Rios we also have a lot of cops who ride bicycles. They get around easier in this congestion, as you can see, and it looks a lot friendlier in a tourist town than having cops driving around in cars all day."

"I guess you're right," she said, "and I don't mind seeing them in those shorts, either."

Derrick laughed. "You would say that."

The morning was already hot and Summer pulled out her sunglasses to soften the glare.

"Music?" Derrick asked.

"Yeah," she said, "why not?"

He switched to one of the local stations and the sound of Reggae music filled the car. Summer was glad for the distraction. She was anxious to get to Linstead but this traffic jam would cost her some of her interview time. At least the music kept her mind off the delay.

Some twenty minutes later they were finally on the Fern Gully Road and on their way to Kingston.

"This road is so winding," Summer said.

"Oh, that's because this is a dried up riverbed. When the Spanish were here they just paved it and turned it into a road. So, of course, it's winding in the very same way that the river used to flow."

"That's interesting, but not very efficient, is it?"

"No, I guess not. But we've lived with it for so long I don't know if they're ever gonna change it."

"Well, I should hope not. It's beautiful." She looked around. "I never noticed it last night but look at all those ferns hanging over. And it's so calm and cool under here."

"It's okay, I guess," Derrick replied.

"Hey, that's where we had dinner last night," Summer cut in, as she pointed out the restaurant tucked away in the bushes.

"Okay, little girl," Derrick laughed, "you remembered."

She punched him on the shoulder. "Stop laughing at me."

"I can't help it," he chuckled. "It's so easy to laugh at you. You get so excited about simple things."

"Alright," she said in an exasperated tone. "Everything here is new to me. Just bear with me, will you?"

"Okay, my sweet. I don't mean to give you a hard time - it's just that you're so funny."

"Humph." She folded her arms across her chest and pouted. "I'll get you. When we get back to Chicago I'm going to take you somewhere you've never been before and you'll be excited too, you'll see."

"I look forward to it," he smiled, "anytime."

Derrick drove along a road which, in Summer's mind, was way too narrow in some places. Still, it was a pleasant ride.

She enjoyed the greenery, and especially going through the small towns where people would be going about their daily business. To Summer the trip was an eye-opener.

When she saw a man riding a donkey with two huge baskets hanging on either side she got excited and Derrick laughed at her all over again. "The man's going to do his work. He's a farmer. That's how he gets around."

"I know. I'm not that stupid. But it's just that you don't see these things every day. At least, I don't; not in Chicago. I like seeing all this new stuff. I mean, it's different. You have to understand, I'm studying Communications. All this is stuff I can use in my work. Don't you see?"

"Whatever you say."

Almost forty minutes later they arrived in Linstead. They turned off the main road and onto a narrow track that led to a small house almost hidden by trees. Derrick drove into the yard and immediately three dogs rushed out, barking madly.

A stout black woman ran around from the back of the house, shouting, "Rex, Prince, get out of here. Go on." She picked up some small stones and threw them at the dogs. "Lady, go look after your puppies."

She broke a switch from a nearby tree and hit them on the rump. They dashed away, still barking. She bent to pick up her hat which had fallen off in the flurry of activity and, with a broad smile on her face, approached the vehicle.

"Well, finally, Mr. Dunn. Courtney call and tell me you coming so I was looking out for you over two hours now. What happen?"

"Traffic backed up on the road, Mrs. Kitson."

She peered into the vehicle. "And this is the nice lady who going to do the interview?"

Derrick nodded. "Yes, this is Summer Jones."

"Welcome to Linstead, Mam," she said, smiling, and took the hand that Summer stretched to her in greeting.

Derrick and Summer got out of the vehicle and walked with her up the pathway to the little blue house.

"I was planning to prepare breakfast but when it get so late and I don't see you I change me plan. I goin' work on lunch instead." She wiped her hands on her apron. "I was jus' aroun' the back trying to catch the chicken but it give me quite a chase, you see."

"Why were you chasing a chicken?" Summer asked, confused.

"For the lunch." Mrs. Kitson looked at her as if she should have known.

"But you can't kill a chicken now."

"Why not? You don't eat chicken?" She looked perplexed then nodded as if in realization. "Oh, you are vegetarian."

"No," Summer said, feeling a little stupid. "It's just…"

"Good," the woman cut in. "You too skinny to be vegetarian; you need some meat on you bones. Come on to the back with me. Let's get a nice, big one and I'll cook a sweet lunch for you."

Before Summer could say another word Mrs. Kitson grabbed her by the arm and dragged her off to the back of the yard with Derrick in tow. As they walked the woman kept up a constant chatter.

"I tell the little boy from next door to catch one for me, you know, but him been running around the yard and not catching a thing, not even fly. Anyway, make we see what him up to."

They walked along the dirt path to the back of the house just in time to see a small boy, no older than eleven years old, holding a chicken down on the ground with a metal basin covering its body, its head and neck exposed. The chicken was flapping violently under the basin and squawking wildly.

He had a large knife in his hand and was just about to swing it down onto the bird's neck when Summer screamed.

"Stop! Leave that chicken alone!"

The boy stopped, his eyes wide, then got up from his knees and backed away. Summer ran towards him knowing she must have looked like a mad woman but she didn't care.

She grabbed the basin off the chicken. It flapped wildly and flew off into the bushes.

"But what you doing?" the woman exclaimed, indignant. "That was your lunch."

"It's okay," Summer said, panting, "I don't need any lunch. I'm fine. Just leave the chicken alone. Please."

"Well," the woman threw up her hands in frustration, "if that's what you want. But I don't see how you can come into my house and I don't give you something to eat. The only other thing I can offer you is some soup."

"Yes," Summer said, relieved, "soup would be fine."

"Alright." She turned to the boy. "Orville, go light the fire under the pot with the goathead soup. Quick, quick." She turned to Summer. "It won't take long – just ten minutes to heat it up."

"Goathead…soup?" Summer asked, feeling her stomach go queasy. "Ah, thank you, but it's okay. I'm really not hungry."

"Not even a little of the soup?" The woman almost looked offended.

"Mrs. Kitson, I thank you so much for your offer," Summer said quickly in an effort to appease her, "but I'm fine."

"Alright, Mam," the woman sighed. "You are a strange one to come to somebody's house and want to go away on an empty stomach but, if that is what you want…" She put her hands up as if in resignation.

Derrick smiled and put his arm around the woman's shoulders. "Mrs. Kitson, it's okay. We're in a hurry right now but next time we pass through we'll stop and eat. Promise."

The woman nodded and beckoned to them to follow her into the house. They entered through a tiny kitchen and into a living room cum dining room. There was a dining table with a floral table cloth and a bowl of plastic fruits on top. A kerosene lamp sat by the fruit bowl although it was obvious that they had electricity. A television was on and a soccer game was in progress. Mrs. Kitson ushered them over to a big red couch and as they sat down she pulled a chair from around the dining table.

"Okay, Mrs. Kitson," Summer said, "I'd like to get started right away, seeing that we have so little time. Can you tell me about Courtney, what he was like as a child?"

"Well, that boy, you see, from baby stage until he was in Primary School coming up, he was a stubborn little boy. And rude!" She opened her eyes wide. "The boy used to give a lot of trouble but I tell you, he was always so loving. Never, never leave me out at all. You see that t.v. over there", she pointed, "he buy it for me. Yes, because he want to make sure that when him on t.v. him mother can see him nice and clear. And he tell me that once things are set him want to buy me a big house on the hill."

"That's admirable. Sounds like you have a wonderful son."

"Oh, yes, and talk about ambitious? That is Courtney. When him was growing up him always used to say, 'Mummy, I going to grow up and have a big job so that I can do things for you'."

Summer nodded thoughtfully and scribbled on her notepad. "And what other interests does Courtney have?"

"Him always love to play cricket but outside of that, music is the thing. I know him jus' start him career but him so hopeful." She nodded and beamed at Summer. "Yes, as I tell you, him say him want to buy him mother a big house on the hill."

"That sounds good, Mrs. K. I'm sure you'd love that," Derrick said, smiling.

"But, of course. You think I don't want a big house to fix up nice-nice? And I know my boy is going to make it."

"So he loves cricket and music," Summer prompted. "Anything else?"

"There's another thing – outside of the cricket and the music him did want to study engineering. Him get a place at the university in Kingston, you know."

"Really?"

"Yes," her face turned sad. "Him never get to enter, though. Me couldn't afford it." She looked thoughtful then shook her head. "Anyway, when him realize that that was not happening him go full-scale into the music and then him enter the talent competition and God bless him, you can see how him is doing now. One day, one day, though him going to finish up the engineering - the musical engineer, that's what him call himself." She laughed at that.

They spent another fifteen minutes with Mrs. Kitson then said their goodbyes.

"You mus' come back again soon, my dear," the older woman gave Summer a hug. "You is a sweet child and I know you going to write some nice things about me son."

Summer smiled and they all three walked to the vehicle.

"Drive safe, now, you hear?"

"Will do, Mrs. K," Derrick said, and held the door open for Summer.

As they backed out of the yard Summer waved and the woman blew kisses at them.

When they left Linstead they drove along yet more winding roads, but this time the scenery was even more beautiful. They were following the path of a long, slow river that Derrick called the Bog Walk Gorge. There was thick foliage all along the way and the water bubbled so serenely by that Summer felt relaxed just watching it.

Derrick drove the car over a stone bridge which had no restraining walls and Summer learned from him that it had been built in the fifteenth century by the Spanish who had occupied the island before the British.

When they finally reached the outskirts of Kingston she was tired and hungry but satisfied at having made such significant progress in gathering data on Super Cool.

"Thanks for a wonderful day, Derrick," she said with a smile.

He smiled back. "No problem."

When they arrived at Big Ship Recording Studio in Kingston Lance and Super Cool were already there. A young woman stood in the voicing booth with headphones over her ears. Lance waved as they approached then continued to give instructions via the mixing board's built-in microphone.

"Give me a little more soul. I'm not feeling you on that last line. Let's hear some real passion, Sharona."

The singer nodded then closed her eyes and, obviously understanding what Lance meant, she sang the line with deep feeling. He didn't hold back the applause.

Summer went to sit on a leather couch at the back of the small room. Derrick watched the engineer at the mixing board then he, too, joined Summer on the only available seat.

Summer sat, fascinated, as the engineer worked the board then she turned her attention to the petite girl whose voice filled the room. She leaned over to Derrick. "Is that one of our singers?"

He shook his head. "No, she's a local girl I found on my last trip here. She'll be doing a duet with Super Cool."

"Will I be working with her?"

"No. Not right now, anyway. If she works out then we'll see."

They remained silent as they watched Sharona. Then Super Cool went into the booth and they spent almost an hour recording lead vocals for their duet.

Summer touched Derrick's arm again and leaned over to whisper in his ear. "Why does Lance come all this way to record music? I'm sure we have great studios back home in Chicago."

He put his mouth to her ear and whispered back, "It's the Jamaican vibes. You need that for Reggae music. You really can't get it anywhere else."

At that moment Lance turned and fixed them with a hard stare. Derrick never even noticed but Summer dropped her eyes guiltily.

Damn! she thought, angry at Lance for choosing that moment to turn and look at them but even angrier at herself for feeling guilty when she was totally innocent. Who was he to be looking at her like that, anyway? He was the one who had sneaked off to see his woman.

Summer raised her eyes and boldly returned his stare. Then as he watched she curved her lips into a smile and turned her face to Derrick's whispering mouth. She pressed her lips against his and his eyebrows raised in surprise. Their contact was brief but when she glanced back and saw the dark look on Lance's face she knew she had achieved her goal.

Derrick sat back and looked at her in confusion then a slow smile spread across his face. She looked back at him but offered no smile in return. He didn't seem to notice. Instead, he leaned over to her again, smiling confidently, and whispered, "I knew you'd come around. You just can't fight this thing between us."

Summer looked away quickly and her eyes suddenly stung with tears. She felt sick inside. What had she done? With that one impulsive act she could have set wheels in motion that could force her into a very uncomfortable position. She could end up hurting not one, but three people with her stupid act.

She glanced back at Lance, wanting to tell him it was all a lie, that she'd only faked it to get back at him. But it was too late. He had already turned away from them and was talking to the engineer. His rigid back was the only clue to the extent of his anger.

The rest of the evening in the studio was sheer torture for her. Despite the presence of others Summer was so aware of Lance that her breath was tight in her chest. Her nipples hardened of their own volition and she struggled not to rub them to ease the tingling. It was as if this new tension between them had set her nerve endings on edge. Every inch of her ached for him.

When the session finally ended and Lance walked out with the singer Summer slumped back into the sofa and sighed in relief.

"Are you okay, honey?"

She opened her eyes to see Derrick standing over her, a look of concern on his face.

"Yes, Derrick, I'm fine." There was a hint of resignation in her tone but she made no effort to sound cheerful. Derrick stroked her arm but she just sat there, eyes closed, not saying a word.

"It's time to go."

It was only when he put his arm around her shoulders that she responded by leaning heavily against him and rising to her feet.

"You're tired." He kissed her gently on the forehead. "Let's get you home."

They went outside and Summer was surprised when Lance waved them over to where he was piling boxes of CD's into the back of his Land Rover. As they approached he slammed the back door and turned to them.

"I've told the others already," he said, "but since neither one of you was here, let me repeat myself. I'm inviting the entire group to dinner tonight at the Blue Mountain Restaurant. We're to meet at eight." He looked at Derrick. "You know where it is, right?"

"Yeah, I've been there before," Derrick nodded. "The food there's pretty good…"

"Hey, Derrick." A yell interrupted him. It was the music engineer, Jerry, who had just exited the studio and was heading for his red Toyota Celica. "Somebody left a pair of sunglasses on the couch; they kinda look like yours. You missing one?"

Derrick patted his breast pocket and yelled back, "Thanks, man."

"I'll be right back," he said quickly then dashed off, leaving Lance and Summer standing silent, staring at each other.

Summer eyed Lance warily then said, "I won't be at the dinner tonight."

"Excuse me?" He frowned.

"You heard me," she said stonily. "I'm not in the mood to go out tonight so count me out."

"May I remind you, Ms. Jones, that you're on a business trip and as such your time is mine," he responded coldly. "I expect you to be at the restaurant on time. What you do after we leave there is your own business."

She frowned at him. The way he'd said the last remark made her feel cheap and dirty and she hated it that his opinion even mattered at all.

"And what's that supposed to mean?" Her nostrils flared and she made no effort to hide her anger.

"You can take that any way you want," he grated, "just don't let me have to come get you for dinner. I can assure you, you would not like the consequences."

"Are you threatening me?" She drew herself up to her full height and glared up at him.

"Let's just say I'm making my position clear."

"It's clear, alright," Summer sneered. "It's clear that all I am to you is a damned employee, nothing more. Don't worry, I know your policy about fraternizing with employees. I know my place."

"What the hell are you talking about?"

"You told Derrick that he should stay away from me because 'management' shouldn't fraternize with employees." When he hesitated she growled, "Don't you dare deny it."

"You idiot," he rubbed his brow as he looked down at her, "I only said that to Derrick because…" He stopped and then his face turned hard again. "That doesn't matter now. You're obviously better able to take care of yourself than I thought."

Disgust was plain on his face and she lashed out at him, wanting to hurt him as much as he'd hurt her.

"Yes, I am. I also know a real man when I see one."

Lance looked like she'd slapped him in the face. Good, she thought, let him suffer. She pressed on. "That's right, a man who isn't just trying to get into my pants."

A cloud of rage darkened Lance's face and Summer took a step back involuntarily. Had she gone too far? Damn this temper of hers. It just wouldn't let her stop.

Before she could move any farther he grabbed her upper arm and dragged her to within inches of his face. "Don't you ever speak to me like that again."

The words were so laced with anger that Summer trembled inside. But she would never show fear. Instead she glared back at him until he pushed her away from him.

Without another word he jumped into his truck and sped away.

Chapter 14

To Summer's surprise the dinner turned out to be quite pleasant. It was Monisha's birthday and Lance had organized special service for their table. A violinist played the happy birthday song for her then, after a delicious meal, a huge birthday cake was brought out. Monisha almost looked teary eyed. Summer could hardly believe this softer side of her.

By the time they got back to the hotel it was after eleven o'clock and she felt drained. They said their goodnights in the lobby and she headed straight for the elevator. She had a feeling Lance was watching her but she was too tired to even care.

When she got to her room she lay back on the bed and threw an arm over her eyes. It took ten minutes of quiet before she felt ready to head for the shower. She lifted her arm and blinked to clear her eyes.

It was then that she noticed the message light blinking on her telephone. Strange, she thought. She wasn't expecting any calls. She groaned as she rolled over and picked up the receiver then pressed the button. When she heard the voice of Doctor Ogobo she sat up straight, heart pounding.

It was about her mother – she'd had a stroke and was at the hospital. Summer trembled as she listened to the entire message.

When it was over she quickly dialed the number for the hospital and waited with bated breath. She didn't get the doctor but the nurse on duty told her that her mother had passed the worst and was resting peacefully. She advised Summer that it would be best not to wake her.

When she'd hung up she sat on the edge of the bed, twisting her hand in her lap. The guilt was heavy on her heart. She should never have left Chicago, she thought. She had to go back right away.

She grabbed her room key and without stopping to call she dashed down the hallway to Lance's room. She rapped urgently at the door until she heard the sound of the locks being opened.

Lance stood before her in nothing but a white bath towel draped around his waist.

"What do you want now," he demanded with a frown, "another pound of my flesh?"

Before he could go on she blurted, "I have to go back to Chicago. My mother's in the hospital."

"What?" He froze for an instant then grabbed her arm and pulled her into the room. He pushed her down gently to sit on the edge of his bed then looked at her, concern written all over his face. "When did you get this news?"

"Just a little while ago. They'd left me a voice message to call the hospital." She looked up at Lance with pleading eyes. "I have to get out of here, Lance. My mother needs me."

"I'll get you out of here as soon as possible. Just hang on." He opened a drawer and pulled out a pair of boxer shorts then grabbed a pair of jeans from the closet.

"Give me just a second", he said as he hurried to the bathroom. He returned in seconds, shirtless and barefooted but wearing jeans.

He stood in front of her for a moment and shoved his hands into the pockets of his jeans. Then he spoke. "We'll go out to the airport by four o'clock. We'll try to get you on the Air Jamaica flight that leaves at six. You'll have to make a connection in Miami but you should touch down in Chicago by at least one in the afternoon."

He rested a hand gently on her shoulder. "You need some rest. Let me walk you to your room."

She rested her hand on top of his and looked up at him. "Thank you, Lance." Her voice cracked and he put a finger to her lips.

"Hush. It's okay."

He went over to the closet, pulled down a shirt and slipped his feet into sandals. He tucked his key into his pocket. "I'll come get you at three-thirty," he said and went to put his arm around her shoulders. "Let's go."

When Lance knocked on her door at the appointed time Summer was packed and ready to go. The trip to the airport took less than thirty minutes and she was only the second person in line. After she had checked in Lance took her arm and lead her to a row of seats nearby.

She sighed as she sat down. She rubbed her eyes and when she looked up again he was looking down at her.

"Did you get any sleep?" His voice was low, almost gentle.

She sighed again. "Not a wink. There was so much on my mind...I just couldn't."

"Here," he pulled her head towards his shoulder, "try to relax a little. I know it's hard but making yourself sick with worry isn't going to help anybody."

She rested her head against his shoulder and closed her eyes. She felt as if her body was absorbing strength from his. A calmness enveloped her and she drifted off in his arms.

Summer woke at Lance's gentle shake. "Time to go, Summer."

When she let go of his hand at the security entrance she felt lost and alone again. But when she got to the other side of the check point he was still standing there, watching her. She waved goodbye and he waved back. Then she turned and headed for the gate.

Lance took his time getting back to the hotel. The sky was just beginning to lighten and the morning air still held the coolness of the night. As he cruised in the Land Rover his thoughts were on Summer. He just couldn't figure her out. One moment she was a feisty vixen, the next she was an innocent then before you knew it, she'd become a real bitch.

And now this. She'd seemed so helpless, so lost. All anger left him the moment she reached out for his help. There was something about her that made him want to protect her and keep her close by his side even though he knew she was an independent woman, used to charting her own life and getting things done on her own.

The problem was, she was always proving to be a real challenge to his peace of mind. He'd never before met a woman who could drive him to such emotional extremes. Lately he seemed to be losing control.

He frowned and set his mouth in a determined line. There was no way he was going to let the little minx get the better of him.

But despite his resolve Lance found himself thinking about Summer all that day. Although he was tired he was first at the studio and by the time the others arrived he'd already started cuing up the equipment. He was not surprised when Derrick approached him.

"Lance, I'm worried about Summer. I was going to bring her over here but then I found out that she checked out. Did you know about that?"

"She got a call last night. Her mother is sick so she had to head back to Chicago," Lance said gravely. "I took her to the airport this morning."

"Is it really bad?"

"Well, her mother is in the hospital so it must be serious...but I guess you'll be calling her so she should be able to give you all the details then."

"I would, but I don't have her number in Chicago. You don't know it offhand, do you?"

Lance was annoyed at the question but he kept his face expressionless. "Call the office. Chantal can get it from the files."

Derrick looked somewhat surprised at his clipped tone but he just walked away, ending the conversation.

For the rest of the day Lance worked hard, pushing the singers to the limit. When Monisha questioned his intensity he fixed her with a hard stare. "If you don't want to be here you're free to leave."

"But Lance, I was just saying…"

"You're not here to speak, you're here to sing," he said bluntly. "Now, if you're not prepared to do that I don't need you wasting our time."

"Geez!" Monisha shook her head but said nothing more.

Super Cool and Derrick looked at each other, eyebrows raised, but remained silent.

After that Lance tried to get a hold on his temper but no matter how hard he tried he kept being distracted by thoughts of Summer. He threw himself into his work and drove the others so hard that they finished two days' work by eight o'clock that night.

"Whew," Derrick sighed as he flopped down on the couch, "I'm beat."

Lance looked over at his cousin but remained silent. Then he said, "So…did you call Summer?"

"I tried a couple of times but only got voicemail. Looks like she was out all day."

"Probably with her mother," Lance said.

"Yeah."

Neither of them spoke for a while then Lance broke the silence. "You like her?"

Derrick seemed taken aback by the question. "You know me, man. The ladies love me."

"That's not what I asked you."

"Alright, man, I'll level with you. That girl's got something on me, man," Derrick was nodding as he spoke, "and I think she likes me, too."

"What makes you think that?" The question came out sharper than Lance had intended.

"She's been giving me these vibes ever since we got to Jamaica," Derrick said smugly. "She likes me, man. I know it."

Lance was silent again. Then he rose. "See you tomorrow." He slung his bag over his shoulder and headed for the door.

Back at the hotel he decided to order room service and go to bed early. He hadn't slept at all after she left his room at almost midnight. He'd been pushing himself all day, trying to drive her from his mind, but without success. Now, as he stood under the spray of water from the shower he let himself relax and allowed his thoughts free reign.

There was no use denying it. He was taken with this woman. He was forced to admit that he had worked hard all day, not just because he was trying to hold thoughts of her at bay, but also because he wanted to finish the project early and get back to Chicago as soon as possible. As much as he would like to deny it, his haste to return was all because of her.

He stepped out of the shower, grabbed a thick towel and rubbed his head vigorously.

"Damn you, Derrick!" he said aloud.

He towelled off then strode into the bedroom. He donned boxer shorts and sweat pants but left his feet and chest bare. As far as he was concerned, the less clothing one wore while in Jamaica, the better.

He unlocked the glass sliding door and went out onto the balcony. Although it was almost nine the air was still warm from the evening sun. A light breeze caressed his skin and brought with it the smell of jasmine. He leaned forward and looked down at the cars and people below.

He gripped the railing. He wanted to call her, to hear her voice. On the other hand he wasn't ready to look like a fool for any woman. After another minute of hesitation he pushed away from the railing and went back into the room. He checked his palm pilot for her phone number then dialed. After five rings her answering machine chipped in and he growled and hung up the phone.

When his food arrived ten minutes later he picked at it then pushed the tray away and lay back on the bed, staring up at the ceiling. What the hell was she doing to him? He was going to have to put a stop to this. The woman wasn't interested in him; it was Derrick she wanted.

He picked up the phone receiver a second time. "Monisha? You still up? Good. Want to go have a drink with me?" He grimaced as the girl squealed her delight. "I'll be right over."

Summer switched on the television then pressed the button, searching through the channels. "See anything you like yet?"

"Keep going."

She continued pressing until Lucy appeared on the screen.

"Yes. That one."

"Mom, it's in black and white."

"So? I'm from the black and white era. And anyway, those are the best shows." Edna took a sip from her glass. "That was when television was television."

"Okay, we'll watch this one," Summer acquiesced. "Lucy is pretty funny."

"And a lot more wholesome than some of the shows they have on TV today. Gangsters, shootings, sex...what else are they going to put in front of our children?"

Summer went to sit in the chair by her mother's bedside. Edna was propped up in bed eating Jell-O from a small plastic bowl. Her legs were covered with a thin white sheet and there was a light green blanket at the foot of the bed. Her face was thin but cheerful and she was obviously enjoying her daughter's company.

She suddenly burst out laughing and turned to her daughter. "That Lucy is something else, isn't she?"

"She sure is, Mom." Summer's calm voice and smiling face hid the turmoil in her heart.

She had come so close to losing her mother that now she spent every available moment by her bedside. Four days had passed since she'd returned to Chicago and, with each passing day, her mother had grown stronger. Doctor Ogobo had even said he might release her in another two or three days. Summer was relieved but she was still scared. She couldn't even contemplate being without her mother.

"How is the thesis coming along?" Edna asked.

"Oh...kinda slow," Summer replied distractedly.

"Summer," Edna looked at her sternly, "you have to settle down. You can't afford to miss your deadline."

"I just lost focus a little bit, Mom, but I'll make it," Summer reassured her. "I've got lots of notes. I just need to actually start writing the report."

"Just don't wait until the last minute," her mother warned. "I would suggest that you spend even an hour working on it every day so you don't have a mad rush a week before the end of the semester."

"Mom," Summer chuckled and rolled her eyes playfully, "I'm not like that anymore. I'm more organized now."

"I'm not so sure, Summer. I remember times when you had to stay up all night reading a book you hadn't opened all semester...for a test next day!" Edna shook her head.

"Those days are over," Summer laughed. "I don't think I can do all-nighters anymore. That was when I was young."

"And you're old now, are you?" Edna joked.

"No. Just older. And wiser, I hope."

When the nurse came at nine o'clock to tell Summer that it was time for Edna to rest she reluctantly kissed her mother's cheek and bid her goodbye. When she got back to her apartment she grabbed her notes, switched on the computer and began to type.

She was engrossed in the introductory chapter of her thesis when the shrill ring of the telephone startled her. Her heart thumped and she hesitated before resting her hand on the receiver.

"Hello?" Her voice was hoarse and hesitant.

"Hello, Summer. It's Lance."

She relaxed with relief. "Oh, Lance, it's you."

There was silence then his voice came again. "Were you expecting another call? I hope I'm not disturbing you."

"No, not at all. It's just that ever since I got that scary phone message about my mother every time the phone rings I get so nervous."

"I see." There was another pause then he asked. "How is your mother doing?"

"She's doing much better now, thanks," she said. "She's still in the hospital but the doctor said he might release her by the weekend. I'm hopeful."

"I'm glad to hear that. I want you to know that you can take as much time as you need to be with her."

"Thanks, Lance. I think things will be back to normal by the time you get back next weekend." She sat twirling the phone cord around her index finger.

"Actually, I plan to be back a lot earlier than that."

"Really? When?"

"This weekend."

"So soon?" Summer clutched the cord, hoping the joy she felt was not transmitted in her voice. "How come? You had all those tracks to get done."

"We've been doubling our efforts and I'm already more than halfway there. If all goes well I should be back in Chicago by Saturday night."

"Wow, that's great," she began to gush then caught herself, "...about finishing up early, I mean."

Lance chuckled. "Want to make sure I don't misunderstand you?"

"No, it's not that. I just..."

"Don't worry about it. I'm just teasing. But seriously, how are you?"

"I'm fine," she said, glad he'd asked. "Now if only my mother were fine, too, I'd be perfect."

"Has she been sick long, or is this something that happened when you were away?"

"Mom has MS. She's been suffering from it for a long time. Now on top of that she had this stroke. That's why I had to rush back."

"You never mentioned your mother's illness before. Is someone helping you take care of her?"

"When she leaves the hospital she'll go back to the nursing home. She's lived there the whole time I was in college," Summer explained. "She's very independent; she didn't want to burden me, she said. But she knows I'd love to take care of her."

"Do your relatives help out? Do you have people supporting you?"

"No. I don't have any brothers or sisters. My mother was an only child too so, of course, no aunts or uncles on that side of the family. And my father's dead."

"So you're all alone."

"I have my Mom."

"I know that. I mean you're the only one she has to rely on."

"Yes."

Lance was silent for a while then he said, "Why didn't you ever tell me this?"

"Tell you what?"

"About your mother being sick. About your being her only family."

"I wasn't sure…" she paused. "…I didn't know if it was appropriate."

"No, I don't think so. I think it's because you thought that if I knew I wouldn't give you the job."

"Well, something like that," she admitted.

"And it was because of your mother's illness that you were afraid to come to Jamaica for two weeks."

"Yes."

"You should have told me, Summer."

"But I was scared. I lost my scholarship, I lost my apartment, and I was trying to get money for my mother's surgery. I was scared I'd lose the job."

"Summer, what kind of monster do you think I am?" he growled into the phone. "I would never have fired you because you couldn't go on that trip. It's your mother we're talking about here. To me, family is the most important thing in life. I would never deny you that."

"Well…I know that now but I didn't know you back then," she said meekly. "And Lance?"

"Yes?"

"I appreciate your saying that."

"I'm not just saying it, I mean it," he said brusquely. "Now what were you saying about losing a scholarship and needing money for surgery?"

"I'm sorry. I didn't mean to blurt all that stuff out."

"But you did, so explain yourself."

"It's just that there was a lot going on in my life all at the same time," she sighed. "You already know about my having to find a new apartment on short notice but on top of that I had to find five thousand dollars to cover my last semester of school. I was also trying to figure out how to get money for Mom's eye surgery."

"I see. No wonder you jumped at my job offer."

"I had to find a way to make more money, and fast," she defended herself. "Now do you understand why I did my best to protect my job? There's a lot counting on my salary."

"I can see that." There was a pause then Lance asked, "So I guess you've heard from Derrick?"

"He left me a couple of messages but no, I haven't actually spoken to him. Is he alright?"

"Your man is fine. He'll be back this weekend."

"He's not my man."

"You could've fooled me. He's been going on about you all week." His voice turned hard. "And last time I saw you guys together I recall a kiss."

Summer bit her lip then muttered, "It's not what you think."

"It doesn't matter what I think, does it? You've made your choice."

"Lance…"

"No, you don't owe me any explanation. Let's just leave it alone and move on." He sighed. "It's getting late so I'll let you go now. Goodnight, Summer."

Long after he'd hung up she still sat with the receiver in her hand staring blankly at the wall, wondering what had just happened.

Chapter 15

"Wow, Chantal. That's beautiful."

Summer gazed at the diamond in admiration.

"I'm so excited. We're planning to go to Grenada for our honeymoon."

"You should have fun," Summer said. "I hear they have beautiful beaches there."

"My cousin went there last year and she said it was great. She got all these brochures and stuff for me." Chantal held a brochure up to Summer.

Summer shook her head. "I'd love to look at them but right now I've got to run. I've only got an hour to finish my presentation. I'm still on for two o'clock with Lance, right?"

"Two o'clock it is."

"Okay, you'll see me then. Catch you later."

Summer had been back in the office for almost a week and was hard at work on the promotional campaign for Super Cool's new album. She had worked late the last two evenings just so she could have the project completed on time. She was almost there but wanted to review it once more before making her presentation.

She was at the computer clicking through the slides when there was a quick rap at the door and Derrick walked in.

"Hi, Beautiful. Been thinking about me today?"

"Derrick, please. I've only got forty-five minutes to finish up this presentation. I can't entertain you right now."

She hoped he would hear the annoyance in her voice and leave. She was disappointed when he just grinned and took a seat in the chair across from her.

"Oh, come on, now. You haven't seen me for four whole days. What – not even a welcome back hug or a kiss?"

"No, Derrick. I'm busy."

"You work too hard, Summer." He shook his head. "You're too young to be such a workaholic. Slow it down, girl."

Summer sighed. "Can we talk about this later? I have to get this done by two o'clock."

"Later it is, then." Derrick slapped his knee and rose. "I'll come get you at six. There's a new Italian restaurant nearby that I want to check out."

"Restaurant? Tonight? I don't have time for a date."

"Well, you did say we could talk later."

"Yes, but…"

"No 'buts'. I'll be back here six o'clock sharp."

Summer nodded in defeat. Anything to get him out of here, she thought. She needed to concentrate. She breathed a sigh of relief when he closed the door behind him.

As soon as Derrick had returned from the Jamaica trip he'd called her and she had agreed to go out to dinner with him. She knew she had led him on and wanted to meet with him face to face and let him down gently. Things didn't turn out quite the way she'd intended. Derrick had been so excited about seeing her again that he chatted non-stop and she just couldn't find the right moment to break the news to him. Then he left for New York two days later and she just never got the chance to do it.

She knew she would have to do something about it very soon. Derrick was becoming something of a pest and she certainly didn't want to complicate things any further by playing with his feelings. Maybe going out with him tonight was not such a bad idea after all. It would give her a chance to set things straight between them.

At exactly two o'clock Chantal knocked on the door of Lance's office and ushered Summer in. He waved her over to a seat and mouthed, "Just a second". Summer slid into the chair and sat quietly, waiting for him to finish his telephone call.

She pretended to be absorbed with the papers she'd brought in but the presentation was the last thing on her mind right then. She stole a furtive glance at Lance.

He was as handsome as ever. Impeccably dressed, as usual, his grey business suit was complemented by a wine-coloured tie and there was the glint of gold on his wrist. As she watched him she couldn't help but note how he exuded the power and grace of a panther. She wondered if she would ever experience that power again.

At that moment Lance put down the receiver and looked up, and Summer quickly averted her eyes. She shuffled some papers then looked back at him and said brightly, "All done, as per instructions."

She leaned over and handed him the folder. He opened it and flipped through the pages slowly. She waited quietly while he read. Finally, he looked up.

"This looks good. Very professionally done," he said, nodding. "You write like someone who's got years of experience in P.R.."

"Thank you," she beamed, glad for his praise. It was the first pleasant thing he had said to her all week.

He had hardly spoken to her since his return from Jamaica and she'd had the distinct impression that he was still very angry with her. They exchanged pleasantries when they met in the hallway or in the lunch room but outside of that they hadn't had much to say to each other. He'd spent the past week locked in his office or away at meetings.

She'd been busy, too. Now that the album was done he wanted her to work quickly on the Public Relations campaign. He wanted the album launched and the music on the air before the summer was over. As he reviewed the document he seemed enthusiastic about her strategies and she was relieved.

"So you're recommending sampling to college radio stations as well?"

"Yes. We have an untapped market of millions of students in colleges and universities across this country. Can you imagine how big this could get if we got even a tenth of them to listen to our music?"

He nodded, a thoughtful look on his face. "And you think college students will buy this type of music?"

"Absolutely," she said confidently. "The more aware people are, the more they appreciate other cultures and expressions of creativity. A lot of the students on my campus have started listening to Lover's Rock and Reggae. I know what I'm talking about. Trust me."

He looked up from the page and gave her an enigmatic look. Summer felt herself squirm a little inside but she steeled herself so that her face would reveal nothing.

Instead, she continued talking as if she hadn't noticed. "When you see stars like Beyonce and Janet Jackson using Jamaican Dance Hall in their music, you know there's a market out there."

"I have no doubt about that. What I have doubts about is whether we'll be wasting our resources trying to pursue this particular group when they have no interest or money to give us the returns."

"I anticipated that. And that's why my college programme is designed to pay for itself. This is where we get maximum mileage at the lowest cost by partnering with other companies who would love to target college students. It's all there in my tactical plan. You'll understand my strategy after you've read it through."

Lance nodded thoughtfully then picked up a silver pen and made a few notes on the corner of the page. "Okay, I'll spend some time going through the details."

"And remember, that is just a small part of the overall strategy. If we execute all that I've planned this album will go platinum."

Lance chuckled at that. "Such confidence. But that's what I like about you, Summer. You're young, full of ideas and so cocksure that failure doesn't even cross your mind."

"I thought that's why you hired me?" She smiled.

"You're right. That's exactly why I hired you. I need someone to bring a fresh perspective to this business and I have no doubt that you're the one who'll do it." Lance leaned back in his chair and laced his fingers together. "I'm going to review your business plan this evening and we'll have a follow up meeting tomorrow, same time. I want to go through it first then you can take me through each element of the plan in detail. After that you'll have two days to make revisions and finalize the presentation. I want you to be ready to present it to the rest of the team and our agency partners by Friday morning."

"Me? I thought...you'd do it."

"This project is your baby, Summer. I need your passion when it's presented. We need everyone's buy-in if this is going to work so you'll have to sell your ideas to them." He smiled at her. "I'm sure you can handle it."

"Thanks." This vote of confidence from Lance lifted her spirits. "I won't let you down."

When Summer left Lance's office she headed straight for the library. She loved a challenge. Lance had, in essence, challenged her to do a top class presentation on Friday and, in the same breath, do what she claimed she could do – make the launch of Super Cool's album a smashing success. She was going to review the tapes and DVD's of Super Cool's past performances and incorporate them into her presentation.

She would wow the team so that they would all rise to the occasion and give this campaign their best efforts. Then, once they were all on board she'd make sure that the execution of the plan was flawless. Even if Lance hated her otherwise, he would have to respect her when she showed him what she could do.

Six o'clock came too soon for Summer. She was so excited about being allowed to present the plan that she wanted to spend her time preparing the best presentation possible. Still, she knew that Derrick was a man who would not take no for an answer so she was ready when he peeped into her office at three minutes before the hour.

"Ready to go, my angel?"

"Ready." She shut the computer down and picked up her handbag and her briefcase. "So where are we going now?"

"Luigi's on the Lagoon. It's new but I hear the food is good."

"The restaurant is by the lake then?"

"You got it. Lakeview while you eat. Not a bad atmosphere when you're in the mood for romance."

Summer grimaced but said nothing. She smiled inwardly at the irony of the situation. Just over a month ago she'd been a waitress serving this man at a lakeside restaurant and now she would be dining with him at one.

The problem was, she would much rather have had the irony of dining with his cousin, the man who had been turning her world upside down ever since she'd met him in The Southern Belle.

"Help you with that?" Derrick stretched his hand and took the briefcase from her then held the door open so she could pass. As she stepped through the door, the thanks on her lips, she looked up and her eyes met the taunting dark ones of the man who had been on her mind.

Her heart plummeted. This was just about the worst possible time for Lance to come out of his office. Although his face was expressionless she could guess what he was thinking.

Just when her spirits were lifting this had to happen. Lance nodded to Summer and Derrick and bid them good evening. Then he picked up a folder from Chantal's desk, went back into his office and closed the door.

As they drove to the restaurant Summer leaned back in her seat and closed her eyes. Derrick made light conversation but although she responded to all his questions she gave him no encouragement. Eventually, he fell silent.

When they got to the restaurant Summer tried to be better company. She laughed at all of Derrick's jokes and even shared a few of her own. She felt sorry for him. He was trying so hard to be charming.

After dessert he sat drinking a cup of coffee while she sipped on green tea. He reached out a hand to stroke her forearm, making Summer jump in surprise. Tea splashed from her cup into the saucer below.

"Sorry. I didn't mean to scare you." He seemed deflated by her response.

"No, it's my fault. It's just that you surprised me, that's all."

She dabbed at the saucer with a napkin then set her cup down and looked up at him. He was still watching her and she began to get uncomfortable under his intense stare.

"Do you mind if I ask you something?"

Here it comes, she thought, but all she said was, "Go ahead. What is it?"

He looked down at his coffee mug and drummed his fingers against the side. Without looking up he asked, "Do you like me, Summer? I mean even just a little bit?"

"Of course I like you," she smiled at him. "You're like the mischievous brother I never had."

"That's not what I'm talking about, Summer, and you know it." Derrick looked up, obviously annoyed. "Now please, do you or do you not have feelings towards me?"

"Derrick...," she struggled to find the words, "...I don't want to hurt you but I have to be honest. I see you as a great friend but...no, I don't like you in the way you mean."

"It's Lance, isn't it?"

"Excuse me?"

"You're in love with Lance."

"Why would you say that? I never said…"

"You didn't have to. Your reaction when he's around says it all."

When Summer frowned he continued. "Whenever the two of you are in the same room you get all tense and breathless and you always look like you're trying to run away. Then he gets all serious. There's definitely something between the two of you."

Summer sat silent, staring at her hands. Finally, her voice came out in a broken whisper. "I don't know what's happening to me. I know the kind of man Lance is. He's got women hanging all over him. I know I don't stand a chance, but…there's just something about him that turns me into a bumbling idiot."

"Don't be so hard on yourself. He has that effect on lots of women."

His sarcasm was not lost on Summer and she looked at him sharply, wondering if the conversation was going to get unpleasant.

But then Derrick just shook his head and sighed. "Well, I tried, but I know when I'm beat." He patted the hand she had rested on the table. "Still friends?"

"Always friends, Derrick," she replied, and squeezed his hand in return.

The next two days were hectic for Summer. She had her follow-up meeting with Lance and he gave her a few pointers on how to structure her strategies to best suit the music industry. Outside of that he had very few changes and she was grateful for that. She had so little time in which to prepare for the meeting that she was glad she didn't have to revamp the whole thing.

She felt guilty when she had to call her mother Thursday night to postpone their planned "Bingo Night".

"I'll make it up to you, Mom. I promise," she said, hoping Edna would understand.

"Don't worry about it, honey," her mother soothed, "I know you'll come over just as soon as you can. You just work hard and present the best damn plan that anyone ever heard."

"Mom, I can't believe you said the "D" word." Summer gave an exaggerated gasp. "I'm shocked."

"Go on and leave me alone, girl. At my age I'm allowed a few curse words."

"You might be the only one left who still calls that a curse word," Summer laughed, "but, for you, it's progress. You used to have a fit when I said 'hell'.

"And don't you think you can start now, young lady."

"Yes, Ma'am," Summer said humbly, then spoiled it by giggling.

Her mother sighed then spoke in mock disgust, "You're a hopeless case. Now just get off this phone and go get your presentation done."

"Okay, Mom. Sleep tight." Summer spoke softly into the phone, then waited.

"Good night, dear." Edna replied then there was silence.

"Hang up the phone, Mom."

"No, you hang up."

"No, you first."

"No, you…"

"Alright, alright," Summer growled, "I'll go first. But next time it will be your turn."

"Alright, dear." Edna's tone was smug.

"Bye, Mom. I love you."

Summer need not have worried so much about the presentation. Her tactical plan for the launch of "Super Cool – A New Era" was so well received that Lance congratulated her afterwards. He particularly liked the way she had brought aspects of Super Cool's life, such as his experiences growing up in the country, into the campaign. He said it lent some credibility to the artiste's image as 'one of the people'.

Her spirits soared at his praise. She walked sedately back to her office, closed the door behind her then punched the air with a celebratory "Yes!" After that she sat at her desk and pretended to be absorbed in her work but inside she was still caught up in the high of the great impression she had made.

Her initial success gave her new impetus. She had so many ideas for other campaigns. She'd been working on one for Top Cat and, buoyed up by Lance's praise, she was anxious to share it with him. She checked her watch. Two forty-five. She had just enough time to do an abbreviated version and pass it to Lance before he left at the end of the day. She knew he often took work home on the weekends and wanted him to review it so she could have his feedback next Monday. Well, if I'm going to get it to him by five I'd better get cracking, she thought.

Summer was close to finishing the summary when she glanced at her watch. She grimaced when she saw that it was ten minutes to five. She didn't want Lance to leave without it. She dialed Chantal's extension.

"Chantal, Lance hasn't left yet, has he?"

"No, he had some teleconference or other to finish up. You know how he is," she said and Summer could almost see her rolling her eyes. "It's almost five o'clock on a Friday afternoon and he's still trying to squeeze the most out of every minute of the work day. I keep warning him that if he's not careful he'll…"

"What time will the conference call end?"

"They usually last around thirty minutes so I'd guess about five-fifteen. You want me to tell him…"

"No, it's okay, thanks." She cut in again, trying to keep the conversation brief. "I'll just try to catch him before he leaves."

"Well, I'm packing up to leave, myself. You have a great weekend."

"Thanks. You, too, Chantal."

At exactly ten minutes after five Summer stapled the pages of her report and dashed down to Lance's office. The door was closed and she wondered if she should knock or just slide it under the door so he would see it on his way out. She didn't want to disturb his call so she bent down to execute her plan B.

She was on her knees, the paper halfway under the door, when it opened and she found herself peering up into Monisha's startled face.

Chapter 16

"What are you doing down there?" Monisha looked at her suspiciously.

Summer felt her face suddenly get hot and she stammered, "I'm...I'm sorry. I was just going to slide something under the door."

She struggled to her feet, trying to be graceful although rising elegantly from such an awkward position was difficult. When she was on her feet she smoothed her skirt then held the paper out to the woman. "Would you mind handing this to Mr. Munroe?"

"I'm right here. You can hand it to me yourself." Lance's voice came from behind Monisha then he appeared, briefcase in hand, obviously ready to leave. "What is it?"

"Nothing. I..." Suddenly, she was tongue-tied. "I...was just going to leave something for you to look at over the weekend...if you had time. But I can see you're busy."

She turned to leave with the document but Lance grabbed her arm. "Wait. I'll take it."

He pulled the papers from her stiff fingers and read the title. He smiled. "You're on a roll, I see. Another business plan. I look forward to reading it."

She nodded and bid them goodnight then walked stiffly down the hallway back to her office.

When she had closed the door behind her she let her shoulders droop in defeat. Her hands trembled slightly and her heart beat fast. She had never been so embarrassed in her life. They were probably laughing at her right now. She grimaced at the thought. Then something else occurred to her

– what if they thought she'd been spying on them, maybe even trying to listen to their conversation? She would have to clear this up with Lance on Monday.

Worst of all, though, was the realization that Lance and Monisha were seeing each other. She had always thought it but Chantal's remarks had made her doubt this assumption. Now she knew for sure. She felt so deflated that she couldn't bear another minute in her office. She had to get out of there, get them out of her mind.

She quickly shut down her computer, grabbed her bag and headed out the door. There was only one place she could go to ease her turmoil. She wouldn't even bother to go home first. She exited the building and headed for the train station.

Edna took one look at her daughter's face and said, "Something's not right with you, Summer. What's going on?"

Summer sat down and rested her handbag on a nearby stool. "Oh, nothing. Just tired, that's all."

"Don't give me that," Edna cut in. "You've always shared your problems with me so don't start holding back now. Tell me what's wrong."

Summer sighed then began. "There's this man… at work. When I first met him I couldn't stand a bone in his body. He just… rubbed me the wrong way, you know? But now…I can't get him out of my mind. I still don't even know if I like him. But…" she looked at her mother with a frown, "…I think I'm in love with him."

Edna nodded slowly then said, "I can see you're confused. You're really attracted to this man but I bet I know what the problem is. He's probably got a very strong personality that's constantly in conflict with yours." When Summer nodded her mother smiled and asked, "So tell me, why do you think you're in love with him?"

"I guess it's because…he's the only man who makes me feel like I want to be around him all the time. But then it's so weird because when I'm with him I end up acting like a complete fool."

"So, let me understand this - you feel you're in love with this man but he makes you feel crazy. So that's why you came in here all depressed?"

"No," she sighed. "I found out he's seeing someone."

Edna looked thoughtful then said, "He's told you he's in a relationship?"

"No, but he doesn't have to tell me that. Just this evening I saw them leaving the office together. I sure don't need any more than that to know what's going on."

"Be careful you're not jumping to the wrong conclusion. Here's a thought," Edna touched her temple and feigned a look of realization, "why don't you just ask him how he feels about you?"

"But that's crazy." Summer was incredulous. "You really expect me to do that?

"It just might work."

"Yeah, and it just might make me end up looking like a worse fool. You've always given me good advice, Ma, but this time," Summer shook her head, "I don't know."

"Well, instead of asking him how he feels why don't you let him know how you feel about him?"

"But it's like the same thing, isn't it?"

"Not really. You don't have to come out and say it. You can just show him in subtle ways. Feel him out. Test the waters, so to speak."

"You mean I should flirt with him?" Summer frowned at her mother.

"Whatever you want to call it, Summer, I just think you need to stop sitting there feeling sorry for yourself and do something about it. Find out how he truly feels about you. Throw him a bone. If he doesn't bite then just leave it alone. But you just can't give up without even trying." Edna shrugged. "That is, if you're really in love with him, like you say."

"I think I am, Mom. But I'm scared."

"Of what?"

"Of getting hurt." She looked away. "Like you."

"Come on now, Summer. You can't think like that."

"But, Mom, I do think about that. I know you loved Dad so much and look what he did to you." Summer bit her lip as the memories came flooding back. "He hurt you so much, Mom, and it was because he knew you loved him too much to leave him. I don't want that to happen to me."

"Hush, child. That doesn't have to happen to you. You and I are two different people so we'll react to situations in different ways." Edna reached over and squeezed her hand. "You're strong. You'll survive. But you can't keep hiding away from relationships because you're scared of getting hurt."

"I know…"

"No, I don't think so. You don't know what it's like for me to know that I'll be departing this world one day, leaving my little girl all alone. That worries me, Summer."

"Mom, don't talk like that," Summer pleaded.

"I have to. It's reality. One of these days I won't be around and I would love to know there's someone there for you. I pray for you all the time." Her voice grew softer. "I pray that, before I die, my daughter will find the happiness that I was looking for."

"Mom, don't."

"No, Summer. Let me speak." She folded her arms across her chest and continued. "I've watched you reject young men who seemed nice and genuine. You can't keep doing that, Sugar, or else you'll wake up one day to find out that you're my age and all alone in the world. I worry about you, Summer."

"Please, Mom, I can take care of myself."

"I know you can, honey. But it's hard being alone." She touched Summer's cheek gently then looked at her earnestly. "Don't get me wrong. I'm not saying you should throw yourself at the man. I didn't raise my daughter that way. All I'm saying is that, in life, we have to go for what we want."

"I hear you, Mom," Summer said softly.

Lance remained silent as Monisha chatted on about her last performance in Atlanta.

"That's my biggest market. I'm sure of it. Those people love me." Lance smiled and nodded as he had been doing all night, trying to look interested.

He still had the plastic smile pasted on his face when she scolded, "Lance, you're not listening to me."

"I heard everything you said." He brought his eyes back to her face.

"I doubt it. You haven't really been with me all evening. Are you alright?" She reached out a hand and stroked his own.

"I'm fine, Monisha. Really," he said, trying not to sound bored. "Now tell me some more about the people in Atlanta who really love you."

"Well, at least you heard that part." She smiled back then began her story again, totally oblivious to his true feelings.

As had been happening all evening her voice soon faded into the background and his responses became mechanical and vague. Despite his calm exterior Lance's mind was in turmoil. His thoughts were on the woman he had left back at the office.

Summer had really impressed him with her work this week. He always knew she would be an asset to his business but she had attacked her projects with such passion and represented herself with a maturity that was beyond her years.

But it was not only her work that he had on his mind. The girl was beginning to grow on him in a way that no woman ever had. He looked forward to seeing her each day he walked into the office although he made sure no-one could ever tell. His interaction with her was nothing less than professional.

"And do you know what she said about me?" Monisha's sharp voice sliced through his thoughts. "She said I was 'ghetto-fabulous'. I could've ripped the face off that heifer, I was so mad."

Not waiting for a response, she went on to give her opinion of her adversary and Lance continued to respond at appropriate times but all he was doing at that moment was wishing that it was Summer who sat across from him. He found her so stimulating. He knew without a doubt that she wouldn't be spending her time talking about some woman and her clothes.

"Lance, you're not listening to me." Monisha frowned at him, then said, "You've been so distracted all evening that I'm beginning to wonder if you want to be here with me at all."

"Come off it, Monisha," Lance said in an exasperated tone.

"No, I'm serious. Am I boring you? Because, if I am, you can just take me home right now. I certainly don't want to be a bother to you."

"Monisha, just calm down," he said firmly. "You don't need to create a scene."

"Well, you'd better take me home, then." She folded her arms and set her mouth in a pout.

He fixed her with a hard stare then sighed. "Alright, then, we'll leave."

He beckoned for the bill and within minutes they were in his car. As he started the engine he glanced at the woman sulking in her seat and saw that her lips were trembling. He didn't know if this was out of anger or hurt but the sight of this new, vulnerable side of Monisha touched him.

Suddenly, instead of feeling angry, he felt guilty. He'd been using her as a mere distraction and she didn't deserve that.

"Monisha, I'm sorry."

She seemed surprised as she looked up at him.

I guess I don't do this kind of thing often enough, Lance thought ruefully.

"I've been a real jerk tonight and I apologize." He gave her a puppy-dog look and smiled. "Forgive me?"

Her face lightened and a smile softened her lips. "Of course, I do. You know I can't stay mad at you." She leaned over and kissed him on the cheek. "Just don't shut me out like that again, okay?"

He nodded and touched her cheek then said, "Now let's get you home."

When they pulled up in front of Monisha's apartment building on Wacker Drive she turned to him. "Why don't you come up for a minute?"

"It's been a long evening, Monisha." He shook his head. "I'm a bit tired and I'm sure you are, too."

"Come on," she cajoled, "just for a minute. I got a gorgeous new painting and I want you to see it."

"You're only saying that because you know art is my weakness."

"Come on."

She spoke in a tiny voice and looked so pleading that he finally said, "Okay, I'll come up. But just for a little while."

The painting really was beautiful. It was done by a local Chicago artist who was renowned for his landscapes and nature scenes. This time he had painted the Chicago skyline in deep purple hues and had accentuated the deep color of the buildings by painting Lake Michigan in silver.

"I must admit, you do have an eye for good work. This is your best one yet, Monisha," Lance said, impressed.

"Thanks. I'm planning to visit the gallery again this month. I need just one more, for the panel at the top of the stairs."

As she spoke she walked over to him and rested her hands on his chest. She lifted her head and kissed him lightly on the lips then pushed against him so that he was forced to sit down in the sofa behind him. "Why don't you just relax and let me make you a cup of coffee?"

The plump sofa was comfortable and warm and he relaxed into its depths. He was just beginning to realize just how tired he was. "Thanks. I could do with some perking up. Keep me awake for the drive home."

As Monisha headed off towards the kitchen Lance leaned back in the couch and closed his eyes. It had been a hectic week for him and he was looking forward to some relaxation on the weekend. He planned to stay at home all day Saturday and drive out to see his mother Sunday afternoon. He had no other plans outside of that and he liked it that way. He could do with a quiet weekend once in a while.

Lance woke up suddenly when something cool touched his face. When he opened his eyes Monisha was leaning over him, her hand on his cheek.

"Wake up, honey. I brought your coffee."

He groaned softly, rubbed his eyes then blinked to clear his vision. It was then that he noticed that Monisha didn't have a cup in her hand but was standing before him in a sheer black teddy.

He began to straighten from his slouched position but before he could move any farther she pushed him back into the couch and pressed her body against his. She raised her lips to his mouth but he gripped her upper arms and firmly put her away from him.

"What are you doing?" Monisha's voice was sharp with disbelief.

"Monisha, I can't."

"What do you mean you can't?" At first she looked confused then her face contorted in anger.

"What the hell is going on?" she demanded.

"I'm tired, Monisha. I just need to go home now."

"Tiredness never stopped you before." Monisha's eyes were like shards of glass as she spat the words at him. "You have some nerve coming up in here and then acting as if you're Mr. High and Mighty and too good for me. I was good enough for you before, so what's with this frontin'?"

"It has nothing to do with you, girl. It's me. I'm just not in the mood right now."

"You haven't been in the mood all night, Lance. Just level with me." Monisha put her hands on her hips. "What exactly is going on?"

"There's nothing going on…," he began, but she cut in abruptly.

"I know what's wrong. It's a woman, isn't it? You've gone and found yourself some woman and now it's time to kick me to the curb."

Monisha paced the floor as she fumed. "I've always known it. It's like I'm not good enough for you. I've never been good enough for you."

"Monisha. Stop it." He tried to sound firm but his voice only came out exasperated.

"Why don't you ever tell me that you love me?"

Lance looked at her face, which was angry and pleading at the same time; he was almost overcome by his feeling of guilt but had no idea how he could diminish her pain. He was not prepared to lie to avoid hurting her feelings. She had known he wasn't interested in a relationship with her but had persisted in starting something and now, despite what she had said earlier, she was demanding more.

"Let's not go there," he said, and got up to leave.

"Where do you think you're going? You can't just leave me like this. I won't let you walk out on me."

"You can't stop me." His voice was grim.

"You bastard," she rasped through clenched teeth. "I hate you."

"Now do you see why I was against this in the first place?" Lance shook his head. "I'm going to leave before we both say something we regret."

Even as he walked out the door Lance could hear Monisha's shrieks but he steeled his heart and kept on walking.

Back in his apartment he lay flat on his back on the bed and contemplated what had just happened. Against his better judgment he'd gone out with Monisha a few times. Then she started getting attached and he backed away. He had succeeded in holding her at bay for months until that night in Jamaica when he'd grabbed at her to save himself from drowning in the dilemma that was Summer Jones.

That was the worst thing he could have done. Monisha became so demanding and possessive that he had to remind her that he never made any commitment to her. That didn't seem to matter. As long as they went out on dates she seemed to think that he was hers. Well, it would end now. After that scene there was no way he could continue down that path.

Lance rolled over onto his stomach and pressed the remote. The television popped on and Steve Harvey came into view. He watched the show for a while but his mind kept drifting off, not to the black-eyed beauty he'd been with tonight but to a petite girl with coppery hair.

Monisha had talked about love tonight. She spoke the truth when she said he'd never told her he loved her. It was a statement he didn't take lightly; and he had no intention of saying it unless he meant it.

Love – what was it, anyway? He'd thought he'd found it once, but then she left him for one of his college buddies. Then he thought of how the memory of Summer made his heart race. Did this mean he was in love with her? He wasn't sure. All he knew was that she was making him crazy just thinking about her. The problem was she'd gone and fallen for his cousin and he was not the type to pursue a woman who was already taken.

Lance turned his attention back to the television. He flipped through the channels trying to find a good movie, anything to take his mind off Summer, but the more he tried to forget the more vividly she came to his mind. He looked at his watch – it was almost ten o'clock. She'd probably be in bed by now, he thought, but still found himself leaning over to reach for the phone. He just felt an urge to hear her voice. He dialed and waited, not anxious but just a little bit nervous. The phone rang once, twice, then by the fifth ring her voicemail chipped in and he knew she was not home.

He slammed the phone down, angry with himself for being such a fool. It was Friday night; the girl was bound to be out with Derrick. He was acting like some love-sick school boy. From now on he was going to leave her alone, he decided. It was no use hiding his head in the sand. She was gone.

Summer pushed the door and entered the apartment. She switched on the light and walked over to the sofa where she threw her handbag in the corner. Her mouth felt dry and she went straight to the kitchen.

She returned to the living room with a bottle of water then sat down and took a long drink. She was so thirsty that the water tasted sweet in her mouth. She downed almost half the bottle before she leaned back, stifling a yawn. The clock on the wall said ten-thirty-two.

No wonder she was so tired. She had left straight from work and had spent the whole evening with her mother. She smiled as she remembered one of the stories her mother had told her tonight – she was always giving her jokes about the old days.

She picked up the phone and punched in her voicemail code. There were two messages. Brian had called to check up on her. She looked up at the clock again and thought about returning his call but then decided it was too late. She would buzz him in the morning instead.

She deleted the message and listened to the next one. Someone else had called but hadn't left a message. The voice message system gave the telephone number and she jotted it down on the pad she kept on the table. She frowned. Somehow the number looked familiar but she just couldn't place it. All she knew was that it was a Chicago number. Probably one of my college mates giving me a buzz, she thought. She could find that out easily enough.

She dug into her purse for her tiny phone book and began to check the numbers of the few people she had in mind. As she searched her thoughts went back to the conversation she'd had with her mother.

What her Mom said made sense, she thought. She had a feeling Lance really liked her and maybe it was time to find out for sure. She had never before believed in leaving things to fate — she'd always believed in creating opportunities rather than waiting for things to happen to her. Why stop now?

As she flipped through the sparse little book she ran into the name of the man who had occupied her thoughts. She smiled as she thought about him then frowned as she saw the phone number beside his name. It was the number she'd been looking for.

Her heart leapt. Lance had called. He hadn't left a message but at least he hadn't written her off. Maybe he was wanting her as much as she wanted him, she thought. Well, she would find out soon enough. She was going to put her plan into action.

Chapter 17

"You look beautiful today." Chantal looked her over as they stood at the water cooler together. "I'm not sure what it is. Maybe it's the color you're wearing, but you just look so...vibrant."

"Why, thank you, Chantal." Summer smiled. "I've never been called 'vibrant' before, but I like it."

"Make sure you get more outfits like this. Hot colours suit you. They bring out your warm tones."

Summer rolled her eyes but Chantal defended her position.

"No, really. For someone with your skin tone the best colours for you are red, orange, hot pink, burgundy and even rich blues. But please, stay away from the pastels. Those will do nothing for you."

"Thanks, Chantal. I appreciate the advice."

"No problem. I like that kind of thing. In my next life I'll probably be a designer or a fashion consultant to the stars." She chuckled, as if acknowledging the futility of such thoughts.

"But that would be great, Chantal. From the first day I met you I really admired the way you dress, wear your make-up, everything. You carry yourself like a queen."

Summer's voice lowered, as if to share a secret. "To tell you the truth, I thought you were a model."

"A model?" Chantal laughed. "I've never been on a runway in my life."

"But you could be. You look better than lots of those models they're going crazy about. But it's not just that. You don't just look good, you know how to make people look good." Summer voice was sober. "Seriously, Chantal, if fashion is what you love I think you should go for it."

"But at my age…"

"At your age? You talk like you're over the hill or something."

"I'm twenty-eight!"

"So?" Summer challenged her.

"So, I can't start over again now. It's too late."

Summer pulled Chantal over to the eating area and beckoned for her to sit down. She pulled up a chair beside her and began to speak earnestly. "Listen, Chantal, it's never too late unless you decide it is. At my undergraduate graduation one of my batch mates was eighty-five years old. Eighty-five! And she didn't think it was too late. She said she'd spent all her life raising children, then taking care of grandchildren, but she'd always wanted to go to college. She decided she was going to fulfill her dream, and she did. And you know what?" Summer's face broke into a smile. "At graduation she announced that she was going on to do her Master's."

"You're kidding!" Chantal looked incredulous.

"Well, you'd better believe it because every word I said is true. Chantal," Summer looked at her intently, "please don't let your talent go to waste. I sincerely believe that everyone has even one special talent in life and if they don't use it then they've cheated themselves and the world of something great."

"Well…maybe you're right."

"I know I am. So you're going to give this some serious thought?"

Chantal nodded, but Summer pressed further.

"Promise?"

"I promise." Chantal nodded emphatically.

"Good. And I'll be your first client."

They both laughed at that then got up and headed back to the main office.

Back in her office Summer wrote her action list for the week as she always did on a Monday morning. Today, though, there was one very unusual item on the list – *Execute Operation L. M.* She giggled, feeling like a mischievous school girl. It was item number four on her list but she was ready – now. She picked up the phone and dialed Chantal's extension.

"Hey, Summer. What's up?"

"Chantal, could you put me on Lance's agenda for today? I just need a few minutes."

"Sure. Just let me check his schedule…he's free at four o'clock. Is that good for you?"

"That's fine."

"O.k., you're on."

"Thanks, Chantal."

That Monday seemed like the longest day in Summer's life. She, who had always prided herself on being so disciplined and hard-working, did hardly anything that day. She just could not concentrate. She started reviewing an agency brief then threw it down in frustration. She'd read the same sentence seven times. She was just not focused.

Nervous as she was, she was relieved when the clock slid round to four o'clock and it was time to execute her plan. Her heart pounded and her palms felt sweaty but she was not going to back out now. She picked up a notepad and pen and, trying to look calm and professional, headed down the hallway towards Lance's office.

He acknowledged her knock with the deep voice that never failed to send shivers down her body. She entered and closed the door behind her, then turned towards him. She was surprised when she saw that he was more casually dressed than she had ever seen him in the office. Today there was no business suit, only a pale blue shirt which was open at the collar. Somehow, seeing him in this less formal attire made her feel just a little bit more relaxed, more confident in what she was about to do.

On his invitation she went and sat in the chair opposite him and rested her notepad on her knee. Lance sat back in his chair and twirled a silver pen in his long fingers. Summer thought he looked a little tired, but as handsome as ever.

"So, what are we discussing today, Summer?"

"I'd like to discuss...us." Summer spoke quietly and clearly.

He raised his eyebrows in surprise and leaned forward. "Us? That's an interesting topic. What about us are we going to discuss?"

She faltered, her confidence slipping a bit, but then she thought of her mother's words and she pressed on. "I'd...I'd like to invite you to dinner...if you're not too busy this evening."

His lips curved into a smile and she could have sworn the look he gave her held some affection. "I'm not busy this evening. I would enjoy having dinner with you."

"Thanks."

She rose to leave but he stopped her, "Wait. What time should I be ready?" Summer could have kicked herself. She'd been so nervous she had forgotten about that part.

"I'd like us to go at seven. Aah...could I ask you a favour?"

"Sure. What is it?" He almost sounded eager.

"I don't have a car yet. Do you mind picking me up at my apartment?" Summer felt a twinge of embarrassment but it had to be said.

"No problem." He nodded. "I'll be there at seven."

When Lance rang the buzzer at seven o'clock she opened up to him wearing a sleek black dress with spaghetti straps. She knew it accentuated the fullness of her breasts and the curve of her hips so she was not surprised when his eyes widened appreciatively.

"Come in, Lance." She smiled what she hoped was a seductive smile as she ushered him into the tiny living room. "I'll be ready in just a second. I'll just need to get my purse."

As she walked towards the bedroom she could feel his eyes on her back and knew, without a doubt, that his eyes were drawn to the sway of her hips. She was wearing high heels for exactly that effect.

As they walked to the elevator Lance rested a hand at her elbow in a protective manner. She could smell the fresh scent of his cologne and felt the latent power in his grip. It made her heart race and her knees weak and she was glad he was supporting her. The sheer masculinity of him was wreaking havoc on her senses and she knew she wanted him now more than ever. If there had been any doubt in her mind before, she knew now there was no turning back.

They arrived at the Peking Restaurant at twenty minutes after the hour and were ushered to the table which was reserved for them. It was in a quiet corner of the restaurant by a huge aquarium full of brightly coloured tropical fish.

After they had placed their order Summer gave Lance her most seductive smile and said, "Thanks for coming on such short notice. I hope I didn't mess up any of your plans?"

"Not at all. I'm glad you invited me."

"And I'm glad you could make it." She smiled again, feeling a surge of pleasure as his eyes roamed over her face.

She knew she was beautiful tonight. Before leaving the office she had asked Chantal for some make-up tips and had followed her advice to the letter. When she was done she was shocked at the dramatic transformation. Her eyes looked bigger and brighter and her lips seemed fuller. She couldn't remember ever looking this beautiful.

"Lance," she caught his gaze with an intense look of her own, "I know you must be wondering why I asked you out."

"The question did come to mind," he nodded slowly in agreement, still watching her intently.

"Well, I wanted a chance to get to know you better. We've worked together for almost two months so I think I know your professional side. Now I'd like to get to know the personal side of you." Summer saw the surprise that leapt into his eyes and, for a fleeting moment, she enjoyed his confusion. It felt great having the upper hand, just this once.

"I see," was all he said and she smiled inwardly as she realized that, at least for the moment, he was speechless.

She pressed on. "Lance, I'm sure I don't need to tell you that...that I'm attracted to you. In fact, no-one has ever made me feel...I mean..." she paused, trying to gather her courage about her, "...feel the way you make me feel," she finished lamely and her face grew hot with the embarrassment.

She had planned her speech so well and here she'd gone and made a fool of herself. She inhaled then tried to salvage what was left of her pride. "I mean..."

Lance leaned forward and rested his hand on hers. "I know what you mean. I feel the same way, too. I'm glad you had the courage to let me know how you feel."

She was grateful that he had rescued her from herself. She didn't know what else she had been about to say but at least she'd been spared. And now she knew for sure that he was attracted to her, too. She smiled softly, "Me, too."

"Summer, I've felt something for you ever since that first night we met."

"In the restaurant?" she asked, surprised. "But you hardly knew me."

"It didn't matter. I knew there was something special about you. That's why I came back alone. I wanted a chance to talk to you."

"Really?" Summer was pleasantly surprised. "But I thought you were laughing at me."

"Not at all. In fact, I admired your spunk. There aren't many women who can stand up to someone like Monisha."

"But I did," she said, glowing in his praise.

"Yes, you did. And I admired that."

Lance looked at her intently and she lowered her gaze, suddenly shy again.

"So how's your thesis coming along?"

She looked up at him, grateful for the neutral subject. "It was going slowly at first but now I'm really on a roll," she said. "I'm past the halfway mark, actually."

"That's great. And what, exactly, is it about?"

"It's entitled, 'The impact of Music on Teenage Communication'. I'm using my new knowledge of the music industry to form the basis of the thesis."

"Sounds deep." He nodded, seemingly genuinely interested.

"Well, I'm trying to make it a paper with substance," she said, encouraged by his interest. "You know sometimes people do studies on subjects that make no contribution to learning or don't even make sense at all. Do you know I read a thesis that was actually about the number of times the word 'river' appears in the works of Mark Twain? Can you believe that?"

"No, I can't," he laughed. "What the heck did that researcher find to say about that?"

"Not much, if you ask me. Just a couple of hundred pages of 'blah'."

At that moment their food arrived. Summer had ordered her favourite Chinese dish – roast chicken in pineapple sauce. Lance had gone for the chow mein with sweet and sour chicken.

"Bon apetit," she said and popped a piece of the succulent meat into her mouth. She ate a few bites then looked across at Lance who was digging into his own meal.

"Lance, I'm curious."

"About what?"

"About you. The real you. I want to know what's behind that exterior you show the world."

"Well, I always thought I was pretty straightforward," he smiled.

"That's not what I mean. All of us have another side to us that's only reserved for the special people in our lives." She laid down her fork. "For instance, I'd love to know what it was like for you, growing up on an island."

"Oh, that's easy. It was probably the best time of my life. But then, childhood is probably the best time in most people's lives, anyway."

When she remained silent he continued. "Until I was thirteen I lived in a little town called Port Maria which is by the sea. I used to get into all kinds of trouble with my friends. In the summertime I'd sneak off with them to the river or spend all day on the beach. It used to drive my mother crazy. She was always scared I'd drown."

"You were a bad little boy," she chuckled. "I can just imagine how you were."

"Let's just say, I was a typical boy. I did the things the boys did there – I'd go into the hills with my friends and shoot birds with my slingshot. Then we'd stay up there in the bushes and roast and eat them."

"Ooh," Summer made a face.

"They were only birds, just like you're eating right now."

"I know, but it just seems different."

"You buy yours in the supermarket, I shoot mine in the wild." He shrugged. "I grew up poor, by American standards. My Mom couldn't buy me lots of toys but in Jamaica, you learn to make your own. We made bows and arrows out of the spines of palm leaves. We made cricket bats from coconut boughs and cars from empty milk cartons. They had bottle caps for wheels."

He laughed as he reminisced. "Looking back I can say that my childhood was a lot of fun. I wouldn't change it for anything. But, enough about me. What about your childhood? I'd like to know some more about you, too."

"I had an okay childhood, I guess," she said, trying to sound nonchalant.

"You guess?"

"Well, it was great when I was very young. I didn't have a lot of friends but I had my books. My summertime was spent mostly at the library. I'd spend hours reading. I devoured books. So I was happy. It was after that....well, let's just say, things got really bad."

"What happened?" His concern was evident.

"My Dad started drinking and then things got really crazy after that. When I was nine he moved out of the house but then he came back about six months later and that's when things really went downhill. He became very aggressive and abusive to my Mom." Her voice grew softer as she spoke. "He would hurt her really bad and I'd beg him to stop. Afterwards he would cry and promise never to do it again." She felt the anger rising in her as she spoke. "But then he'd do it again, and again. I wanted to kill him."

Lance squeezed her hand in his warm one but remained silent, looking concerned, but not interrupting.

"I hated him so much. I was glad when he died. My mother cried but I could only feel relief. She loved him so much even after what he'd done to her. When I saw that I decided there and then that I would never love any man that much. I was scared of getting hurt, like my mother."

"Summer," Lance said, finally breaking his silence, "all I can say is, I'm sorry. You had a rough time, baby, but I hope I can help you regain your trust in men. I'll be there for you, honey. You can trust me on that."

Summer felt teary-eyed as she smiled into his eyes. The tears were not for her father, but for what he'd just said. At this moment she felt that she loved him so much. It made her feel vulnerable and she was scared. She said not a word but simply accepted the kiss he gave her on the forehead.

It was a little after nine o'clock when they left the restaurant. They talked very little as Lance drove back to her apartment, each lost in thought, enjoying a comfortable silence in each other's company.

When they pulled into the parking lot Lance leaned over and gave her a peck on the cheek. "Are you alright?" he whispered.

"I'm fine," she smiled. "Why don't you come up for a drink?"

"Sure you're not too tired?"

"I'm sure."

They rode the elevator to her floor but this time she felt so much closer to him, as if they had known each other for years. She felt that, in opening up to him, he had shared the experience with her. Outside of her mother she had never expressed her feelings to anyone, but now he knew that side of her and she knew another side of him.

When they had entered the apartment she directed him to the sofa then headed for the kitchen. She brought back two glasses and handed him one, an apology on her lips.

"Sorry I don't have anything stronger – it's only wine cooler."

"That's fine." He took it and sipped slowly, not taking his eyes off her.

She suddenly felt nervous all over again and said, "Let me just get rid of these high heels. I'll be right back."

She escaped to the bedroom and returned a minute later, her feet bare. She padded over to where he stood, his back to her. He was looking at her CD rack but as she approached he turned toward her.

"You've got some good music here." He pointed to a Toni Anderson CD. "You seem to be a Lover's Rock fan. I didn't even know you listen to Reggae outside of the office."

"I've got a few albums. Some of it's a bit hard but I love Toni's songs 'cause she gives a kind of jazzy feel to her Reggae." She pulled another CD from the rack. "I don't feel like listening to Reggae now, though. Want to hear some Brian McKnight?"

"Sounds good."

She inserted the CD into the machine and as the soulful voice filled the room Lance gently pulled her into his arms.

"Dance with me?" he whispered, and began to rock his hips to the music as he pulled her into him.

Without her shoes she was just tall enough to rest her head where the hair of his chest peaked out from the v of his shirt. She relaxed against him and followed his lead, losing herself in the feel of his body against hers. She could hear the slow, steady beat of his heart and wondered if he could feel her own. It was pounding so hard in her chest. She closed her eyes and let the strains of 'She Gives Me Crazy Love' fill her being.

She kept her eyes closed even when Lance put a strong finger under her chin and tipped her head up so that he could brush his lips against hers. He teased them, nibbling on them then sucking gently, until she began to respond to his expert mouth. He kept on moving while his kiss grew more insistent, more urgent until she could think no longer, but only feel – the luxurious warmth of his sinewy body, the firmness of his muscles beneath her fingers, the hard length of him against her body.

She didn't resist when he guided her gently over to the couch where he lay down and pulled her on top of him. They didn't break the kiss. She pressed her body against his and stroked his arms as they embraced.

Then she pulled away from the kiss, but only to move her lips across his cheek to nibble on his right ear lobe, then down his neck to his chest. She slid her body down his so that she could have access to him and brushed her lips in the springy hair at the opening of his shirt. With trembling fingers she opened the top button, then the next, until she could slide her hands in and caress the broad expanse of his chest. She lowered her lips and gently licked one nipple, then the other, until his breath came fast and a moan escaped his lips.

He gripped her under the arms and pulled her back up to his hungry mouth. He held her head in his large hands and ravished her mouth so sweetly that she shivered with desire.

Suddenly he stopped. He pulled back from the kiss.

"Summer, wait," he whispered hoarsely. "I don't want to rush you into this thing."

She glared at him. "Don't you dare stop this time."

"Are you sure you want…"

"More than anything," she whispered.

He pulled her back into his arms and kissed her again, this time more gently than before, then slid his legs to the ground and rose with her in his arms. She put her arms around his neck and rested her head on his chest as he strode purposefully towards the bedroom.

As Lance laid Summer on the soft quilt of her four poster bed he lowered his head to kiss her deeply, and as he kissed her his warm fingers slid slowly and seductively down her leg where they caught the hem of her silk dress. Just as slowly, the fingers slid back up her thighs bringing the hem of her dress with them.

It was only when the garment was gathered around her waist, fully exposing her slender legs and sheer black thong that Lance pulled away to stare admiringly at her almost naked body.

"You're beautiful," he whispered, and bent his head to plant a kiss right where the undergarment disappeared between her trembling legs. She sucked in her breath at the shock of the intimate contact and her eyes widened as she felt pleasure flow through her body like molten lava. She had never before experienced anything so sensual, so sweet as this, and she gave herself up to the pleasure of it.

His hand moved to the space his mouth had vacated and he stroked and caressed her until she felt she would scream with pleasure. Her breath came fast and she panted, "Oh, Lance. Now, please..." but he just kept stroking till she felt like she was on fire. He was kissing her eyes, her neck, her lips, driving her insane with the pleasure of it all.

"You're sure?" he growled softly into her ear.

"Yes, oh yes," she sighed and she slid her hands up his neck and pulled his head down to capture his lips with hers.

He raised her up gently and pulled the dress over her head then sighed at the sight of her uncovered breasts. She tugged at his shirt and he accommodated her by pulling it free of his pants and shedding it right where he stood. The muscles of his dark body glowed in the light cast through the half-open door and they rippled with each move he made. He slid out of his pants and lay on the bed beside her then gathered her again into his arms and kissed her passionately.

While he kissed he slid a thumb under the string of her bikini then released her mouth to slip it down her legs, leaving her bare to his gaze. She felt so ready for him. She was dying with the wait. She dug her fingers into his sides then slipped them down to his boxer shorts, trying to push them over his firm buttocks and down his legs.

"Hold on, honey, no need to rush," he whispered and pressed her back into the pillows while he pulled the offending garment down his legs. Then he turned back to her and she felt the rock-hard length of him against her leg and for a moment her heart froze in sudden fear. But then he claimed her mouth again and she lost all thought except for the feel, the taste of him.

He stroked her down there again, driving her wild with wanting, making her writhe with desire. Just when she thought she could take it no longer he slid a firm leg between her thighs and opened her to him. He positioned himself over her and, with a groan, he entered the deepest part of her being.

For a moment she stiffened and clung to him, digging her nails into his back. Then, at his soft whisper, "It's okay, honey, just move with me," she relaxed and received him with all the longing that she'd had and with all of her pent-up passion.

When it was over she lay in his arms, enjoying his large hand caressing her hip and her waist, feeling her heart brim with love for this man who had taken her to such heights.

Now she knew. She loved him. There was no longer any doubt in her mind. As his caresses slowed then stilled, and as his body relaxed against her in slumber, she stroked the arm with which he still hugged her to him, glad that he'd fallen asleep before he could hear her whispered, "I love you."

Chapter 18

It was a perfect September afternoon. The sun was bright but there were just enough small clouds to reduce the heat and make the temperature comfortable. The students were already three weeks into the new semester at Chicago University but this Saturday they would get a treat, compliments of Summer Jones. This was the first stop in the College Campus Tour she had designed as part of her public relations strategy.

The party was set up on the south lawn of the campus and, although it was still two hours before the show, several groups of students had already camped out in front of the huge stage in an effort to secure the best spot. Others were milling around the booths, checking out books on music, signing up for free voice coaching, and dropping off applications for the Munroe Scholarship Programme that Summer had launched. Music boomed from speakers and the DJ from WCUW, the campus radio station, was hamming it up and getting everyone into a fun, party mood.

Summer had strategically positioned the campus parties as a great way to raise money to fund scholarships for students, as well as an excellent publicity opportunity for the institutions themselves. Because of this she received so many requests that she had to promise several of them that they would be included the following year.

This time around she could only execute seven such events. However, she had arranged for the first show to be broadcast to all sixteen schools. For two solid hours the campus party would blast the airwaves of these college radio stations as well as five community radio stations across the country.

Summer felt a surge of pride as she stood in the shade of the staff trailer and watched as more and more students gathered on the lawn and collected the free education materials being distributed at the booths. This was her project, her baby, and it had come to life. She was particularly glad of the way she'd done it – rather than just using the campus parties as a tool to promote the music she had also found a way to make the tour benefit the students in a tangible way.

She came up with the idea of forming associations with institutions and businesses that had goods and services that students would need. First Colonial Bank had offered to provide free financial counseling to seniors who would soon be leaving for the world of work, Safari Bookstores agreed to donate books to the libraries of each of the participating schools and Salome Beauty Corporation was providing free consultations for make-up and grooming, particularly for students preparing for job interviews.

Munroe Productions was sponsoring voice lessons for aspiring singers as well as offering two five thousand dollar scholarships. Summer even got a sponsor to provide free soda pop for the afternoon.

Her thoughts were interrupted when she heard a wolf whistle. She turned to see Lance heading her way, his arms full of heavy-duty extension cords. When he got close enough to be heard only by her he said, "Good job, honey. It's going great."

She smiled her thanks and watched as he hurried off in the direction of the stage.

By the time the first singer hit the stage at five o'clock the south lawn was full of people. Crystal, a petite and vivacious teenager ran onto the platform, five dancers close behind her. She belted out the first couple of lines of her song a capella then the music started and her dancers fell into step with her. An appreciative roar went up from the crowd as the performers executed intricate dance steps. Then Crystal launched into her first song and they went wild. She had an R & B groove that appealed to the audience and she soon had them rocking to her music.

Super Cool entered twenty minutes later and proceeded to wow the crowd with a performance which was a combination of Rock and Roll and Reggae. He pranced from one end of the stage to the other, first rapping in Jamaican dialect then switching smoothly into American slang. He rapped about the girls and their 'bumpers' then he did a remix of Bob Marley's 'Lion, Zion'. He had the crowd with their hands in the air, singing and chanting the words of the song as he performed.

His twenty minutes on stage were filled with dance moves, antics and a capella rhymes that kept the crowd chanting and laughing the whole time. When he finally ran off the stage they screamed for more. He came back and did a three minute encore then left amid shouts and applause.

The crowd was still screaming when the MC, Master Mike, came on stage. "Hold up, hold up, y'all," he shouted and put his hand out to calm the crowd. "That was a great performance by Super Cool." The crowd roared in agreement.

"And now we're gonna make it even better for y'all. We have a special performer who's gonna hit the stage and drive you crazy. Are you ready?" he yelled.

"Yes!" the crowd screamed.

"Are you ready?" he shouted again.

"Yes!" was the response, louder this time.

"Well, if you're ready, if you're really, really ready," the MC shouted while striding up and down the stage, "put your hands together...for...the man of the moment, the lover man, the girls' treasure," he waved at the crowd, "put your hands together for Chicago's very own," the crowd screamed as he built up the excitement, "Mr....Top... Cat!"

Summer clapped her hands over her ears as the crowd erupted in a loud roar in greeting for Top Cat. The band struck a chord and started playing and within a minute of the background music going, a tall, slim young man wearing a leather jacket, jeans and his cap turned backwards sauntered onto the stage. Summer didn't think it was possible but the crowd got even louder as he strolled to the front, tilted his shoulders back and shouted, "Whaddup, Chicago?"

They went crazy. The girls at the front screamed and one of them flung a bra onto the stage. Another one threw a rose.

Summer, who all this time was backstage watching everything that was going on, could not hold back a smile. She had one hand covering her ear and the other, her mouth. She was amused as she watched the girls on top of their boyfriends' shoulders screaming at another man, albeit a performer, on stage.

Top Cat launched into a rap about girls who should 'back that thang up' and the crowd went wild. As if that weren't enough his dancers ran onto the stage and, turning their backs to the crowd, bent over and started to shake their behinds, demonstrating how to 'back that thang up'. Then they turned facing front and started some choreographed dance moves that Top Cat matched, step for step; some of them he did even better than his professional dancers.

Then he launched into a second rap piece about 'gangstas' and the men roared in response. His third piece was a rap of love to women and, in the middle of it, he started gyrating his hips making very sensual moves. At one point during the song he turned his back to the crowd and when he turned back around he ripped his shirt off and flung it into the crowd. There were screams and women reached to grab it. Then the band launched into his fourth piece. The performance lasted twenty ear-splitting minutes but Top Cat left the stage with the crowd begging for more.

When the lights were shut down at eight o'clock that night Summer breathed a satisfied sigh of relief – one down, six more to go.

Summer got her reward next day when Lance picked her up at the apartment and drove along Lake Shore Drive to the most scenic part of Lake Michigan, not far from where she used to live. They got out of the car and held hands while walking along the shore line.

"I'm proud of you, Summer," he said. "Your idea paid off. I couldn't have asked for a better launch strategy."

"Thanks, Lance," she beamed. "I'm glad you're satisfied."

As they walked along they watched couples jogging, rollerblading or just hugging as they strolled along the pavement. It made Summer remember the day she had thought this was not for her. Now she felt lucky that she had found love.

"Want to have some fun?" Lance broke into her thoughts.

"Sure." She brought her attention back to him. "What did you have in mind?"

"Come on," he said, with a roguish smile. "I'll show you."

They ran back to his car and he drove to Navy Pier where he convinced her to get onto the Ferris wheel with him. She screamed as the wheel went high into the air and screamed again as it went down.

He had mercy on her for the next ride; for this one he chose the merry-go-round. That, she could manage. When they got off the ride he teased her for being a baby and she ran after him, trying to pelt him with some of her popcorn.

"Hey, Lance. Summer. What's up?"

They pulled up short and turned to see Derrick waving at them. He had a blonde woman on his arm. "Looks like you guys are having lots of fun."

"As a matter of fact, we are." There was an air of caution in Lance's voice.

"This is Shari." Derrick pushed his companion forward gently. "Shari, this is my cousin, Lance, and …a mutual friend, Summer."

They greeted the woman and chatted with Derrick for a few minutes, then he took her arm and they strolled away.

Lance and Summer looked at each other quizzically then Lance spoke. "Well, he seems happy enough. A pleasant change from all the sulking he's been doing around the office lately."

"I'm glad for him," Summer said, and she meant it. She'd hated to see how depressed he had been, especially because she knew it was because of her. Although he had his faults she thought Derrick was a really nice guy and she hated that he was hurting. She felt relief to see that he'd finally gotten over her.

Then another thought came to her and she blurted out, "Lance, do you think Derrick will tell the others about us?"

"I don't think so. He may be a talker but he's not one to discuss my personal business in the office. I don't see why he should start now." Lance sounded confident.

"Oh, good," she sighed.

"And anyway, what if he did?" He shrugged.

"Then they'd all hate me."

Lance laughed at her. "I doubt it."

She remained silent but thought, Well, I know at least one person who would.

They got more popcorn and strolled down to look at the boats. Suddenly a fat drop of water splashed on Summer's cheek. Then another.

"Rain's coming – run!" Lance yelled, and grabbed her hand. They ran all the way back to the entrance and were lucky to get onto the second tram heading back to the distant parking lot.

By the time they arrived at the car the rain was pouring. Both of them were dripping wet and Summer gave a little shiver.

"You look like a very wet rat," Lance said as he dabbed her face with a handkerchief. When she made a face he added, "A very cute one, though."

He put away the handkerchief and started the car. "Let's get you out of here. I can't afford for you to catch a cold now. Things are on a roll and I need you back in the office tomorrow."

"Slave driver," she growled and pinched him on the arm.

"Ow! I'm going to get you for that."

She laughed at him, knowing fully well that he could do nothing as long as he had his hands busy steering the car through the Lake Shore Drive traffic.

But later he had the last laugh. As soon as they got back to his apartment he grabbed a towel and began to rub her hair vigorously. She had to yell at him to stop. By the time he was done her hair was dry but it had turned into a huge afro that made her look like one of the Soul Train dancers from the seventies.

Lance laughed at her and she ran after him with the towel, trying to catch up to him so that she could whip it at him and give him a stinging slap. He turned on her and wrestled the towel from her fingers then hoisted her onto his shoulder and carried her, kicking and yelling, into the bedroom.

He threw her on top of the bed and, before she could make a move, he pinned her down with one hand and began to unbutton her wet shirt with the other. She squirmed and wriggled but he kept going until he had her shirt wide open to reveal her heaving bosom and bare stomach.

"We don't want to die of a cold, now do we?" he whispered, as he raised her up to pull the shirt from under her. He undid his own buttons deftly and threw his shirt on the ground beside hers. He turned back to where she still lay and leaned over her, his mouth mere inches from hers. She opened her lips to speak but all she could do was moan as he captured her mouth in a bruising kiss that sent tremors down her spine.

When he finally lifted his head his eyes burned with the intensity of his desire. She could feel the pounding of his heart, his quickening breath against her cheek, his hardness against her body.

"Thought you'd gotten away from me, huh?" he growled teasingly into her ear. "Now it's time to pay."

He lowered his mouth to hers again, but this time he was gentle, teasing. As he kissed her he gently circled a nipple with his thumb until he had her arching her back, begging him not to stop.

She reached up to caress his face with trembling hands then slid them down his shoulders and his sides until she got to the barrier that was the waistband of his jeans. She slid her hands to the front and wrestled with the top button until Lance eased her frustration and undid it himself then pushed the damp pants down his legs. She reached behind and undid the clasp of her bra to release her breasts to his view.

She had an enticing view of her own. He stood dark and tall, the muscles of his arms and stomach firm and taut. But it was another muscle that held her gaze. His desire was plainly evident and her heart beat hard in anticipation. He took her hands in his and pulled her up to stand in front of him. Then he knelt in front of her and lifted his hands to unbutton her jeans and pull it slowly down her legs. He kissed her stomach and tickled her legs with his lips. He bent to kiss her knees then slid his tongue up the inner part of her thigh until her legs trembled and she felt as if she would collapse.

Just when she felt she could take no more he rose and slid a strong arm around her waist and tilted her back until she was lying flat on her back. He covered her body with his own and as she opened to receive him he captured her mouth in a searing kiss. She rose to meet his every thrust and was soon riding the waves of passion until the bubbling volcano inside her erupted into hot streams of liquid fire.

Later as she curled up in the darkness beside him she drifted off to sleep, a satisfied smile still on her face.

Chapter 19

"I don't know about that," Top Cat growled as he sucked on a cigarette.

"If it's inconvenient…" Summer began then caught her breath and coughed violently as he blew a cloud of smoke across her desk and right into her face. Her eyes watered and she pulled a tissue from her pocket to dab at them, still wheezing.

When she finally caught her breath she looked pointedly at the cigarette in the young man's hand.

"If you don't mind," she said sternly, "I would appreciate it if you would put out that cigarette."

He gave her a sullen look but stubbed it on her desk then flicked it in the direction of the waste basket. He missed and it fell onto the carpet. He made no move to get up to discard of it properly.

Summer swallowed a reprimand. She looked down at her notepad then back at the rapper who sprawled in the chair in front of her.

"Okay," she said, not hiding her annoyance, "let's try this again. When can I come see you on your own turf? You tell me where and when. It's totally up to you. I'll make myself available."

"So you wanna hang out with Top Cat, huh?" he said, as he smiled smugly.

"I'm afraid not," she said coldly. "It's a lot more than just hanging out with you. My purpose in wanting to spend time with you in what I call your 'environment' is to get a feel of who you are, outside of what the public sees on stage."

"The human interest thing you were talking about, huh?" he asked casually, as he picked his teeth.

"Exactly," she said, trying to ignore his unsavoury behavior. "I want to see something of your personal side. Now, come on," she leaned forward and tried to smile encouragingly, "you've got to give me something."

"There ain't much to say," he shrugged, "except I grew up in the projects and I ain't there no more."

"Okay," she said in a coaxing tone, "what else?"

"I live downtown."

"Uh-huh," Summer encouraged, "go on." He wasn't giving her much to work with.

"Listen," he said, "I ain't into this interview thing. I ain't the talkative type. You said you wanted to see me in my 'environment' so I'll just take you to the projects. That's where I came from so I guess it would make sense to start there."

"That sounds like a great idea," she nodded, leaning back in her chair.

"Tomorrow – be ready for two o'clock." He looked at the thick gold watch on his wrist and the many rings on his fingers glistened in the light. "I gotta split. I got things to do and people to see."

"Well, thanks for your time. I'll be ready at two."

"Cool." He got up and padded in his sneakered feet to the door. "Catch you tomorrow," he said and closed the door behind him.

They pulled into the parking lot of the State Street Homes around two-thirty next afternoon. Top Cat was dressed in a large sweatshirt and jeans that fell low on his bottom. He wore a large cap pulled down over his face and sunglasses. His two bodyguards had traveled in the Land Cruiser with them and Summer was told that he'd chosen this vehicle so that he wouldn't be recognized quickly. He was in no mood to be mobbed by fans today.

When they entered the building Summer was immediately hit by the dank odor and the darkness of the hallway. They headed for the elevator and Top Cat pushed the button for the sixth floor. They exited and there was the sound of a child screaming in the first apartment they passed.

"I'm gonna to take you down to where I used to live," Top Cat said to her in a low voice. "The guy who lives there now with his Mom, he's my homie. We're real close so he's probably the best person to tell you about me."

As they walked down the hallway they passed a group of teenage boys who fell silent and looked up at them guiltily. Their attitude told Summer they were up to some mischief. The boys eyed them but seemed not to recognize Top Cat. He knocked on the apartment door.

"Yes?" A hoarse female voice came from inside.

"It's Michael," Top Cat said. "Craig inside?"

"No," she responded.

There was the sound of locks and the door opened to reveal a woman of about forty-five years with curlers in her hair. "Come in," she said with a smile. She stepped aside to let them into the apartment.

The room was very small and dark and the smell of cigarettes stained the air. The woman clutched a dark blue robe around her body. There was a picture of Martin Luther King and one of Malcolm X on the wall, and the black and white portrait of a bride and groom was on the coffee table. The furniture looked old but there was a flat screen television and a huge stereo system in the living room.

"So where's Craig, Miss Pete?" Top Cat asked.

"Down by the basketball court, where he always is. Been there for the last couple of hours."

"Everything alright with you?" Top Cat looked around the room as he spoke.

"Yeah, I'm doin' alright." She nodded and her rollers bobbed up and down. "Craig's taking care of me now."

Top Cat nodded his head in Summer's direction. "This here's Summer Jones from the office. She's trying to do a story on me so she wanted to meet some of my friends. That's why I took her here, so she can meet Craig."

The woman turned to Summer with an interested look. "Craig can tell you all kinds of things about this boy. They grew up together. But I can tell you stuff, too."

"Yes," Summer prompted, "like what?"

"Like this boy is one of the nicest boys you will ever meet." She smiled as she looked across at Top Cat. "The boy has the kindest heart. You know, I had to do surgery last year for my heart and its Michael here, who paid for it. He never stopped looking out for us. And there are at least three kids in this building who he's sending to college. Is it three Michael?"

"Four," he said offhandedly, as he looked out the window at the grounds below.

"See what I mean? Chile, you ain't goin' find nobody kinder than this boy."

"I certainly appreciate that information," Summer said earnestly.

"Anyway, you run down to the court now. You'll see Craig down there."

"Yeah, he's there," Top Cat said, peering out the window. "I see him."

They went downstairs and as they approached the basketball court Top Cat pointed Craig out to her. There were only four of them and he was the tallest and lankiest of the players.

"Hey, Craig," Top Cat shouted and the man looked over at them. His thin face split into a wide smile.

"Hey, man, what you doin' here?" He sauntered over to them. "And who's this foxy lady with you?"

He whistled as he came up to her. "Hey, baby, you got one sweet bumper on you."

Summer was so taken aback by his outspokenness that she couldn't respond.

"Hey, hey, hold up," said Top Cat. "This here's a lady from my office, so you mind your mouth round her, a'ight?"

"Sorry, man, my bad." Craig raised his hands and backed away, grinning. "Sorry, lady."

"Summer's doing a story about me so she's gonna ask you some questions. Wants to get to know my personal side, she said," Top Cat explained. "Come on, let's go sit over there and you can bring her up to speed."

They headed for the park bench and sat down to talk. By the end of her interview with Craig, Summer had found out that Top Cat, or Michael Parker as he was known to his friends and family, had been a quiet little boy who never got into trouble but as he got older he became more outspoken and was dubbed as a rebel in school. He was always the ringleader of any student action and he was always there to defend people. He was known to beat up a few bullies in his day.

He had a softer side, too, because he took care of his family and friends. The people in this building, his old home, respected him a lot and were proud of the achievements of one of their own.

Top Cat had dropped out of school at the age of fifteen and started hanging out with rappers on the south side. He was pretty much unknown until a couple of years ago when he did a demo tape and sent it in to Munroe Productions. They called him in for an audition and he was immediately taken on board.

Now, two years and three albums later he was a success story. One of his albums had gone platinum and now he was in the middle of promoting the third.

After the interview was finished and Craig had returned to his basketball game Top Cat pulled out a cigarette and took a draw.

Summer turned to him. "How do you feel about the demonstration that took place after the launch of your last album?"

"I heard about it." He leaned his head back and let out a long cloud of smoke.

"Yes, but how do you feel about it?" Summer shifted slightly to avoid the smoke.

"Nothing I can do about it," he shrugged. "I can't stop them from demonstrating if they want to."

"But these are your fans and their parents. Don't you care about that?" She frowned.

"I can't let these people phase me, a'ight. I'm just doin' my thing," he said, nonchalant. "If they wanna demonstrate that's their business."

"But what if all the fans had the same concerns about you, then where would you be?" she demanded.

He was silent. He sat forward on the bench and rested his elbows on his knees as he stared out in front of him.

Summer spoke again, more gently this time. "It's the fans who've made you the success you are."

Top Cat nodded. "Yeah, I know." He looked sober.

"That's why it's important for the fans to get to know the other side of you," she explained.

"But what's my private life got to do with them?" He frowned. "It's none of their damn business."

"Of course, we won't get too personal," Summer agreed, "but the more they get to know about you the greater the connection they'll have with you. Do you understand that?"

"Yeah, I guess."

He flicked the cigarette onto the pavement then said, "Let's go. This place is getting to me." He stood up. "Want to get to know me? Come see my crib. That's where you'll get to see the real me."

"Fine." Summer accepted his invitation. He had a point. She couldn't dwell too much on his past although she wanted to gather all the background information she could. She would also have to look at the man as he was now.

They drove to a building on Ohio Street which was known for its luxury apartments. The lobby was spacious and luxurious with marble floors and walls. There was a huge chandelier in the middle of the ceiling and roses on a round glass table in the center of the room. The attendant greeted them and they took the elevator up to the penthouse suite.

It was even more exquisite than the lobby. As she entered the apartment she was struck by the rich elegance of the decor and the obvious high quality of the furniture. The beige carpeted hallway led into a spacious living room with a massive cream coloured leather couch behind which open drapes provided a spectacular view of the city and lake below.

"You have a beautiful apartment," Summer said, as she walked over to stand by the window.

"Yeah, it ain't too bad up here. Come on. Let me give you a tour."

His kitchen was about the size of her entire apartment and the master bedroom had a huge four poster bed with a sheer gold canopy. She raised her eyebrows when she saw it but made no comment. There was a Jacuzzi in the bathroom. He had a personal gym and a library, as well as a mini music studio.

"Wow, I'm impressed," Summer said.

"Thanks," he said. "I had the designer fly in from Europe to do all this."

She nodded, still looking around. Then, she said, "Could we begin the interview now?"

"Sure, why not? Have a seat. I'll be right over." He spoke to the bodyguards who had made themselves comfortable in the living room. "Y'all can give us a break now. I'll give you a buzz when I need you."

After they had left he turned to her. "Sometimes I need a little more privacy. After having them around all day they get on my nerves."

Summer smiled sympathetically. "I understand. I don't think I could have people around me twenty-four seven."

"Want something to drink? Wine, Martini?"

"I'll just take a soda, please," she said.

"Got some Pepsi."

"That would be fine, thanks," she nodded.

While he got the drinks she pulled her notepad, pen and Dictaphone out of her briefcase. He came back with the drinks in a couple of minutes and handed her a glass then sat at the other end of the couch. He reached over to the lamp and dimmed the lights.

She looked up, frowning. "I need the light, please. To write."

He rested his glass on the coffee table then leaned over and pulled the notepad and pen out of her hand and slid along the couch until he was very close to her. He rested his arm on the couch behind her head and whispered, "You don't need to write anything down. Just relax and I'll tell you everything."

She straightened up quickly and pulled as far away from him as she could.

"You're attractive, you know that?" He sidled closer still. "What are you doing, working for Lance Munroe? He's too old for you. Wanna come work for me?"

Shock had Summer speechless for a moment then she recovered and became filled with outrage.

"What the hell do you think you're doing?" she demanded, fixing him with her most severe frown. "I'm here to interview you. Nothing else. Now please take your arm from behind me."

"Come on, baby. I can do a lot for you; I got the money to give you whatever you want."

"I'm not interested in your money. I'm here on a professional basis and I would thank you to remember that." Her voice was filled with disgust.

He pulled back, suddenly angry. "You know how many women are falling all over themselves to get me? You think you're so high and mighty. What makes you so special?"

"That's not important. I'm here to do an interview. Now do you want me to interview you, or don't you?" Her voice was cold as she stared at him.

It seemed to have no effect, as his face relaxed again, "Yeah, you can interview me…if you're gonna be nice."

She rose and spoke in an indignant tone. "It's obvious that we're getting nothing done here. As I told you, I want nothing from you. I only want to get this story."

"You're worried about a story?" He gave an ugly sneer. "You'd better be nice to me, girl, or you'll have lots more to worry about. Just a word from me and Lance will kick your butt out the door."

"Really?" she laughed. "You run right along and go cry to Lance. We'll see how far that gets you."

He hesitated, as if thrown off by her lack of fear. "Yeah, I'll talk to him…"

"You just do that," she said, cutting him off.

She picked up her briefcase from the coffee table and turned to look down at him. "I think it would be best for both of us if I go now."

He glared up at her. "You can find your way out."

She shrugged, "Not a problem."

She whirled and strode confidently out of the apartment, leaving him sitting with his arm still resting on the back of the couch.

As she rode the elevator down to the first floor she smiled at herself in the mirrored walls and shook her head. She was actually proud of how she had handled the situation.

Just a couple of months ago she would have lost her cool and flown into a rage, but she was improving. She'd certainly changed a lot in a short while. Well, she was glad. She knew that in her line of work she would need to call on this new-found composure quite often – working with 'prima donna' singers was no easy task.

It was Friday evening and Summer had made it to the library. At last. She'd been trying all week to get some work done on her thesis but she had worked late almost every evening. Now she really had to get cracking or she'd be in serious trouble.

Lance had left for Florida two days before and she planned to get a lot of work done before he got back. She walked slowly down the aisles collecting books for her project then took them to a nearby table where she had pencils and sheets of paper ready to gather notes. She sat down, opened the first book, and began to scribble quickly.

She was engrossed in her work when she heard a hiss and looked up to see a petite fair complexioned girl approaching her table.

"Hey, Summer. Long time no see. What you been up to?"

"Hey, Keisha." She gave a little wave. "I've been around. Just not living in the library like I used to."

"Last time I saw you, you were job-hunting. How'd you make out with that?"

"I got a job down at The Southern Belle. But I left after a couple of weeks. I'm with Munroe Productions now."

Keisha paused, thinking, then said, "Never heard of it. What kind of a place is that?"

"It's a music management and production company. The office isn't too far from here."

"Hey, wait a minute. Music. Munroe? This doesn't have anything to do with Lance Munroe, does it?"

"Yes, that's who I work for."

Keisha let out a squeal then covered her mouth quickly. She slid into the chair opposite Summer and whispered, "Girl, you're so lucky. How did you ever land a job with Lance Munroe? He's a hunk."

Summer smiled and nodded but said nothing, afraid to even mention anything to the college gossip. Keisha seemed not to notice her lack of response.

"Come on, girl. What's he like?" she prodded.

"He's a very nice man. Very professional." Summer was nonchalant.

"That's it? I know you don't expect me to believe that's all there is."

When Summer hesitated she pressed on. "There's something you're not telling me. I can feel it."

She stared intently at Summer's face then, as if she had been given a revelation, she exclaimed, "He hit on you, didn't he?"

"No, he didn't."

"I bet he did. I know the type. Big shot mogul, I bet he hits on all the women who come through his door. So come on, girl," she urged, "stop being so tight. Let's hear it."

"Keisha, please," Summer said, getting exasperated. "There's nothing to tell."

"Come on, Summer…"

"Keisha," her tone was suddenly cold, "I have an urgent deadline to meet so, if you don't mind, I'd like to get back to my work."

Keisha glared at Summer. She pushed back her chair and grabbed her purse. "Well, you try to be friendly to some people…" She stalked off, her mouth set in a pout.

Summer sighed with relief when she saw the girl disappear through the main exit. She was the most annoying person on earth. And the nerve of her to be badgering her with questions about Lance. There was no way she would ever betray him like that. She cared too much for him and he'd said he cared for her, too. She could never jeopardize that.

Three hours later, tired and sleepy, she was ready to go. She knew it was useless to go on when she'd read the same line four times and still couldn't remember what it said. She stacked the books on the table, gathered up her papers and her purse, and headed for the exit.

When she got home a message from Lance made her immediately forget her tiredness.

"I'm back." His voice, even on a recording, could still make her shiver. "I have a surprise. Come on over to my apartment in the morning around nine. I'll make you breakfast. See you tomorrow."

Next morning Summer arrived at Lance's apartment ten minutes early. She was so anxious to see him that she couldn't have stayed home a minute longer. He buzzed her up. When she got to his door she knocked and waited, a smile on her lips.

The door opened and Summer's smile froze. She found herself staring down into the big brown eyes of a tiny girl.

Chapter 20

Summer's eyes widened in shock. The child standing in front of her wearing pink shorts and blouse said hello but she could do nothing except stare. The little girl could only be the one she'd heard of, the one from Jamaica.

Lance came up behind the child, smiling. "Summer, I'd like you to meet Michelle. I brought her in from Jamaica with me. Say hello, Michelle."

"Hello," the child said, then ducked her head shyly.

Still speechless, Summer could only nod. The nerve of him. What did he expect her to do? Welcome the child with open arms? And what about the child's mother?

"Are you going to stand there all day? Come in."

Lance walked away down the hallway, Michelle skipping along behind him. Summer entered hesitantly and closed the door behind her. She peered down the hallway, wondering if the child's mother was at the end of it.

"I'm in the kitchen, Summer." Lance called out to her. "Come on down here."

The little girl ran off towards the living room and Summer followed slowly, feeling as if the life had gone out of her. She entered the kitchen and sat on the stool nearest to the door.

Lance had his back to her, his hands deep in a bowl of flour. He stopped kneading and turned to greet her.

When he saw her face he said, "Honey, what's wrong? Why the long face?"

Her lips trembled and she could not speak.

Lance washed his hands quickly and went over to sit on the stool beside hers. "Talk to me, Summer. What is it? Is it your Mom?"

"No." Her voice was sharp with anger but she tried to keep it low so that the child could not hear her. "It's you! How could you do this to me?"

"Do what to you?" He looked confused.

"You…you know how much I care for you but now you've made it clear that it's hopeless."

"What's hopeless?"

"Us. There can never be an 'us'."

"But, why not?"

"Why not?" She was incredulous. "How can you even ask that question? You're in a relationship. You have a child."

"Summer, wait…"

"Don't even try to explain. I was the stupid one. I heard you had a child in Jamaica. I knew you must have had ties with someone, but I was in denial. I wanted you so much that I hid my head in the sand and pretended none of that existed. You were in my life and that's all that mattered."

"Summer…"

"Why didn't you just push me away when I told you how I felt?" She was sobbing freely now, not even caring if the child heard. "Why didn't you put me out of my misery? Why this?"

"Summer, will you shut up?" Lance grabbed her upper arms and shook her hard. "You're hysterical."

He grabbed a paper napkin and handed it to her. She took it quickly and dabbed at her eyes then blew her nose. She sniffed and tried to regain her composure.

"Now that you're calm," he stroked her shoulder comfortingly, "we can talk. You have this all wrong." He turned her around to face him. "Look at me, Summer."

She raised tear-filled eyes and felt her heart ache at the thought of losing this man.

"I don't have a child, Summer. Nor do I have another woman. There is no other woman but you."

Summer was confused. "How can you say that? Your daughter is sitting right there in the living room."

"She's not my daughter, Summer. Michelle is my godchild. Her Dad and I grew up together in Port Maria and even when I migrated to the United States we were still best friends. He died two years ago in a car accident. I've been looking after Michelle ever since."

Summer frowned, her mind still unable to wrap itself around this new revelation. "So...Michelle isn't your daughter?"

"That's what I said."

"Are you telling me the truth?"

"Look into my eyes, Summer. Look at me and you'll see I'm hiding nothing from you."

"But there's still something I don't understand. You said you were going to Florida, not Jamaica."

"I did go to Florida. I was there until Thursday. I went down to Jamaica on an impulse and got Michelle. I'd called and she started crying for me. I just couldn't stand it so I asked her mother if I could come get her for a few days," he explained. "When she said yes I just flew down and got her, and here we are."

Summer was awash with a mixture of emotions. Relief came first, then shame at her rush to judgment, then admiration for him, then love. "Oh, Lance, I'm so sorry."

"Hush," he whispered. "Don't worry about it."

Summer hugged him then went into the living room and sat on the floor where the little girl was playing with her doll.

"Hi, Michelle," she said gently. "My name is Summer."

Michelle turned big eyes up at Summer and gave her a smile that melted her heart.

After a meal of fried dumplings and sPiñach Lance and Summer relaxed on the balcony while Michelle sat at their feet, playing with her doll. He had his arm around her shoulder and as they sat looking at the city below he toyed with a stray curl that had come loose from her scrunchie. She rested her head on his shoulder and closed her eyes, reveling in his warmth against her cheek.

"I was thinking," his voice rumbled against her ear, "you've told me about your mother and what she's been going through. From what you've said she seems like a brave lady."

"She is." Summer nodded. "No matter what she's going through she never complains."

"I'd like to meet her."

Summer lifted her head and looked at him. "Really? You're not just saying that to get on my good side, are you?"

He laughed, "Of course not. And anyway, I thought I was already on your good side."

"You are." She smiled back. "But seriously, how come you want to meet my Mom? I wouldn't have thought that was your cup of tea."

"Why not? Because I'm a man? Or is it because you think I'm an arrogant brute who has no feelings?"

"Well, I must admit, I did feel that way about you - once."

"What?" Lance drew back in mock indignation. "That's what you think of me?"

"Not anymore." She squeezed his arm and gave him a peck on the cheek. "You're my sweet, sweet man who's loving and kind. You're the best man a girl could ever want."

"Wow, why such kind words?"

"Because I...just because." Summer was glad she'd caught herself just in time. She had almost said 'Because I love you'."

"So what about today?"

"Today? For what?"

"To meet your mother."

"Oh, I guess today would be good," she said. "Maybe I could give her a buzz, let her know we're coming."

"Of course. You can go call her right now."

"What time should I say we're coming?"

"In another couple of hours. Let's say noon."

As Summer rose to go and make the call he added, "And ask her to dress to go out. I want us to take her to lunch."

Summer raised her eyebrows in surprise then flashed him a bright smile of gratitude.

When they got to the nursing home Edna was dressed and waiting for them. She was wearing a bright blue summer dress and a wide-brimmed straw hat.

Summer leaned over and kissed her mother's cheek then said, "Mom, I'd like you to meet my special friend, Lance Munroe. Lance, this is my Mom, Edna Jones."

"I'm very pleased to meet you, Mrs. Jones." Lance extended a hand and greeted her with a smile. "I've heard a lot about you."

"And I, about you," Edna replied.

Lance raised his eyebrows, still smiling, and looked across at Summer.

"I've said nothing but good things about you. Promise." Summer laughed at his comically concerned expression.

"And this," she looked down at the little girl by her side and took her hand and pulled her forward, "is little Miss Michelle Davis. She's Lance's god-daughter, visiting from Jamaica."

Edna leaned forward and took the little girl's hands in hers. "Hello, Michelle. I'm very pleased to meet you."

Michelle smiled shyly but said nothing. She looked up at Lance as if for reassurance.

He knelt down beside her and spoke softly. "Miss Edna is Summer's Mommy. Aren't you going to say hello to her?"

Michelle turned her brown eyes back to Edna and, with a more confident smile, said, "Hello. My name is Michelle."

"Hello again, Michelle. My name is Edna Jones and I'd like to be your friend. Do you think we can be friends?"

"Yes." The child nodded gravely. "I have a friend and his name is Toby. He lives next door."

"That's nice, honey."

"And I have a puppy. Her name is Shi-Shi."

"Now that's an unusual name."

"That's my dolly's name, too."

Lance laughed. "She named all her dolls Shi-Shi. I don't know where she got that name but somehow she's fallen in love with it."

As he spoke he went behind Edna and rested his hands on the wheelchair. "Okay, guys, let's get going. It's a beautiful day and I want us to enjoy as much of it as we can."

Summer took Michelle's hand and Lance pushed Edna as they headed for the elevator. As it traveled slowly from the fifteenth floor Edna reached up to pat Lance's hand which was resting on the bar of her wheelchair.

"I want to thank you for this kind gesture, Lance. I really appreciate it."

"No problem, Miss Edna. It's my pleasure."

"You can call me Edna."

"I prefer Miss Edna, if you don't mind," Lance said. "Being from Jamaica, it's sort of ingrained in me to address you like that. Plus, if my mother ever heard me call you just 'Edna' she'd really put me in my place."

They all chuckled at that. Summer was silent for a while, pondering yet another side of Lance that had been revealed to her. She peeked up at him as he stood beside her, strong and tall. He caught her glance and smiled down at her, making her heart jerk. Dear God, she prayed as she smiled back, please don't make me love him so much.

For Summer the afternoon could not have been more perfect. Lance was the perfect gentleman to both Edna and her, and the most accommodating godfather that Michelle could have asked for. He entertained the women with stories of his experiences in the music industry and made them laugh at stories of the things he went through with erratic musicians. Edna was not to be outdone. She shared stories of her early life in Chicago and had them cracking up when she related some of her experiences as a young teacher.

After lunch they went for a drive along Lake Michigan then, just for Michelle's benefit, they stopped at the Children's Museum at Navy Pier. She enjoyed herself so much that Lance had to pull her away and, to stop her from crying, he let her ride on his shoulder all the way back to the parking lot.

It was after six o'clock when they returned a tired but happy Edna Jones to her room at the nursing home. There were tears in her eyes as she bid them good evening.

"My dears, you've done my spirit a world of good. I haven't had so much fun in a very long time."

"I had fun too, Miss Edna. You're a great storyteller." Lance took her hand as if to shake it but she pulled him down and gave him a quick hug.

"I'm glad you had a great time, Mom." Summer was a little teary-eyed herself at seeing her mother so happy. "I'll give you a call tonight, okay."

"Okay, dear. Tell the little angel 'bye for me."

"I'll tell her," Lance whispered as he took the sleeping child from Summer.

He positioned Michelle on his shoulder and waved farewell to Edna as Summer kissed her goodbye.

Summer looked out the tiny window at the heavy cumulus clouds below. It was only six in the morning and the rising sun had turned them into pink, peach and gold cotton candy. She smiled at the thought then turned to look at Lance. He had reclined his seat and lay back, eyes closed. Poor guy, she thought, he looks so tired.

Michelle, who sat between them, was also fast asleep. Of that, she was not surprised. They had been up since three that morning and by three forty-five they were on their way to the Chicago O'Hare Airport.

She was glad Lance had convinced her to join him on this trip. He was taking Michelle back home and was planning to take an extra day off to recuperate from his hectic schedule of the past few weeks. She could do with the rest, too. She hadn't realized how much the college tours would demand of her and this trip, short though it would be, was a welcome break.

She leaned back in her seat and closed her eyes. It would be another three and a half hours before the plane landed so she might as well catch up on her sleep, too.

Summer awoke to a gentle shaking and opened her eyes to see Lance smiling at her. Michelle was up, too, although still sleepy-eyed and yawning.

"We're here," he said softly, and smiled wider as she rubbed her eyes. "You look like a kid when you do that. Now I'm stuck with two little ones – Michelle and Summer."

She rolled her eyes at him and thought, 'Corny, but sweet'.

Lance rented a minivan at the airport and drove the forty-six miles of winding road to the small town of Highgate. He pulled into the driveway of a sprawling bungalow. As they drove up a tall, dark-skinned woman with a short afro came out of the front door and waved.

"Mummy!" Michelle yelled and bounced up and down on the seat.

"Whoa, hold on little pony," Lance said, "we're almost there."

He pulled up under a big shady mango tree and jumped out to open the back door for Michelle. He lifted her from the seat and as her feet hit the ground she dashed away and into the arms of the smiling woman.

He went around to Summer's side, opened the door and gave her his arm so she could jump down to the ground. She landed slightly off balance and he threw an arm around her waist and steadied her against his body.

The tall woman had risen from hugging the child and stood waiting for them, her hand on Michelle's head.

"Jennifer, there's someone special I'd like you to meet." Lance pulled Summer forward. "This is Summer Jones from Chicago. Summer, please meet Michelle's Mom, Jennifer Davis."

Summer extended her hand and was surprised at the strength of the warm hand that enclosed hers.

"Good to meet you, Summer." The woman's accent was thick, much deeper than Lance's, or even Derrick's. "I hope you enjoy your visit to the island. This is your first time here?"

"No. Actually, this is my third trip. Last time I spent almost a week here."

"Really? But I bet this is your first time to such a rural part of the island, right?"

"I drove through the country once – we stopped in Linstead. But I'm mostly familiar with the tourist areas like Ocho Rios and Montego Bay. And I've been to Kingston, of course."

"Great. Well, come on in. I've prepared some lunch for you." Jennifer took Summer by the hand and walked her up to the house. "As long as you are Lance's friend you are welcome in this house."

Jennifer had prepared mackerel and boiled green bananas and slices of yam. It was served with a strong black brew that she called 'cocoa tea' but it was nothing like any cocoa that Summer had ever tasted. It was almost bitter but Jennifer and Lance seemed to be enjoying it immensely, even going back for seconds. When Jennifer saw the face Summer made when she tasted it she laughed and poured her a glass of milk.

"You're just like Michelle. Can't take the taste of this strong Jamaican cocoa tea."

"But everything else is delicious," Summer said quickly, hoping she hadn't offended her hostess.

For answer Jennifer only looked across at Lance and they both laughed. After that Summer decided to stay quiet and eat her food.

After lunch Lance strolled down to the bottom of the garden where a goat was tied. Two goat kids frolicked around the Nanny goat but she just continued clipping away at the grass at her feet, not seeming to notice them at all. Summer stayed behind to help Jennifer wash the dishes. She watched

Lance through the kitchen window as he bent to stroke the goat's back.

"He really loves animals," Jennifer said, and Summer quickly took her eyes off Lance's back and looked at her hostess.

"He always did," she continued, "even when we were in primary school."

"You've known him since that time?"

"Yes. Lance and Trevor, my late husband, were in the same class from the second grade right up to the sixth. They were one grade ahead of me and they never let me forget it."

"I imagine Lance must have been a rowdy little boy," Summer said, trying to picture him.

"Not so much rowdy as bossy. Boy, that Lance used to boss me and Sophie around. Man!" She shook her head as if still suffering at the hands of the child tyrant.

"Who's Sophie?"

"His younger sister. She and I were in the same class at primary school. She lives in Indiana now. Their mother lives with her."

"He never mentioned a sister."

"Lance is private that way. But me, I don't have that kind of problem." They both giggled at that. "She was actually an Olympian. She got a silver medal in eighty-nine. In the two hundred meters."

"Wow. He's from an athletic family."

"You see how tall he is? Well, she's nearly as big. They're from a tall breed."

"Hmm," was all Summer said as she stared at the man, wondering if their children would be tall like their father or petite like she was. She caught herself and looked guiltily across at the other woman as if she could read her thoughts but Jennifer was busy tucking the dried plates into the cupboard above her head.

When they had finished with the dishes Jennifer said, "Come. Let's go keep him company." She opened the back door that led to the garden.

"But what about Michelle?"

"Michelle is alright. She's fast asleep. We won't hear another peep out of her for another hour, maybe even two after that long flight. Come on."

Summer needed no further encouragement. She slipped out the back door behind Jennifer and followed the dirt path which led to the bottom of the garden.

There, she joined Lance in stroking the goat's rough hide. She tickled the kids with a tiny stick and bent to admire the fragrant flowers in Jennifer's garden.

Suddenly, a terrible sound came from across the fence and Summer jumped and moved closer to Lance. "What was that?"

He laughed and rose, then hugged her close to him and kissed her on the mouth. "That was only a donkey. You're so cute when you're scared."

"I wasn't scared," she pouted.

"My apologies, Ma'am." He lifted one eyebrow as he looked at her. "That wasn't you who just scampered over to me when the donkey started braying?"

"Okay, you got me." She punched him on the shoulder. "But it was only because I wasn't expecting it."

"Alright, I'll accept that," Lance said, then called out to Jennifer who was busy with a long bamboo, jabbing mangoes down from the tree. "Jen, we're going to run now. I want to get back to Kingston by five."

"Just give me a minute. I'm trying to get some mangoes for you guys."

"Sounds good. You know Julie mangoes are my favourite."

The trip back to Kingston was a hair-raising experience for Summer. On the way to Highgate she'd been fast asleep but throughout the journey back to Kingston she was wide awake to see the narrow winding roads and precipices. She clutched her seat and stared straight ahead, trying hard not to show her fear. She had embarrassed herself enough for one day and was determined not to feed Lance's amusement any further.

She breathed a sigh of relief as they arrived at Manor Park which was at the outskirts of Kingston. Lance drove them straight to their hotel.

As they were checking in Lance said, "I'm sure you need some rest. Let's meet in the lobby around seven, okay?"

"Oh, I'm fine," she said, not wanting to seem like a wimp. "I'm not tired at all."

"Well, in that case, I'll take half an hour to freshen up then we'll hit the road."

"I'll be here."

Summer could not have asked for a more enjoyable evening. Lance drove her out to Hellshire Beach which was just thirty minutes away. There they sat on a bamboo bench under tall palm trees and ate fried bammies and escoveitched fish as they watched the waves beat against the shore. The beach was practically deserted except for a small boy and two fishermen who were bringing their boats in for the night.

Summer rested her head on Lance's shoulder and watched the setting sun as it sank slowly behind the horizon. She had never felt so peaceful in her life. She wished she could stay just like that, in Lance's arms, forever.

The evening ended too soon for Summer. When Lance told her it was time to go she begged him to stay a while longer.

"You know we'll have to be up by three in the morning again," Lance reminded her.

"I know," she sighed.

"I want you to get some rest."

"Just fifteen minutes more and then we'll go, okay?"

"Alright, honey," he acquiesced. "Whatever pleases your little heart."

Summer relaxed against him again and closed her eyes. This was her heaven.

The flight back to Chicago next morning was uneventful. Summer had been home only a couple of hours when the telephone rang. It was Lance.

"Good news, Summer." His voice was edged with excitement.

"What is it?"

"Monisha's album was nominated for the World Music Awards. I just got the news."

"Wow, that's great."

"Do you know what this can do for us? It's our best P.R opportunity yet."

"Don't I know it," she agreed. "I'm going to start working on a plan right now."

"Hold on, little Missy. You're off today. Don't let me hear you say another word about work until you get into office tomorrow. Understood?"

"Yes, sir, Captain, sir."

"And no more of your cheekiness or else I'll have to come over there and punish you."

"Anytime," she chuckled as he groaned and hung up the phone.

Chapter 21

Lance hung up the phone and turned to Derrick who lounged in the couch in the corner. An unlit cigarette hung from the side of his mouth. Lance raised his eyebrows and looked pointedly at Derrick.

"Don't tell me you've taken up smoking again?" Lance's tone was disapproving.

"Not really." Derrick plucked the offending item from his lips and held it between his second and third fingers. "I'm just experimenting with it again. Looks cool when I'm kicking it with the honeys."

"I'd suggest you stop acting like some freshman trying to impress the senior girls. You know how Aunt Jean feels about you smoking. That's what got you in trouble in the first place."

"Aw, Mama worries too much. A couple of cigarettes are not going to kill me."

"I think her biggest worry is that it will lead you to do other things. Like last time. Don't tell me you've forgotten already."

Derrick shook his head and had the decency to look ashamed.

"I promised your Mom I'd keep your nose clean," Lance continued. "You've been doing pretty good. Don't let me down now."

Derrick nodded and flipped the cigarette into a nearby trash can.

"Derrick," Lance leaned forward as he spoke, "I get on your case because I care about you. Even if I hadn't made any promise to Aunt Jean I would still be on you. You know that, right?"

"Yeah," Derrick said, with a sigh. "I know it. I'll stay out of trouble. You've got my word on that."

"Good. Now let's talk business. When are you leaving for the Kingston show?"

"Monday. What about you? You should be heading to Los Angeles soon, right?"

"Yeah." Lance nodded. "Leaving Monday, just like you."

"Think we're gonna bring it home?"

"I think we have a pretty good chance," Lance replied. "We put a lot into Monisha's album. There aren't many companies that do that much for one singer."

"Yeah, but we're up against some big names. You think we can beat them?"

"Let's just say, I think we can give them a good run for their money."

"You know I'll be watching from Jamaica. Good thing practically everybody there has cable. I'm looking forward to seeing you and Monisha on t.v."

He rose to leave then paused. "By the way, you're taking Summer too, right?"

"Can't. It's come down to the crunch for her and that thesis she's working on. She's got to turn it in next week or they won't grant her the degree."

"Ooh, I know she's pissed. After working so hard on promoting that album she's got to be going crazy, not going."

"Naw, she's okay. One thing you should know about Summer – she doesn't get all excited about stuff like that. I wish she could come but she's cool about it."

Derrick sat down again and said, "Don't say I'm nosy but I know you and Summer have been seeing each other. Things going okay between you two?

Lance paused before answering, trying to read Derrick's expression. He knew his cousin had been taken with Summer and he didn't want to hurt him if he didn't have to. But

Derrick seemed not to have suffered from having lost Summer. His expression was open and curious, and there was no trace of bitterness on his face.

Lance cleared his throat then spoke. "Actually, things are going pretty good between us."

"Yeah? So you're doing the steady thing with her, then?"

"It's...it's more than that." Lance tried to keep his voice calm but lately, even the mere thought of Summer got his heart to pounding. "It's a whole lot more than that."

"And what the hell is that supposed to mean?" Derrick gave him a puzzled look.

"She got me, Derrick. But good."

"You sound serious," Derrick said.

"I am. I've fallen for this girl. Hard."

"You? No way. Not you, the lady killer." Derrick sounded doubtful. "The man who swore he'd never be caught dead tied to only one woman?"

"I said I'd consider it – after I'm forty."

"Well, you're still some ways away from forty, my good man."

"I know, but this girl..." he said, putting his hands up in a gesture of helplessness, "...this girl, man, she just grabbed my heart and ran away with it. There wasn't a damn thing I could do about it."

"I can see you're a lost case." Derrick said then frowned. "Wait a minute. What about Monisha? Didn't she have a thing for you?"

Lance shook his head, slightly embarrassed at the reminder. "She never loved me, man. She was infatuated with me. And I guess I couldn't turn down such a pretty package. But she's okay. She's seeing that guy from Alexis Agency."

"No kidding."

"Yup. He's got the dough and she's got the flow. They make a lovely couple."

"I guess. Anyway, man, I gotta run. Catch you later."

Lance watched him leave then leaned back in his seat and tapped his pen on the desk. Soon, he was lost in thought.

Now why in the world had he told Derrick all that? Some of the stuff, he hadn't even thought about. It just came out. When it came to Summer it was as if he couldn't help himself.

"Now it's my turn to go under the knife?" Monisha's tone was sarcastic. "Do we really have to do this?" She rolled her eyes, obviously annoyed.

"Monisha, all I'm trying to do is get to know you," Summer said. "Just give me a little of your time. Please."

"Oh, alright," Monisha finally said, "but I just want you to know you're being a pain."

Summer sighed. She would really have preferred not to have to do this and the thought had even crossed her mind to ask Lance to let her skip over Monisha but she killed it as soon as it came into her head. Her sense of responsibility prevailed. She had a job to do and she would execute it, painful or not.

"Come on, then," Monisha said roughly. She stepped out of the office and down the hallway, not waiting for Summer. She pressed the elevator button and Summer had to rush to jump in before the door closed.

The chauffeur was waiting for them downstairs. They climbed into the Hummer and sped off to Burn Ridge where Monisha's parents lived. The driveway curved towards a stately house with long, white columns that rose into the air. The lawn was immaculate and roses filled the huge flowerbeds that were under the windows.

When they got out of the car Monisha let her in the front door.

"Good day, Miss Monisha." A tall young woman in black slacks and a white blouse approached them.

"Tell my mother she's got a visitor," Monisha said curtly and walked off, leaving Summer standing in the entrance, staring at the woman.

"Please follow me, Miss," the woman said pleasantly, and walked ahead of her into a huge, sunny sitting room. "Please have a seat. I will get Mrs. Stone in just a moment."

As Summer sat she looked around the elegant room and could see that this was a home that was well cared for. The mahogany paneling gleamed in the light. Everything had a polished look.

"Hello." A deep female voice startled her and she looked towards the entrance.

A slender woman in a floral lounge suit entered the room. Her black hair was caught on top of her head in a bun and her face was perfectly made up. She was like an older version of Monisha.

Summer stood up quickly. "Hello, Mrs. Stone."

"I understand you are here to interview me?" The woman looked at her enquiringly.

"Yes. I'm with Munroe Productions. I'm sure your daughter would have explained that I'm trying to do a story on her, and I'd just like to gather as much information as I can."

"Okay, I'll see if I can help," the woman said. "Have a seat."

Summer sat down again and Mrs. Stone settled into a chair across from her.

"Is your husband available also?" Summer asked, not wanting to start without him.

"No," she said, shaking her head, "he's away on business at the moment. You may speak to me."

"Thank you." Summer nodded and pulled out her notepad. "I just wanted to find out what Monisha was like as a child growing up here?"

"Oh." The woman seemed relieved. "She was a cute little girl, always running around in ribbons and ponytails. She was a talented child; started playing the piano when she was five. That's when we started sending her to do voice training, too."

"That's interesting." Summer scribbled on the pad. "And she got all of this training here in Chicago?"

"No, we also sent her to finishing school in Europe, and that's where she really blossomed." The woman spoke proudly. "She was a straight A student and we always made sure to stay on top of her so she wouldn't slack off in her studies."

"That's great," Summer said. "Now, can you tell me what her likes and dislikes were, as a child?"

"Well..." the woman was silent for a moment and seemed to be thinking hard, then she said, "...I guess like any other child she would have liked dolls and candy, and things like that. I'm not really sure. The nanny took care of all that."

"Yeah, that's right." A sharp voice came from the entrance.

They both turned to see Monisha standing in the doorway.

She came into the room and said, "Tell her about my likes and dislikes, Mom – if you can really say anything from the little you know about me."

She turned to Summer. "They were always shipping me off to boarding school in New York, London and Paris. I was supposed to be anywhere but here at home."

"We were only trying to give you the best..."

"Yeah, right." Monisha scowled. "Always trying to improve me. I was never good enough, Mom. So now somebody comes and asks you a simple question about me and you can't even answer because, guess what, I was never here."

She turned back to Summer. "They were always trying to make me sing better, make me play the piano better, make me speak French."

"But Monisha..." Mrs. Stone had her hand at her collarbone and looked very distressed.

"Oh, forget it." Monisha turned her back to her mother. "I don't know how much you're going to get out of her about me," she sneered, "because that woman knows nothing about me."

She gave her mother another glare and stalked out of the room.

Summer sat silent, shocked. She looked at Mrs. Stone and the woman's eyes were glassy with tears.

"Mrs. Stone…" she started to speak but the woman seemed not to hear her. She just covered her face with trembling hands and her body shook with her tears.

Summer felt sorry for the woman but had no idea what she could say to make her stop crying. So she said softly, "I'll see myself out."

Summer slowly walked out of the house and went to look for the chauffeur. All she could think about was the hurt and pain in Monisha's eyes. In that short space of time she had learned more about the singer than in all the time she'd been working at Munroe Productions.

It was Monday evening, four days before Summer's deadline to hand in her thesis. She had requested the week off from work so that she could finalize her research, get her paper typed and submitted by Friday at noon.

Now she sat in her usual spot in the library and surveyed the piles of books in front of her. She felt like screaming. The thesis was coming along, but so slowly. The days, on the other hand, seemed to be flying by. She felt like she needed a personal assistant, a secretary and a typist just to get it all done.

She looked at her watch – six o'clock. No wonder she felt so hungry. She'd been there since ten in the morning and hadn't had a bite to eat all day. She packed her books neatly at the end of the table and slung her purse over her shoulder. She would have to get something to eat or she would not be around to submit a thesis at all.

She was heading for the campus cafeteria when she remembered that she had planned to call Brian on Sunday to wish him a happy birthday. With all the stress she was under it was no wonder she had totally forgotten. Oh well, she thought, she would just call him when she got to the cafeteria.

Calling Brian was one thing. Convincing him to let her get off the phone was another.

"Come on, Summer. I haven't seen you in ages."

"But we've spoken on the phone. We've both been busy so it just wasn't possible."

"Well, you know I'm off on Mondays so I'm free now. What say we get together for a drink?"

"Not this evening, Brian. I'm busy." She sighed, almost sorry she had bothered to call him. "I only slipped out of the library for a few minutes so I could grab something to eat. I've got to go back in a little while."

"I have a great idea," he said. "You just wait by the front entrance and I'll pick you up and we can go grab something together. I'm only five minutes away from CU. I'll be there in no time."

"Alright," Summer said slowly, still doubtful that it would make sense for them to meet. Still, she didn't want to disappoint him, especially since she had missed his birthday. "I guess we could do that. But only if you're really quick."

"I'm on my way."

Brian was true to his word. Within minutes he was pulling up beside Summer in his black convertible Mustang. As soon as she saw him she ran down the steps and hopped in, and he roared off.

"Hey, you," he grinned as she settled into the seat. "You're looking good."

She rolled her eyes. "No, I'm not. I look awful. Can't you see the bags under my eyes? They're almost big enough for me to carry my books in."

"Oh, be quiet. You know you look good."

"Well, you don't look bad yourself. You look kinda more…muscular." She studied him, then asked, "Have you been lifting weights?"

"Remember I told you I was going to join a gym? Started last month. Lost eight pounds already," he said proudly.

"It shows," she said, impressed. "You look good."

"Thanks," he said, and she was amused at his bashful smile.

The closest restaurant outside of the campus was Wendy's. Brian pulled up by the drive-through window and ordered chili and a salad for Summer and a hamburger and fries for himself.

"Hey, what about the diet?" Summer teased.

"Yeah, well, you can't be good all the time," he grinned.

He drove to the park nearby and they pulled up under a huge elm tree. They reclined the seats and pulled out the bags of food.

"So, how's it going with you?" Brian peered at her as he bit into the burger. "Last time we talked you were just coming back from Jamaica."

"Has it been that long?"

"Yeah, it's been that long. You abandoned your boy," he scolded. "Once you got into the company of them big shots you forgot all about me."

"Oh, Brian, don't say that. I haven't abandoned you. I've just been busy, that's all."

"Yeah, yeah. Don't worry about me. I'm just giving you a hard time."

"You're so wicked to me," she complained and made a face at Brian. "You make me feel so bad."

"I said don't worry about it," he said, his mouth stuffed with French fries. "I'm cool."

"Sure?"

"Absolutely."

She gobbled down a mouthful of lettuce then asked, "So how are things going at the restaurant?"

"Same as always," he replied. "Jackson's still on the rampage. I'm thinking of leaving that place."

"Really?"

"Yeah," he nodded. "I'm good enough to make it on my own. I just need a little start-up capital, that's all."

"So you gonna get a loan or something?" she asked, taking a sip of her Pepsi.

"I haven't thought that far yet. I just know I want to do my own thing."

"I think you should jump on it right away. You're a great chef. And if you ever need a P.R. consultant you know where to find me."

"So what about you? What's new on your end?"

"Well, the job has been really interesting so far and I get a chance to travel. Now if only I could get this damn thesis out of the way I'd be a happy camper."

"And that Munroe guy. You managing okay with him?" Brian looked concerned. "I heard he's not the easiest person in the world to work for."

"I'm getting along with him quite well, actually. In fact..." she paused, dying to share her joy with her friend but scared of saying too much.

"In fact?" Brian prompted her, his curiosity obvious.

"In fact, we work well together," she ended lamely.

"Oh, no, you don't. I know that wasn't what you were going to say. You're not gonna get away that easy. In fact, what?"

"That was it. Now stop hounding me." She dipped her spoon into the chili and pretended to be absorbed with its consistency.

"Summer, if you don't come clean with me I'm going to keep you in this car and then you won't get to finish your work."

"You wouldn't."

"Try me." He folded his arms across his chest and sat back, still watching her. "Now cough it up."

"Brian," she whined.

"That won't help. The only way I'm taking you back to the library is if you tell me exactly what's going on."

"Alright," Summer sighed. "But it's just because I absolutely have to get back to my work. Otherwise you could never bully me."

"Whatever." Brian rolled his eyes. "Now talk."

"I...I think I've fallen in love with him."

"What? I thought you were going to say he made a pass at you, or something. But falling in love? How did that happen so quick?" Brian stared at her as if she were crazy.

"I don't know, really. I mean, I didn't even like him at first. But as I got to know him I found out that he was so real, so down-to-earth." She became pensive. "He's so different from what I first thought."

"Meaning he's been generous with his gifts, huh?"

"Brian, I can't believe you just said that." She frowned at him. "It has nothing to do with what he can give me. In fact, he's not given me a single thing except my salary that I work hard for."

"Then what the heck would you want with a man like that?" he demanded.

"Will you shut up and just listen?" Summer glared at Brian. "Lance has shown me a side of him that's impressed me more than money or gifts ever could. He's shown me that he's kind and caring, and not just to the women he's pursuing. I saw how he dealt with his little god-daughter. And you should have seen him with my Mom – she loved him."

"Your mother? This must be really serious for you to take him home to Mom."

"It was his idea, really. He was the one who asked to meet her."

"Hmmph." Brian looked skeptical but said nothing.

"Anyway, it's almost seven," she said, looking at her watch. "Can you take me back to the library now?"

"Alright. I know you haven't told me everything but I'll get you next time." He revved the engine and they drove off.

'Yeah, right,' Summer thought, 'you'd have to kidnap me for a week before I tell you anything else'.

She didn't get home until almost eleven that night. Her head pounded and she felt like just throwing herself down on the bed and sleeping for a week. She dropped her book bag on the ground and headed straight for the bathroom where she splashed water on her face then stared in the mirror at her disheveled hair and tired eyes. She was glad Lance was not around to see her right now.

Lance. She hadn't heard from him all day. He had left for Los Angeles early that morning but she should have heard from him by now. She dabbed her face with a soft towel and padded over to the phone. Yes, there was a message. She smiled. She knew he hadn't forgotten her.

She sat on the couch, punched in her password and leaned back to listen to the deep mellow voice she loved so much.

Instead, a sharp female voice assaulted her ear. "Miss Jones, this is Amy Spence from the Serenity Nursing Home. You need to get in touch with me right away. Your mother had another stroke and had to be rushed to the hospital. Please call me as soon as you get this message."

The phone receiver fell from nerveless fingers. It was happening all over again. Dear God, her mind screamed, what are you doing to my mother?

She was sobbing as she dialed the number for the nursing home. The phone rang eight times before someone came on the line. By then, Summer thought she was going mad.

"Where is she? Where is my mother?" she blurted out between sobs.

When the warden had calmed her enough to find out who Summer was talking about she said, "She's at the City of Chicago Hospital. You need to go there right away."

Chapter 22

"Amazing grace, how sweet the sound that saved a wretch like me."

Summer bowed her head and dabbed her eyes as the singer's voice filled the church with the mournful sounds of the song. Her heart was filled with pain and she felt that she could not go on any longer. She couldn't believe her mother was gone.

She wiped the tears that kept flowing down her face and looked at the coffin in front of her, covered in flowers, and thought of how her mother loved flowers so much and now she would never see them again.

As she stared a small sob escaped her lips and Brian put his arm around her shoulder and pulled her close. Summer put the handkerchief to her face again and wept. She leaned into the solid mass of him and shook from the intensity of the sobs racking her body.

When she finally got control of herself she sniffed then drew a deep breath, straightened her back, and looked forward steadily at the pastor as he rose to give the message. She tried to be strong. She knew her mother would have wanted that.

Summer's nightmare had begun the moment she had got the message from the woman at the nursing home. As soon as she'd spoken with her she immediately called a cab and rushed over to the hospital. When she got there she rushed over to the front desk where the nurse was on the telephone.

Summer tapped on the counter trying to get her attention but the woman totally ignored her.

"Hello. I'm here to see my mother. Edna Jones."

The nurse continued talking.

"Excuse me. I'm here to see my mother. It's an emergency."

The nurse covered the mouthpiece and said, "I'll be right with you. Let me just finish this call."

"I have to see my mother now. She's here in this hospital. Just tell me where she is."

She clenched her fists in frustration and was about to let the nurse have it when she heard a familiar voice.

"Miss Jones."

She turned quickly and saw her mother's doctor standing at the entrance.

"Dr. Ogobo." She ran over to him. "What's happened to my mother? I got a call that she had to be rushed to the hospital. Where is she? Is she okay?"

Dr. Ogobo put his hand on her shoulder and pulled her over to sit on a nearby chair.

"Please calm down, Miss Jones. Your mother was rushed in last night because she had another stroke."

"Yes, I know that, but how is she?"

"She's in very serious condition right now."

"Oh, my God...," she moaned in fear.

The doctor patted her hand. "As I said, the situation is serious but we have her stabilized and we're monitoring her closely."

"Can I see her right now?" Summer asked anxiously.

"I'll take you to her room but I must warn you, she cannot respond to you. She won't know you're there but you may come and sit with her for a while."

As Summer followed Doctor Ogobo to her mother's room her mind was in turmoil. She was so scared. And she felt so guilty.

She normally called her mother at lunchtime every day but today she'd been so focused on getting her thesis done that she had decided to skip the call just this once so that she could get her work done. She knew that she could never go on the phone and spend less than an hour with her mother so she had decided to forego the call until next day. But it was not to be.

Summer couldn't help wondering if she had made that call if it would have made a difference. Maybe she would have realized that something was wrong, and then she would have gotten her mother to the hospital earlier. Maybe.

When Summer entered the room she almost didn't recognize her mother. Edna lay in the bed, thin and frail. She had tubes in her nose and needles were stuck in her arms. A bag of saline hung beside her bed.

Summer approached slowly and peered at her mother, almost afraid of what she would see. She looked so still. Her heart beat hard in her chest and she touched her mother's hand.

"Mom."

There was no response. A sudden fear gripped Summer and she touched the hand again.

"Mom."

When there was still no response she turned quickly to the doctor, "She looks so still. Is she…"

"She's alive. But she's in a bad state."

"Oh, my God," she cried, and turned back to look at the woman she loved so much. "Oh, Mom. Why did this have to happen?"

"Miss Jones," the doctor approached her and rested his hand on her shoulder, "please, try to calm down. Right now your mother needs to recover. She needs your strength. Be brave, for her sake."

"Yes, doctor." Summer nodded, but her legs felt like they were collapsing under her. Doctor Ogobo seemed to realize how weak she felt because he pulled a chair over and helped her into it.

"You may stay here by your mother's side," he said. "Just try not to get too upset. She needs you to be strong."

Then he slipped out through the door.

Summer turned back to her mother and stroked the frail hand. The tears welled up in her eyes then broke free to run down her cheeks. She didn't care. All she knew was that her beloved mother was lying in this hospital bed, fighting for her life.

"You can do it, Mom. You can make it. I'm here for you," Summer whispered through the tears. "Just, please...don't leave me. Don't leave me alone here. I love you. I need you, Mom."

Silence. But she prayed that, even in the silence, her mother was hearing her.

Summer sat by her mother's bedside the entire night, sometimes drifting off momentarily into a doze but always waking and looking anxiously at her, hoping to see some signs of life.

When the sun came up next day she was still sitting in the chair, holding her mother's hand. The nurse came in and greeted her then asked her to leave the room so that the doctor on duty could examine her mother. She was reluctant to leave and begged the woman to let her stay but her request was gently denied and she went slowly from the room.

Summer leaned against the wall outside the door and rubbed her eyes. She was so tired but so afraid. She could not lose her mother, the only person who loved her. She didn't know how she would survive if she lost her. She felt so alone that she decided she had to talk to someone.

She walked over to the pay phone and dialed Lance's cell phone number. She knew he would still be in California but she just needed to talk. But there was no answer. All she got was his voicemail. She quickly left him a message that her mother was in the hospital and that he should call her at the hospital's main number and ask to be put to her mother's room. When she hung up the phone she felt empty inside.

The nurse and the doctor came out within a few minutes and told her that she could go back in, but they advised her that it would do her good to go home and get some rest because there was no change and it would not make sense for her to stay there and suffer. She needed to keep her strength up so that she could be there for her mother.

Despite her reluctance to leave she spent another hour with Edna then headed for home. She planned to just freshen up, get something to eat, and head right back.

When she got home she checked her voicemail just to see if Lance had returned her call but there was nothing. It didn't make sense for her to call the office because it was closed. It was the day before Thanksgiving and Munroe Productions had given all employees the day off. Still, she tried, just in case. As she expected, all she got was voicemail.

The only other way she could think of reaching Lance was through Derrick but he had told her that he was going to be in Jamaica for the whole week so she knew he was out of reach. As a last resort she tried Lance's cell phone again. Still just voicemail.

She left him another message. "Lance, this is Summer again. Please. Get in touch with me as soon as you can. My mother had another stroke so she's in the hospital. I'm home right now but I'm heading back there in a little while. You can reach me there at the main hospital number, just ask for room 231. Ask them to connect you. Just please, get in touch with me."

Summer showered quickly and stuck a microwave meal in the oven. She gobbled it down as fast as she could, pulled the comb through her hair, grabbed her purse then dashed back out the door. She didn't want her mother to wake up and not find her there.

She caught a cab and, within two hours of leaving, Summer was striding down the corridor, heading back towards room 231.

"Miss Jones."

She turned at the sound of a female voice and saw the nurse approaching.

"Miss Jones, just wait a minute, please."

"Yes?" Summer looked at her questioningly.

"Please come with me. The doctor would like to talk to you."

"Talk to me? Is...is my mother worse?"

"Just follow me, please. Let me take you to his office."

"No, tell me now. What's wrong?"

"Miss Jones. Please." The nurse was insistent. "Come with me and the doctor will explain everything."

She turned on her heels and quickly walked away and Summer was forced to run to catch up with her. The nurse ushered her into Doctor Ogobo's office then left, pulling the door shut behind her.

The doctor indicated that she should have a seat. She sat on the edge of the chair and stared anxiously back at him.

"What's the matter, doctor? Are you going to have to operate? Is she worse? What's going on?" The words tumbled out of her.

"Miss Jones," he paused and looked very uncomfortable and sudden fear gripped Summer's heart. "Miss Jones, I'm sorry, but we lost her."

"Lost her?" Summer stared back at him in confusion. "Lost...her?"

"Yes. Your mother passed away shortly after you left this morning."

"My mother...is dead?" She stared back at him, bewildered.

"I'm sorry."

"My mother is dead?" she said again, not believing what she was hearing.

"Yes. I'm really sorry but she's gone."

"But...but I was just here. I was with her." Her voice rose with each statement. "She was sick but she was still alive."

"I know, Miss Jones, but she was very weak. She couldn't fight it. She tried but her body gave up."

"But...why didn't somebody call me?"

"We knew you were heading right back and I didn't want to give you such news on the phone. I wanted to speak to you face to face," the doctor explained gently. "I'm very sorry but your mother was a very sick woman. With the Multiple Sclerosis and two strokes her body just couldn't handle it."

"No, no. I can't believe this." Summer shook her head then looked pleadingly at Doctor Ogobo. "Tell me this is all a mistake."

"I'm sorry. I can't. She's gone."

"Oh, no. Oh, God." When the doctor went over and put his arm around her she clutched at him as if she were drowning. "Oh, God. Mom."

Summer remembered very little else except being led to a room where she was put to lie down. When she awoke an elderly lady was by her side.

"Are you feeling better now?" The woman's voice cut through her daze.

"Yes. Who are you?" she groaned, blinking as she tried to focus.

"It's Amy Spence, from the nursing home."

"What…what do you want?"

"Miss Jones, I know this is a difficult time for you but I'm here to discuss funeral arrangements. For your mother."

Summer remained silent and just stared at the woman as if she were senseless.

"You have nothing to worry about," the woman continued. "Your mother arranged it all. After her first stroke she discussed it with me and put everything in place."

"Discussed it with you? "Summer repeated, still dazed.

"Yes. She planned her funeral arrangements and already paid for everything. She told me that you were pretty much alone and she didn't want you to be burdened at her passing so she asked me to be in charge of everything."

Amy Spence straightened her spectacles on her nose and continued in a very businesslike manner. "I am organizing the funeral for tomorrow evening, according to her wishes for a speedy burial. She said there were no relatives who needed to be advised, but I just want to confirm that with you. Is there anyone who should know about this?"

"No." Summer shook her head. "I don't have any family. It's only me."

"So it's only…you?" The woman still looked doubtful.

"Yes. I said I don't have anyone else," Summer said, exasperated. "Please just do what you have to do."

"Alright, I understand." The woman nodded and stood up. "I know this is rough for you. I'll take care of everything."

As Amy was about to leave Doctor Ogobo entered.

"How are you feeling now?" he asked, placing a cool hand on her forehead.

"I'll live," she muttered, not looking up.

The doctor sighed. "Well, you may go if you feel up to it. I'm sure you'd prefer to be with family and friends right now."

"I'll take you home," Amy said quickly, turning back towards Summer. "I don't think you're up to finding your way home in your condition," she said as she helped Summer out of the bed.

"Thanks," was all Summer could say as the woman took her arm and led her out of the room.

When Summer got home she locked the door, threw herself on the bed and burst into tears. She still couldn't believe it. She had lost her mother. She would never see her again. She didn't know what to do.

She thought about Lance, thought of calling him again. She got up and went to check her voicemail. Nothing.

It was like she was living her childhood all over again. Just like her father, this man she loved had abandoned her. Just when she needed him most he was nowhere to be found.

The tears started rolling again, faster and faster, and she sat on the floor and leaned her head on the wall and bawled.

She just needed somebody right now and there was no-one near. Lance had let her down. She'd left messages, she'd reached out to him in desperation, and he hadn't even bothered to call back. He was no friend of hers. She couldn't rely on him.

She never wanted to see him again. As far as she was concerned he was nothing to her, and never would be anymore.

She sniffed loudly and wiped her eyes then picked up the phone and dialed Brian's number.

Chapter 23

For Summer, going home after the funeral was the hardest part. She had just said goodbye to the only family she had left and now there was nothing, no-one. After the ceremony some of the nursing home staff had come around, trying to comfort her, but she hardly knew them and she just wanted to get away.

The only person she still leaned on was Brian. He was the one who drove her back to her tiny apartment and held her to him as they took the elevator upstairs. He was the one who took the keys from her trembling fingers, opened the door and led her gently over to the couch so that she could rest. It was Brian who took her shoes off and rested her feet on the couch and told her to rest while he went to make her some supper.

Right now he was in the kitchen opening cupboards and banging pots on the stove. Summer didn't care what he made her. She did not even feel like eating anything at all. She was just empty inside. Her heart felt as if it had turned to stone and there was no feeling left inside her.

She lay on the couch and stared up at the ceiling and thought about her mother. Her mind went back to all the agony that her mother had suffered at her father's hands and she hated him all the more now that her mother was dead. She had always resented her father for his abuse but now that her mother was gone her hatred for him intensified.

She had always wanted to do so much for her mother, just to make up for all the suffering she had gone through, but now the chance was gone - forever. She hadn't even graduated yet. She had wanted to start a real career so that she could afford the big house she had always wanted to buy for her mother, the boat cruise she had wanted to take her on. None of that had happened. And now Mom was gone.

Her greatest happiness had always been to make her mother happy. Now that was gone, too. She felt cheated of the chance she had always wanted to grow up, become successful, make her mother proud and do everything she could to make the twilight of her life her best years.

She sighed as the thoughts raced through her mind. She felt like she would never be happy again.

Some time later, Brian peeped out of the kitchen and said, "I've got some soup for you, Summer. Come on over. You need to have something in your stomach."

Summer stared at him for a moment, still absorbed in her thoughts, then she dragged herself back to the present and all the sadness that came with it.

"Come on, honey. You have to eat."

He walked over to her, stretched out his hands, and took hers in his. He pulled her up and led her gently to the stool then pushed the bowl of steaming soup under her nose.

"Oh, Brian." She looked at him mournfully. "I don't think I can eat. Not even a spoonful."

"You have to try, Summer. You have to eat or else you'll get sick."

"I don't care."

"But I do. Come. Have some of this soup."

He dipped the spoon into the bowl and held it up to her lips. She took a sip and the hot liquid burned a trail down her throat and into her stomach. It growled.

"Now, you hear that? You're starving. I'd bet you haven't had a thing to eat all day."

"I didn't want anything."

"Well, you're going to have something now. I'm not gonna let you starve to death." He dipped up another spoonful and put it to her lips and she swallowed. She was able to have almost half of the bowl but as soon as the sharpness of her hunger was dulled she pushed his hand away and refused to have anymore.

"I'm alright Brian. I don't need any more."

"Okay, honey." He took the bowl to the sink then turned to her with a questioning look.

"Hey, how come you haven't mentioned the boyfriend? Where is he, anyway?"

"I don't want to talk about him." Her answer was curt and she refused to meet Brian's eyes.

"But…I don't get it. Shouldn't Lance be here with you right now? I would think…"

"I said I don't want to talk about him," she growled. "I never want to hear that name again."

Brian turned surprised eyes to her then, without a word, turned back to the sink.

"Brian, I'm sorry." She dropped her head into her hands. "I'm sorry. I just can't take any more of this."

He dropped the spoon back into the sink and gathered her into his arms. She was enveloped in the warmth and bigness of him and it made her feel so safe, just for a moment, that she burst out crying all over again.

"Alright, honey, alright. I know it's tough but you just gotta hang in there."

Brian stayed with her until almost ten that night. Then he lifted her in his arms and carried her into the bedroom. He laid her gently on the bed then covered her with a blanket.

He kissed her on the forehead then said, "Try to get some sleep, alright? And if you need me you know where to find me."

She pulled the blanket over her face but she stayed that way for over an hour before sleep mercifully came to her.

Summer woke up with a start. A noise had woken her. It was the telephone. Her heart pounded. Who could it be? Something must be wrong, she thought. Was it her Mom?

Then suddenly, she remembered. It would never be her Mom anymore. She was gone. There was no-one left for her to worry about. No-one left who would worry about her.

She glared at the phone and felt like throwing it off the nightstand. It was always the bearer of bad news. But she had got the worst news of her life two days ago and there was nothing else that could phase her right now.

The clock winked eleven forty-eight. Maybe it was Brian checking up on her, she thought.

She picked up the receiver and spoke.

"Hello." Her voice was deadpan.

"Summer, I'm sorry to call you so late but I wouldn't do it if this weren't an emergency."

It wasn't Brian at all. This was a heavily accented female voice.

"Who is this?"

"It's Jennifer. Remember? Michelle's mother."

"Jennifer from Jamaica?" Summer was confused. Why would this woman be calling her? And at this time of night?

"Yes."

"What is it, Jennifer?" Summer knew her voice was not very friendly but she didn't really care.

"I'm calling to tell you about what happened to Lance."

"Lance? Has something happened to him?"

"Yes. Derrick called me just this evening and told me that Lance was in a car accident. He's in the hospital. Derrick called me from the airport. He was actually on his way there but he told me about it and asked me to get in touch with you. He didn't want to be the one to give you the news." She paused then said hesitantly, "He said he was afraid you would get emotional on him."

"When did this happen? Today?"

"No. It happened Tuesday night but Derrick didn't hear about it until yesterday and so he left Jamaica today to head straight for California."

"But Lance…is he alright?"

"No, Summer. It's really bad. He's in a coma right now."

"Oh, God."

"Yes, they say he was thrown out of the vehicle and sustained head injuries."

"So he's all alone there now?"

"No, his Mom and sister flew down yesterday and, as I told you, Derrick is on his way. In fact, he should be in California by now. I'm trying to get a flight out by tomorrow or Saturday. So he'll have family around him. But we just wanted you to know."

Summer willed herself to stay calm. "Jennifer, do you know what hospital he is in?"

"Yes, Derrick told me. Just hold on a minute."

Jennifer came back within seconds. "It's Atlantic Christian Hospital. I don't know the room number but I guess you can call the hospital and they can put you through. But remember, he can't talk."

"No, it's okay. I won't call. I just need to get down there."

"Alright, Summer. I'll let you go now because it's late but I just wanted you to know."

"Thanks, Jennifer." Summer hung up the phone and put trembling fingers to her mouth.

Oh God, she thought. Not another one. I can't lose two of them at the same time. Then another thought struck her. There she had been, hating Lance for not calling her back, when all this time he'd been lying in a coma.

The guilt swept over her. She felt like she was being punished for her sins. She had hated him, and now she was in danger of losing him altogether.

She got out of the bed and opened the closet. She pulled out a small suitcase and threw it on the bed. There was no way she could sleep now. She began to pack. She was going to catch the first flight out to Los Angeles.

Chapter 24

Lance opened his eyes slowly, painfully, but the glare of bright lights made him close them again quickly. He had a splitting headache. It was as if a thousand drums were beating in his head. He waited a while then slowly opened his eyes again.

He squinted, trying hard to focus, but everything was swimming and blurry. He closed his eyes a third time then opened them again, this time forcing his eyes to remain open. He let out a groan as he felt sharp pains in his head.

Immediately, a brown face came into view. It was a woman. She was fuzzy but he could make out that there was a look of concern on her face.

"Lance?" she whispered and peered into his face. He struggled to speak but no sound came.

"Lance?" she called again. Then he was staring into deep brown eyes.

She turned quickly away and he heard her say, "Go call the doctor," then she was looking back at him. He felt that he knew this woman but his mind was so muddled that he was totally at a loss as to who she was.

Then vague memories slowly drifted into shape inside his head and the face became clear. He knew her. He knew her intimately.

"Summer?" His voice was hoarse as he struggled to speak and it came out as a croaking whisper.

"Yes, Lance. I'm here."

"Where am I?" His eyes searched her face but all he saw there was relief and gladness.

"You're in hospital, Lance. You've been unconscious for four days."

"How..."

"You were in a car accident. You got head injuries and you've been in a coma ever since."

"I don't ...remember," he groaned.

"Shh. Honey, don't try to remember anything. Just lie back." She stroked his face as she spoke. "I'm just so glad you've come back. I thought...you might not make it."

"Was I...that bad?"

"Yes. The doctors said they did all they could but then they could only leave it up to your body to heal itself. Thank God you've come back." Summer leaned over and hugged him gently so she wouldn't disturb any of the needles in his arms.

At that moment the doctor rushed in with Lance's mother and sister right behind. Doctor Francis walked over to his patient and greeted him. "Mr. Munroe, you had us scared for a while."

As he spoke he lifted Lance's eyelids then checked the monitor. "I'm glad you decided to rejoin us in the world of the living."

He turned to Summer, Maggie Munroe and Sophie. "Could you leave us for a little while? I need to examine Mr. Munroe and make sure that everything is alright."

When the women had left the room Lance settled back down into the bed and let the doctor do his examination. By that time the nurse had come in and they were checking his vital signs. Gradually, he was able to gather his thoughts and he began to remember what had happened.

He'd left the music awards ceremony and had dropped Monisha and her friends at a nightclub and was heading back to his hotel. He stopped at a traffic light. When it turned green he began to move off and that's when it happened.

All he remembered was a horrific crash and then blackness.

The doctor and nurse finished their examination and helped him to dress again in his hospital gown. They tucked the sheet up under his chin and then they left. Immediately his mother, Sophie and Derrick rushed into the room. His mother was first to his side.

"Lance. Thank God, you're safe. We were so worried about you."

Sophie gave him a lopsided grin that was just a little bit wobbly and said, "Hey big brother. What d'you mean by scaring us like that? You nearly drove us crazy with worry. Don't you ever do that to us again."

He laughed softly and said, "Well, I didn't plan this. It just happened."

"We're glad to see you back, old boy," Derrick said from the foot of the bed. "It's good to see you awake, man."

Lance nodded gingerly. "It's good to be awake. I have no intention of leaving this world just yet."

"True word," Derrick said. Then, as if by way of explanation he added, "Oh, by the way, the doctor said only three of us could come into the room at one time so you'll see the others in a bit. Jennifer's here, you know."

"Yeah? She flew in?" Lance asked, touching his head.

"Of course. As soon as she got the news she booked a flight. What did you expect?"

"Yeah, that's Jennifer," he said, then paused and looked up. "But Derrick, you were supposed to be in Jamaica."

"Yeah, but when I heard what had happened you know I had to be here. I wasn't going to let my boy be suffering in the hospital and I'm not by his side."

"I really appreciate that."

"Man, you've done so much for me. I couldn't leave you out in the cold."

"Mom," Lance turned to Maggie, "I'm sorry I put you through all of this."

"You didn't put me through anything, Lance. You're my son. Didn't you expect me to be here by your side?"

"Yeah, but I'm still sorry you had to go through all this," Lance said.

Then he turned to Sophie. "So who's watching those kids of yours?"

"Robert's at home with them. He's always good with the kids," she replied. "He told me he'd take care of everything and I should just come to you. He's been real worried about you, Lance. In fact, I'd better go give him a call right now and give him the good news."

"And I'll touch base with Chantal and those guys from the office," Derrick said. "They've been worried sick about you."

After the two had left the room Maggie stayed with Lance for several minutes more.

Then she said, "Alright, I'm going to give you a break. I'm sure Summer and Jennifer are dying to see you and talk to you so I'll be back later. The doctor said not to let you overdo it so I won't let them stay long, okay?"

"Sure, Mom. You can send them in."

"And Lance," his mother said, smiling, "I think you made the right choice. I like her."

Summer was the first to dash through the door and over to Lance's bedside. She leaned over and kissed him on the forehead and he could see that there were tears in her eyes.

"Oh Lance, you don't know how good it is to see you with your eyes open."

Jennifer, who had come in right behind her, stood on the other side of the bed and smiled. "Lance, I'm glad to see you're back with us."

"Hey, Jennifer." He smiled weakly. "I'm sorry I dragged you all the way over here."

"No, no, you didn't drag me. I wanted to be here for you just like you've been there for me and Michelle."

"Thanks, Jen."

"No problem, Lance."

Lance turned to Summer who sat in the chair beside his bed. She was holding his hand in hers. She sniffed and seemed to be struggling not to cry.

"Honey, I'm back. What are you crying about?"

"I don't mean to cry. It's just...it's just that I'm so glad I didn't lose you, too."

"Lose me...too? What do you mean?"

"Oh, Lance. It's my Mom. She died."

"What?" His heart leapt in shock. "When? What happened?"

It was the day after your accident," she said sadly. "She had another stroke Tuesday night and was rushed to the hospital. I was with her but I went home to change and by the time I came back she was gone."

"Oh, no. Oh, my darling." He stroked her soft cheek. "How did you manage all alone?"

"It was very hard but I tried to be strong," she sighed. "The funeral was on Thanksgiving Day. The nursing home arranged it all. Then that night I got the call about you and it was as if my whole world went crashing down around me all over again."

"My poor Summer," he soothed. "I'm sorry, baby. I'm sorry about your Mom; so sorry I wasn't there for you."

"You couldn't help it, Lance," she smiled sadly at him. "You were struggling for your own life. I just wish I'd known."

"Well, you're here now and that's all that matters."

Lance looked up as Jennifer came up to the bed and leaned over and kissed him on the cheek. "I knew you'd make it, Lance. You're a fighter. I'm gonna step outside for a while. I have to call home to see how Michelle is doing. And I..." she looked at Summer then back at Lance, "I think you two need some time alone."

When Jennifer left Lance reached out and took Summer's hand and pulled her close to him. "I'm so glad you're here."

"Nothing could have kept me away from your side," she replied. "Not now. Not when you need me."

"But I wasn't there when you needed me."

"It wasn't your fault, Lance. I survived. I can't say it's been easy but I'm still here. And you're still here. And I'm grateful for that."

Lance looked at her gravely. "Summer, my dad always used to say, if you're going to do something for someone, don't delay. It took a near-death experience for me to really understand the wisdom of his words. Summer, there's something I've wanted to tell you for the longest time but I've been foolishly putting it off."

"Yes? What is it?" She looked so concerned that his heart ached for her.

"Summer Jones...I love you. With all my heart, I love you."

"Lance, are you sure? You're not just saying that because of my Mom, your accident..."

"I've never been more sure of anything in my life. I was just too much of a coward to tell you before. But now I'll tell the world...I love Summer Jones."

"Oh, Lance." The tears came to her eyes again. "And I love you, too. So much, it hurts. And I thank God for bringing you back to me."

"There's something else," Lance said, and Summer stared at him curiously.

"What else could there be?"

"I had a secret, but now I want to tell you."

"What is it?" she asked and the anxiety was back in her eyes.

"After the music awards I was heading for home but all I was thinking about was you. I was thinking about the surprise I planned to have for you when I got back to Chicago. You see, I'd ordered a ring for you and I was wondering how you would react when I gave it to you. I wasn't sure how you really felt about me, but I guessed that you cared for me, at least a little bit."

"Oh, my goodness. You got me a ring?" Her face melted in pleasure but then she frowned. "But you were thinking about me just when you had the accident; you had the accident because of me!"

"Not at all." He shook his head. "In fact, that's what probably saved my life. Normally as soon as the light changes I hit the gas and I'm off but this time I was a little bit slower. Maybe if I'd been as fast as I usually am, instead of the front of the car taking the blow I'd have probably taken the full force myself. Summer, let's not talk about the accident anymore. I want to talk about us. Come over here."

He pulled her close and kissed her then put her away from him and looked deep into her eyes. "Summer Jones, I don't have that ring with me but, will you marry me?"

She hugged him tight, then with the brightest, sweetest smile ever she said, "Yeah, mon."

Epilogue

R & B music filled the room as people mingled in the hallways with cocktails and others swayed to the rhythm pulsating. The main room was gaily decorated. The draperies on the walls were festooned with royal blue and silver chiffon and the tables were covered in navy blue cloth with silver napkins atop them.

There were at least thirty people in the room and they were all chatting and laughing. It was obviously a festive occasion.

Summer rested her arms comfortably around Lance's hips and swayed with him, dancing to the sweet tenor of Luther Vandross. She raised her head to look at him and he smiled down at her, filling her heart with joy. He was handsome, as usual, in an elegant suit of silver grey. It was the perfect complement to her own shimmering silver gown. She'd chosen their outfits for the evening and she knew they looked good.

Suddenly a man's loud voice came through the microphone and they all turned towards the podium. Lance pulled Summer close to his side as they stood and waited for the announcement.

"To all our friends and family members, thank you for coming," Derrick said. Summer was impressed with how handsome he looked with his newly trimmed down figure in his black tuxedo. Shari had really done a good job with him.

"We've all had fun this evening, the music was great and the food was delicious, so now that we've had our fill it's time to congratulate the lady being honoured this evening."

He raised his glass. "Let's raise our glasses in a toast to Mrs. Summer Munroe."

They drank to her then Derrick beckoned to her to come forward and there were loud cheers and applause as Summer slipped away from Lance's side and went to stand beside Derrick. He stepped back and directed her to the podium.

"Thanks, Derrick," she said as she leaned forward to the microphone, "and thanks to you all for coming. I really appreciate your being here to share my joy. It took a long time coming, actually an extra year because of my leave of absence, but now I'm glad to say I have my Master's Degree."

"Yeah!" someone at the back shouted, and then others joined in with "woof, woof". Everybody laughed at that, then they clapped so long that Summer had to hold her hand up to silence them.

"I've finally achieved one of my goals in life," she continued, "and I thank all of you who have been there to support me, but I must thank a very special man in my life, the one who has kept me focused and stopped me from throwing in the towel. I want to say thanks to my dear husband for throwing this wonderful graduation party for me. Lance, I love you."

There were more cheers as Summer left the podium and walked back into her husband's arms.

The DJ started the music again and Lance and Summer had one dance. Then she left him to go and mingle with the crowd.

After a few minutes she was surprised when he came and took her arm, excusing her from a group with which she was conversing.

"Come here, you," he growled playfully into her ear, "I don't want you away from me for even a minute. You're all mine."

"Oh, you baby," she teased, following him, "I'll always be yours."

He walked quickly towards the French doors and went out onto the patio with her close in tow. Then he turned her towards him and caressed her upper arms.

"I don't want you running off to Iraq covering news stories now that you have your degree," he said. "I want you here with me."

She smiled up at him and put her hand to his cheek. "Oh Lance, this is where I want to be. I'm not gonna run off and leave you. Remember I once told you that my interest was in people rather than just the news."

"Yeah? So?"

"So that means I have enough to do here. I don't have to go anywhere. There will always be people around me. And anyway," she looked up at him slyly, "I have another big project I'm working on, right here at home."

"Really?" He looked curious. "You never mentioned it before. What's this project about?"

"About you, and me, and our love."

He looked even more confused. "What are you talking about?"

"I'm talking about getting things ready for a very important guest." She laughed and hugged him tight when he still looked bewildered.

"I'm talking about our child – you're going to be a daddy."

Lance looked at her, incredulous, then he gave a whoop of joy and lifted her into the air and spun her around.

The people who stood by the doors looked out and saw the joyful couple and smiled at their antics but Lance and Summer didn't care who was watching.

They spun round and round, laughing and lost in the joy of their love.

About the Author

Judy Powell has always been an avid reader of romance. Having sampled all genre – from Gothic, to Historicals, to Regency to Contemporary – she decided to focus on an area which she feels has not yet been fully developed – the Multicultural Romance.

Judy is Jamaican by birth but has lived and worked in various countries including France, Puerto Rico, the USA and Canada. She has also traveled extensively in the Caribbean and Latin America. In addition to English she speaks Spanish, French, and a smattering of German. She holds a Bachelor of Arts in Foreign Languages/ International Business Administration as well as a Master of Arts in Spanish and an M.B.A. in Marketing. She is working on a third Master's Degree in Humanities/ Literature. Judy is a member of the U.S.A. Honour Society, Phi Beta Kappa.

Her love for people, world cultures and music led her to write *Hot Summer*, which is set in both Chicago and Jamaica, and is a combination of African American and Jamaican cultures. The novel is a celebration of the diversity and the multiplicity of cultures, even among peoples of African descent.

Judy enjoys talking to her readers so feel free to send her an e-mail at info@judypowell.com or visit her website at www.judypowell.com.